The Scene

MARK LAKERAM

ISBN: 978 0 9957929 2 0

To my mum

CONTENTS

PROLOGUE

The two gigantic white feathery wings sprouting from his back spanned a greater distance than his height. Using them, he was able to take to the air easily, soaring above to look down on the world he felt had betrayed him. Using the air currents made flying effortless. It was like surfing, he imagined, having never surfed, catching onto a wave or air current and allowing the surfer's body to follow where nature commanded. While he flew, he made adjustments to the wings that were part of him and manipulated certain feathers to catch the wind in their own unique way, which enabled him to fly as he wished—unrestrained. He began his vigil over the people below, wondering who was like him, who needed help, who was bad, and who would just love him for being himself. This was when he felt the most liberated and happy in life, in the imaginings of this safe haven and alternative reality. However, this daydream always ended the same way, with the clouds above parting and a gigantic hand, what he presumed to be the hand of God, coming down. He always looked up to try to see a face, but only a hand was ever visible to him. Before he knew what was happening, unable to stop himself, he would fly straight into the open palm. The warmth from the hand felt good and stopped his feathers from bristling; the caresses made his whole body shake with joy. Then the hand would ever so gently close around him and his former ecstasy would turn into panic and claustrophobia. Suddenly, the gentleness would be gone and the hand became a vice. Before any pain registered, the real horror would come from the sound of the bones of the humeri and the digits in the once-mighty wings being crushed. Then the hand would open, and he would fall unceremoniously to the ground.

Marco opened his eyes and put his iPod on repeat to hear the song again. The lyrics sang out about wings being broken in hands and the singer feeling unable to speak the words inside him. As the music started again, Marco felt the song spoke to his seventeen years of life so far, capturing his feelings and desires to be saved from his unhappy existence. This past year had been difficult for him. He knew it could have been a lot worse, but he felt that the lives of all the other students at his school were easier than his; for that, he was jealous. The song's second time around, he did not daydream, because he was only half paying attention to the lyrics. A tennis match between a man and a woman was distracting him.

He had come to Clapham Common to kill some time, so he was sitting on the grass enjoying the kiss of the sun on his legs, taking in the atmosphere, and generally people-watching. This newly acquired skill for basking in the sun and observing the world go by had been honed earlier that summer when Marco's dad had insisted he go to Italy to spend time with his relatives for summer vacations. When Marco was much younger, he used to love the "Italian jobs," which was how he and his English mother used to refer to their Italian vacations. But that was back when all he had to worry about was eating delicious food, playing silly children's games, and just being a kid. Now things were so much more complicated. Hanging out with his

2

cousins no longer involved stealing biscotti from Grandma's kitchen; life had become full of intricate games of cunning and intrigue.

An example of such a game had taken place ten days earlier at the Garden Bar, a coffee shop in Milan. Being only half Italian, Marco always considered that his full Italian cousins regarded him as somewhat of an unknown entity—not quite one of them but someone they had to include. He had survived the vacation on lies, telling them what they wanted to hear and providing himself a suitable alibi so he would not have to participate in the regular hunt. The group of four had just ordered a round of coffee when four girls walked past. The blondest of the girls looked back at the four young men, smiled, then turned and whispered something to her friends. They all started giggling. Bardo, Marco's first cousin, leapt up from the table and pursued the girls, who had not gotten far. Marco was sure if the blondest girl had not looked back, his group of guys would have still hollered "beautiful compliments" at the girls to impress them and make them fall instantly in love—or at least delude them long enough to allow the guys to be guys, but the look and the giggles had secured a full-on assault of charm. Nico, Bardo's younger brother, who was the same age as Marco, was already moving to another table, while Taide, a second cousin, was grinning in the direction of the girls even though they had their backs to him. Within two minutes Monica, Anna, Linda, and Alice had changed their plans and joined them in the cafe.

The charm offensive continued, and the four American tourists were lapping up the attention and stories three of the guys told. As this continued, Monica looked at Marco. "You're not like your cousins, you're much quieter," she stated, then threw her head back and started laughing, flashing her brilliant white teeth.

"Erm...I have..."

"What Marco was going to say is that he's upset this is his last weekend here before he has to go back to London," Nico interjected.

"Lunn-dan," Linda squealed. "How exciting."

"Yes, I guess he's disappointed he won't get to show you all the sights of Milan, but you girls must come to his leaving party tonight. It's at this new club everyone is talking about. Will you let us take you?" Bardo added.

The guys got up to get more drinks, ignoring the waiter service, to give the girls a bit of privacy to mull over the newly presented option.

"Look Marco, I know you are going to go on about your really fit girlfriend back in London. But we need you to make up numbers, so no protesting, complaining, or wussing out. We all have girlfriends, apart from Taide who needs to get laid, so you are in. Your London girlfriend will never know what happens out here," Bardo enthused.

"So where is this new club anyway?" Taide asked.

Nico smiled. "Don't be a special case; we'll just take them to any of the usual clubs. They won't know."

Bardo winked and signaled they should return to the girls. "So what is it to be, ladies?"

"Sure, we'd love to go to this club with you," Monica said. After another half an hour of finalizing the details for the night and general flirting by the majority of the group, the guys and girls separated until later that evening.

Looking at the tennis match currently playing before him, Marco realized the female player reminded him of one of the American girls, the one he hated. That stupid bitch had embarrassed him and brought unwanted attention. Suddenly very angry, he thumped the ground with his fist.

After the guys had finished getting ready for the night out, Bardo and Nico looked even more like brothers. They were both wearing tight white t-shirts, which showed off their bodies and accentuated their tanned dark looks. Black trousers finished the look. The only difference was that one was wearing Armani and the other was in Prada. Taide had tried to achieve a similar look as the brothers but on a budget. Marco made what his Italian cousins deemed an insufficient effort in blue jeans and a thin black shirt with the sleeves rolled up. When the guys picked the girls up at their hotel, the first few moment were awkward, as they all assessed each other and decided who they liked or wanted the most.

In a bar, the group had a few drinks courtesy of Bardo, to get to know each other better, and then started to pair off. Marco went for Alice; she declined the alcohol, and he thought he would be safest with a sober girl. As he got to know her better, he found himself liking her more. Even when they moved on to the club and they could not exactly hear each other, being in her company was easy. Nico had swapped partners in the club and sat with Monica on his lap, which Marco thought was a bit tactless since Bardo had been her partner at the beginning of the night. However, Bardo was not bothered and seemed very content with Linda. As they were pushing their faces together one of his hands was rubbing her back and the other one was stroking her leg. Taide, who was not behaving with the same urgency as the brothers, was dancing with Anna, and Marco thought they were getting on, laughing and joking together.

Marco had excused himself from Alice and gone to the bathroom. He'd wondered if he had overthought the situation earlier; the night was actually going well, and he was having fun. When he had finished, he found Alice waiting for him.

"Would you mind walking me back to the hotel? All the others have gone, and your cousins said you wouldn't mind."

"What do you mean gone?"

"Bardo and Nico have taken Monica and Linda somewhere else. And Taide and Anna went for a walk, and she didn't want me tagging along. You don't mind, do you?"

They had found themselves walking back to the hotel. They ended up walking along the bank of the Darsena, which was quite romantic, but Marco appreciated the scenery more than the company. As they approached the hotel, Alice asked Marco again for the names of places to check out in London and if he would mind writing them down, as she could not remember them. If it was up to the other girls, they would just end up in all the usual tourist spots, she explained. So, Marco found himself in Alice's hotel room writing a list of places for the girls to visit in London. Alice left him to it and went to change out of her clubbing clothes. Suddenly, she burst out of the bathroom in just her underwear.

"I know you have been a gentleman with me, but I really find you attractive."

Before Marco could respond, Alice was on him, using her tongue to pry open his mouth and thrusting it in. Marco was surprised and found himself responding. She moved his hands onto her breasts and tried to undo his jeans. When he realized what was happening, he'd tried to push her away.

"What is wrong? You don't have to worry, I'm on the pill."

"It's...it's...it's just that I have a girlfriend back home who I love, and I don't want to cheat."

"That's fine, I don't care. I just want some fun, and I know you do too," she purred. She'd managed to open the buttons of his jeans and put her hand inside his underwear. Marco attempted to get her off him.

"Why don't you want to? Are you a virgin? Your girlfriend must be really boring not to let you have any fun. I can be your first, you will really like it."

"I really don't want to. I am going to go."

"Why are you still soft? What is wrong with you? Do you not like girls?"

"What...er...no..."

"Oh my God, you are GAY!"

That one word ran through Marco's head alongside his irrational hatred for the female tennis player. Her opponent took his top off. That got Marco's full attention. He felt something stir in him, the very something that Alice had held and mocked. He found himself staring at the guy as he arched his body to serve, and wondered why it couldn't have been that guy in that hotel room instead of

Alice. He wondered what his cousins would think of him if he confirmed Alice's malicious gossip by dating a guy. He had managed to defuse the situation then, but he was not sure if everyone had believed him.

After Alice called him gay and made other derogatory comments about his sexuality, she'd texted Monica to tell her that Marco was a faggot. Monica and the other girls, declining offers for furthering Italian-American relationships, were with the cousins having late night coffees near the hotel. Monica took great pleasure in telling them what Alice had texted her. The guys had realized they were not going to get laid and left the girls soon after receiving this piece of information. When they met Marco later, he'd lied to them. He told them he fucked Alice, but she did not want her friends to know and think her easy, so they had agreed to tell the girls he was gay and nothing happened. The guys seemed to buy this story, especially as they had now deemed the other girls frigid.

Bardo slapped Marco's back. "Good man. I knew you would not let me down."

Now, on Clapham Common, Marco found himself getting really turned on by the topless tennis player. He wanted to stay and watch him, but he had to meet his friend, so once his excitement was no longer obvious he left. Thirty minutes later he was knocking on the door of Robert Ashton's home, still thinking about the guy from the tennis courts. When Bobby, or Bobs as everyone called him, opened the door, Marco was surprised to see his friend had lost weight and gotten a tan since he last saw him at the end of term. The two friends greeted each other and went to the kitchen to get a drink. They talked about the new summer blockbusters that had been released and the hotness of the female stars. Marco based his part of this conversation on the hotness of the male stars and which of the actresses he wished he could replace with himself, to get with their male counterparts. Then the talk moved to their respective holidays; Bobs had just come back from two months in the south of France with his family. Marco looked across at his friend, and deemed that he must have lost at least a stone.

"Well, friend, the vacation seems to have suited you well."

"Ha, you mean I'm no longer a fatty. Well, I thought I'd make myself more attractive this summer for our last year at school." Bobs grinned.

"So did you get any over the summer?" Marco asked. He knew this was a loaded question that would eventually require him answering the same. Bobs knew he did not have a girlfriend, so that excuse would not work. At least he felt he could now embellish some of his Italian escapades.

Bobs explained that while he hadn't gotten any, there was someone he'd met and liked.

"Is she from school?" Marco asked.

Bobs shook his head.

"Did you meet her on vacation?"

Bobs was starting to look a bit flushed, and Marco remembered what it was like when his cousins badgered him for information about his pretend girlfriend. He decided to let it lie. Bobs said it might be easier if he showed him, and left the room.

Marco looked through the kitchen window at the

Ashton's garden. He could tell that Mrs. Ashton, some sort of interior designer, took real pride in it. He wondered if Mr. Ashton ever helped her, because from what Bobs had told him, he was not around much due to his high finance job. Marco had felt a bit more apprehensive the few times he'd met Bobs's father because he seemed really strict, like his own father. He knew both the Ashtons were currently at work and wondered how they would react if Bobs did something of which they did not approve. This in turn made him think of his father and how he could never tell him the truth about himself. Besides, he sometimes kidded himself that maybe gayness was just a phase, but deep down he knew it was not. Maybe he could move to a foreign country to study abroad, or maybe he could find a woman to settle down with and somehow make it work. All these thoughts started to depress him.

Bobs came back into the room with his laptop and put it on the kitchen countertop; he opened the machine and started to boot it up. While they were waiting, Bobs asked the inevitable question of Marco. "So what about you, you Italian stallion?"

"I am only half an Italian stallion, but I did manage some on holiday. There was an American girl and we sort of..."

Before Marco could finish the story he had developed in his head, Bobs interjected, "Girl? I always thought you were gay."

Marco felt his heart racing; there was that word, the word that everyone wanted to use to define him. Time seemed to stop. He looked out the window, then back at his friend and wondered what he should reply. He suddenly felt himself at a crossroads—he could lie, which he was sure Bobs would accept, or he could tell the truth for the first time. His heart was beating so fast he was certain that Bobs could hear it. It felt like too much time had passed. He had to say something.

The laptop screen jumped to life with color and sound, asking for a password. They looked at the screen, then looked at each other, making eye contact for the first time since the forbidden G-word had been mentioned.

"Well, actually, I am sort of bi." Marco knew that he was not bi, but it seemed like the best way to test the waters for Bobs's reaction. He felt this gave him the out to say, "I am still one of the boys, I like girls too."

"So am I," Bobs also lied, feeling slightly cheated that his mate, who he always suspected was gay, had chosen to say he was bisexual.

These gay friends, even though they continued the lie to a certain extent, felt an immense sense of relief; suddenly, the world did not seem that bad. Marco felt a sense of comfort, but he still felt he had to sell his lie in case this was some kind of trap. Bobs might out him when school started back, making him the school leper, or tell Mr. and Mrs. Ashton, who in turn might tell his dad. So he went ahead with the rest of his Alice story, telling Bobs how he was in this American girl's hotel room and they were fooling around, kissing, touching her breasts, and how they eventually had sex and he liked it. Why wouldn't he? He was bisexual, after all. He gave the story all the bravado a teenager would when telling his friend about the time he lost his virginity.

Bobs listened and started to believe his friend, but he

honestly did not really care if it was true or not. He wanted to talk about guys, not girls. "Cool, so what have you done with guys?"

Then Marco decided to be truthful. "I've only ever looked, imagined, fantasized about doing stuff with guys." Bobs looked at him thoughtfully. "But due to a lack of opportunity and being too scared, I have never done anything. Look, you are the first person I have admitted this secret to, and if truth be told, I'm only just coming to terms with it myself. Today is the first day I have actually said the words out loud."

"I've talked to guys about this online, but you are the first person I've ever said those words to out loud too. I hope you know how difficult this is for me."

"So tell me about your online guys."

"Well, there is this one guy that I frequently chat to. I am thinking about meeting him in person."

Marco felt the tiniest pang of jealousy. He had lied about being with a girl and here was his quiet friend doing what he had not worked up the courage to do himself.

"Let me show you some pictures of my friend. He is not currently online, but I have saved a few photos on my computer. Just look at the guy's well-toned torso, and one of him in white Calvin Klein boxers with the outline of his cock showing."

"What about the face?"

"He's not out and wants to save the face reveal for when we meet up."

Marco was concerned that his friend had been chatting to a 25-year-old man whose face he had not seen. He wanted to subtly express these feelings, but he realized

Bobs would not hear them at this moment; it was a conversation that would have to be revisited.

"Marco, we should try to find you an online friend." Bobs logged onto a site called Manchat and before Marco knew it, they were looking through profiles of men, or lots of headless torso shots.

"Change my age. I don't want to speak to guys our age because I don't want to run into someone from school. What if the entire rugby team is sitting around pretending to be gay on a site like this, to find out who is gay at school? They can spend the entire school year making that person's life a misery. Remember what they did to the effeminate, Dan, who they forced out of the closet." After about half an hour spent online, they kept getting requests for their own pictures, with strangers trying to entice the young men to show their faces. Some of these people even went as far as unlocking their own private pictures, which showed erect cocks. Both Marco and Bobs found themselves getting turned on but felt uncomfortable admitting this to each other, so they agreed to stop chatting. But each made a mental note to go back online in the privacy of his own bedroom.

"I always thought you were, that's why I gravitated towards you."

"Really why didn't you say something sooner?" Bobs asked.

"At least we now have each other to talk to."

"What do you think your parents will say?" Bobs asked.

Macro cringed at the thought. "I'll think about that later."

"I have always suspected the School Captain is gay.

What do you think?"

"If he is he would rather die than admit it," Marco answered. "He is good-looking though."

"It's always the athletic, outgoing, loud, obnoxious types." While Bobs spoke, he suddenly wondered if Marco found him attractive. "So am I fit?"

This took Marco by surprise. When he thought about it he realized that Bobs was not unattractive, especially now that he had lost some weight. "I think of you as a close friend, not in that way."

"Yeah, I feel the same way about you."

"However, I do not want my first time to be with a stranger from the Internet and come across like a totally inexperienced virgin," Bobs told Marco. "And as you have already done stuff with a girl, maybe you could give me some pointers. I have never even kissed anyone before."

Marco realized what Bobs was implying. The more he thought about it the more he decided that it would be really cool; he had never kissed a guy and his first kiss ever had been forced upon him by someone who'd turned out to be very nasty. He was turned on by the topless male tennis player, by talking about the guys at school he fancied, and looking at all the pictures the Internet men had shown them. Marco stood up, walked over to Bobs, and hugged him. From the hug, the two best friends started kissing each other. As the kisses continued, their hands started moving over each other's bodies. Then Bobs took Marco's hand and led him upstairs to his bedroom.

By the time the young men reached the bed, both were very turned on, but neither was exactly sure what to do, so they continued kissing and touching. Then their clothes started coming off and their naked bodies started rubbing against each other. Bobs took the initiative and starting doing the things to Marco that he wanted done to him, and Marco responded by doing these same things to Bobs. After they both finished, they lay together and continued kissing. Then they decided to have a shower. In the shower, Bobs enjoyed soaping Marco's slim body and let his hands wander down to the Italian's firm ass, as they continued showering and exploring one another.

Once they left the shower and dried off, they returned to Bobs's single bed, which due to the size meant one had to lie on top of the other. They continued kissing, but this time, they talked as well.

"I'm happy we shared this learning experience."

"Yeah, it has strengthened our friendship."

Bobs looked at the clock. "We have over two hours left before either of my parents will be home." Bobs moved his hand back down to Marco's ass. Marco, who was fantasizing about the tennis player to really get himself going, wondered if the player was gay too and then thought, how can you tell if someone is gay?

1

HE LOOKS AT YOU FOR JUST A
LITTLE BIT TOO LONG

On a bench on Clapham Common, I'm staring at the symmetry of the imposing white structure with its magnificent wrought iron balconies and high windows. I cannot believe I am about to move into the French Renaissance Grade II building. I am trying to figure out if the apartment can be seen from my current position. This task might be easier if I were to go inside and look out a window, but I am finding that too daunting at the moment, so I just prefer to stare at it. I remember reading about Nightingale Hall when my girlfriend's dad first bought her the apartment a year ago and she told me she would be moving to London. I had searched the name of the property to see how expensive the apartments were, but what I had been more interested in was a headline from eight years ago linked to the building: "Sinister fire kills three in historic building." The article had lots of pictures of the burnt-out shell and quotes from local people saying it was a tragic loss of life, a beautiful building had been destroyed, and the area would never be the same again.

Despite public opinion at that time, a careful and deliberate reconstruction of the building saw Nightingale Hall rise up from the ashes and become fully restored to its former glory. Some people even said the building looked better than it did previously, but somehow, it does not seem right to me that my first home in the capital should be better than anything in which I have previously lived, including my parental home in Nuneaton. I had always planned to live in the city, but thought I would share an apartment or a house with some cool strangers somewhere out in zone four. However, Carmen, my girlfriend of three years, insisted I move in with her. We have been having a long distance relationship for the past year, since she started working as a trainee accountant in a top London firm and I remained in Cambridge to finish off a Master of Philosophy. I really do want to live with her, but not in the place her dad had bought. However, the decision is made now—I am moving in, which could be a good thing because I don't have a steady income yet.

As I am mentally preparing myself to walk over to the building and enter it as a resident instead of a visitor like I had done on previous visits to London, a couple of strangers come along. The two men walk hand-in-hand past the bench. As they go by, I hear one of them say to the other, quite audibly and without any shame, "Bench guy is quite cute." When they get further away from me, the one who had spoken turns and stares. For some reason, I feel embarrassed and just stare at the ground. When I look up, the man who is looking at me asks, "Look, mate, are you lost? You can always come and spend a few hours with us." At that point, his friend asks me more seriously if I am okay. Once I have assured them that I am fine and that I am not a soldier returning from the Afghanistan war who has suddenly experienced post-traumatic stress disorder, a suggestion wishfully made by the starer due to my large trekking back-pack, the couple laugh and go on their way.

I carefully pick up another one of my bags and cautiously secure it on my back so the contents will be safe; the other two bags I grab and head over to Nightingale Hall.

"Hello, Mr. Clarke," Maurice, the concierge, greets me. He has remembered me from my previous visits. Then he off-loads the two bags I am carrying in my arms and tells me he will escort me and the bags up to Miss Howard's; she has left the spare keys with him to pass on. On the journey to the flat, the concierge goes through the opening times of the building's gym and swimming pool, new features added in the refurbishment. When I am alone in the apartment, I carefully remove my oversized backpack and place it with my other bags on the floor. I decide to unpack after some lunch. Carmen has stocked the fridge well and has left little notes reaffirming how happy she is that we are living together again and how much she loves me. I am halfway through eating a chorizo sandwich when there is a knock at the door.

I open the door to a guy, but before I can say anything he says, "Welcome to the Phoenix."

"Thanks. The Phoenix?"

"It's a sort of affectionate nickname us gays have given the building, reborn from the ashes into glory with a gym and all that. I'm Tim Douglas, I live in the apartment next door. Carmen told me to pop by and check that you are settling in okay and have everything you need."

"Come in then."

"So, Richard…"

"You can call me Ricky."

"Do you have everything you need?"

* * * *

Ricky starts to go on about straight man stuff. I stop listening. I am wondering why Carmen had kept him to herself; he is hardly amazing, so she would not have had to worry about any of us cruising him. However, while Ricky is not obviously good looking, there is something there. If he spent some time in the gym and toned up his lean frame he would be a lot hotter, and he needs to spend a little more time grooming and preening; a little bit of wax in his hair would look good, like the quiff I have. His good points are his slenderness—he is taller than me at about five feet ten inches—his jet-black hair—mine is dirty blond—and large green eyes. These things make him stand out. After enough time has passed so it will not be rude, I decide to make my excuses to leave. "I need to go and prepare for a party tonight to celebrate the boyfriend's promotion at work. You and Carmen must come over; no excuses will be accepted, as you only live next door."

* * * *

When Carmen arrives home, she is so excited about us living together that we don't speak and just head to the bedroom. After we finish having sex a couple of times, I get out of bed and go over to the chest of drawers which Carmen had cleared out for me, and take out a large black box with a red ribbon. I present her with the box and join her back on the bed. We both sit naked; she opens the gift and says she is delighted by one of my framed prints. It is from when we were on holiday in Helsinki—an abstract rusted iron structure shot from below where I had to lie on the ground.

We doze in each other's arms for a while until we fall asleep. When I wake up, I point out that it is ten o'clock and we have probably missed the gathering next door. Carmen points out that they are a gay couple and it's Friday night, so the party probably hasn't even started yet. We get up and get ready to go—if we had had to travel farther than the ten meters required, I would not have bothered. I wear dark blue jeans and a baby blue shirt with a sweater, the staple dress code of nearly every party I had been to in Cambridge. Carmen looks hot in a tight purple dress, which suits her petite frame. She grabs a bottle of champagne from the wine rack, and we head out the door.

She knocks on the door with the number six and turns the handle; it opens. Music, sounds of people chatting, laughing, and general merriment hit us. I turn around in the hallway, and with my free hand—the other is intertwined with Carmen's—I go to close the door, but it re-opens in front of me and hits me flush on the face. I briefly see the guy who pushed open the door; he looks mortified. I move my hand under my nose and notice it is red and wet. Carmen is asking me if I am okay.

The guy offers to take a look. I instinctively tell everyone I am all right, but my cupped hand under my nose is now full of blood and starting to overflow. Carmen, who is squeamish at the sight of blood, has backed away. I try to stop the blood flowing down my front and onto my new neighbors' floor by tilting my head back. I instantly regret this, as the blood goes down my throat and makes me gag. The guy pulls down his jacket sleeve and moves it up to my face, gently squeezing the soft part of my nose.

* * * *

I see my guests Carmen and Ricky arrive while I am walking from the kitchen to the living room and I go over to check why they are loitering by the front door and not showering my cheeks with kisses. I see blood, which has seeped through Ricky's fist and landed on the doormat. I can't help but let out a little yelp. I realize the situation is being handled, and think the best thing I can do is to find them a nice quiet area in which they can sort themselves out. This, I decide, will be best achieved in the sanctuary of the injured party's own apartment, particularly since they are right by the door.

Sweeping the three guests including Taylor Farrant, the one who had opened the door on Ricky's nose, back into Carmen and Ricky's apartment, I feel more at ease. When the four of us are in the bathroom, Ricky puts his head over the sink, letting the blood drip out as instructed by Taylor, who is standing next to him. I assess that the situation is now in hand and off my carpet, grab Carmen's free hand (the other is clutching champagne), and say we should go back to the party.

"Dr. Farrant will take care of Ricky and bring him over when they're done."

Ricky, I guess feeling like a complete idiot for all this attention on him after just meeting all of us, looks in the mirror and nods to Carmen to go.

Carmen looks ill at the sight of blood; she is probably deliberating whether to leave or not when Taylor says, "I just need to check the bleeding has stopped, assess if he feels faint, and then we will be over."

"See, an excellent doctor. Your hubby is in good hands." I put an arm around Carmen's shoulder and escort her out of the apartment.

As we are leaving, I ask, "Bitch, how could you have kept that cutie hidden all this time?" I notice a picture on the wall; it was not here earlier. I stop and stare at it, as it is mesmerizing. Carmen exits the apartment, saying she needs to get a drink. I say I will join her in a minute. As I look at the picture, I hear the two men in the bathroom talking.

"So, are you really a doctor?"

"I know my dashing good looks don't make me seem old enough to be a doctor, but for my sins I am, so you are actually in good hands. I'm Taylor, by the way. Also, as a gay man, I know how to take care of clothes, so take your top off and I will get rid of those blood stains."

Taylor pops out of the bathroom and goes to the kitchen, so I go in to ask Ricky if he took the picture. He is taking his top off, which catches me off guard. He has a trim torso that looks natural.

"Excuse me, Tim." Taylor returns with a makeshift ice pack and without his own bloodstained jacket. He moves next to Ricky, sets the ice pack down on the sink, and asks to have another look at his nose. The two men are standing face to face. Taylor is two inches taller than Ricky, and bends down ever so slightly to examine the damage.

Ricky is staring into the dark blue eyes of his assailant, I guess looking for a clue to whether anything is seriously wrong because, although he has not admitted it, I bet his nose hurts like hell. Taylor moves his own head so Ricky does not have to move his. He holds both his hands on Ricky's face, first on his cheeks, checking for broken bones, then moves them to his nose. He gets Ricky to remove the blood-soaked tissues to see if the flow has stopped. He sees there is still a bit of spotting, so he gets his ice pack from the sink and places it on the back of Ricky's neck. Ricky jolts forward at the shock of the sudden cold; Taylor still has one hand on Ricky's face, so luckily does not get head-butted. He suggests he will move the ice pack to Ricky's forehead because it might not feel as cold there. When Taylor moves the ice pack, a few drops of cold water drip onto Ricky's chest. I watch as the man's nipples cannot help but get erect, and decide to give the doctor and his patient some privacy.

Next door, I find Carmen in a group of four, listening to Nathan Lockwood, whom she has met a few times through us. Nat is describing how a new intern at his job likes him. Before coming to the party they had been out having a few after-work drinks. The intern sat next to him and kept pushing her leg against his. One of the other people in the group stops the story at this point to ask why Nat is still not out yet at work. Nat just rolls his eyes and continues with his story.

Carmen asks, "How can the girl be so naive as to like a gay man?"

"So her leg is pressed against mine, then she has a sip of wine and places her arm strategically next to mine, and I start getting a semi," Nat says.

"Whatever. I wouldn't even be able to get it up for a woman," one of the group rebukes him.

"It's likely because he hasn't had sex in ages," another

adds.

Nat gets a bit defensive. "I'm being serious. I have never tried it with a woman, and I'm curious to see what it would be like. Maybe I'm bi."

"If you are talking about bi guys, get that man of mine to tell you about his bisexuality," I interject.

Someone gently slaps my ass. I turn around and kiss the face of my smiling boyfriend Bobs. Carmen comes up to him to congratulate him on his promotion. After they embrace, he asks her, "So where is he?"

"I am not telling you, until you, Mr. Bobby Ashton, tell me all about your bisexual past. I never knew you had been with women before."

"Ha ha. Don't worry, I haven't. It's only when I came out to my best friend nine years ago, I said I was bisexual. It's a gay thing. Some of us find it easier to sugarcoat being gay by saying we are bi. It seems less dramatic and everyone accepts it more readily. My dear Timothy never lets me forget the story, because he came out as a fully-fledged homosexual at the age of thirteen. Anyway, I personally believe and know many gays and straights that believe bisexuality doesn't exist, so I think Tim is also mocking 'my un-pc' views. I think a bisexual is just someone who is confused, or wants the best of both worlds, or is happy living the lie because it is easier."

The group we are with move off together after a bit of whispering and motioning to each other, leaving Nat, Bobs, Carmen, and me. Carmen takes this opportunity to ask Nat about the girl at work who likes him. "I can't fathom how a woman could like a gay guy beyond the aesthetics, as the guy wouldn't be providing any sustenance in terms of feelings."

What Carmen does not see is Nat's inherent quality, which make some people, both male and female, fall for him straight away. He is better-looking than average, topped off with a killer smile which is usually on display (behind his back, Bobs and I refer to him as the Joker). However, he is ignorant of the full extent of his charms. He thinks people are just friendly, and is childlike in his belief that it is always a case of "just friends." Of everyone at our party, he has caused the most heartache for suitors without knowing it.

"Well to be honest, I think she likes me because I am nice to her at work and show her the ropes and everything," Nat responds to Carmen.

"But would you really have a sexual relationship with her? Bobs was just saying how he didn't believe in bisexuality."

Bobs decides to back up his opinion by cutting in. "Our dear Nat is not bisexual; he's in love with J..." The stare Nat shoots him is enough to tell him he had better not finish his sentence.

"I am not bisexual, but I would like to try it with a woman just once. That way I'll get to fully confirm my homo status. Bobs is just being a bitch, because he has only been with two guys, because that's all who would have him."

The last dig is payback for Bobs's unfinished sentence.

We are about to be treated to a full on gaat or gay spat, but Carmen asks, "So who were those guys we were chatting to earlier? The mixed-race guy who wanted to know why you aren't out at work seemed nice."

Without answering, Nat downs the remains of his drink and goes off to get another. Bobs smirks, links his arm through Carmen's, and says it is about time she introduces him to "little or big Dick."

The initial group has moved off and are in the master bedroom. I join them to speak to Jason Vaughan, Nat's J, or Jas. Jas is in the en suite with the door open, and the other two are in the bedroom discussing the best place to go for the after-party. Jas is checking himself out in the mirror; he is playing with his hair. It is slightly longer than usual, which means he has to style it more. I think he looks better with shorter hair. I notice his complexion does not have the healthy milk-coffee glow it usually has, and he looks a bit washed out. However, it does make the freckles on his nose stand out more. His brown eyes are surrounded by mildly bloodshot whites, which makes me think that after this weekend someone should tell him to lay off the party scene for a while.

"I need to pee," he announces. The other two come into the bathroom from the bedroom. He undoes his jeans and pulls down his underwear slightly. He fiddles inside his boxers and pulls out a plastic bag and puts it next to the sink. The pouch in the boxers, which is there for a guy to place his cock to make it look bigger, obviously has a different use for Jas. He looks like he is going to pee, so I leave. I hear the door being locked behind me.

Bobs is on his way to the living room where the majority of our guests are. There is a knock at the door. Bobs opens the now locked door to let in our new guests and is greeted by a familiar face and that of a stranger. Bobs kisses Marco and thanks him for coming, albeit late;

both Marco and his friend have wet hair.

"You should be grateful that I came at all because you know how much I hate this place, this Phoenix. We, only came to celebrate your promotion. Anyway, this is Richard, a guy I met earlier."

"Hello."

Bobs hugs Richard and looks like he got a damp ear for his effort. Once they have entered the apartment, Marco and his man start kissing passionately.

Carmen, who joins us unexpectedly, gasps out loud, which makes the kissers stop and look up. Richard looks totally ashamed and goes bright red. Marco pulls away from him and comes over to Carmen, who is standing next to me. He kisses her on one cheek and whispers in her ear, "Tonight, I am Carlo."

He winks a hello at me.

She kisses his other cheek and whispers in his ear, "Marco, what are you like?"

"Carmen, let me introduce my new friend, Richard."

"Sorry for my initial reaction, it's just that was such a passionate embrace and Carlo said that you guys had only just met."

"That was nothing, if you wanted to see passion you should have come down to the pool ten minutes ago where we were fucking."

"Yeah, right, the pool is not open at this time of night," she replies, but realizes she is wrong when she notices they are both slightly wet. Richard goes even redder.

"Anything is possible when you know the right door code," Marco replies.

"That's our, er 'Carlo'," Bobs says.

We move toward the living room and the rest of the guests. The party is starting to wind down. Some guests have their jackets on and are now coming over to say 'bye.

Marco goes to Carmen and thanks her for playing along. "You know how I don't want guys I'm not going to see again to know personal details about me."

"You could always see him again," the romantic in Carmen says.

Marco replies, "It's tempting, he was a great lay in the pool, and I'm definitely going to have sex with him a few more times tonight, but I really don't see any sort of future."

Richard, who has returned to his normal color, stops at the door to the living room where Bobs has led him. He stares at Carlo/Marco, whom he had met earlier in the night and with whom he'd just been intimate.

Carmen says she is going to look for her Richard.

"Maybe he's in the kitchen with the drinks, Carmen," I tell her.

"More likely he probably just went to bed, I haven't seen him here at all."

On our way to the kitchen, we meet Jas's friends. They are in their coats and seem louder than before. One of the men, who is very chirpy and seems to be skipping down the hallway, asks if we want to go to Vauxhall with them to continue the party.

Jas escorts us the rest of the way to the kitchen because he is looking for Nat. In the kitchen, we see Nat and a few others but no Ricky. I need another drink, and pour myself a glass of champagne from an open bottle of Dom. I have a sip, make my way out of the room, and hear Jas asking

Nat to come to the club with them. I slow down to hear the response, but there is none. I turn around. Nat has his hand on Jas's face and is looking into his eyes. Finally, I think. They are about to make out.

"Jas, I'm not going to be able to make it to the club tonight." Nat gives him a peck on the cheek. "I'll make sure I'm free next time." Jas hugs him and giggles, then exits.

"Are you okay?" I ask Nat.

"I'm fine, just tired, and I need to go home."

I head out to the hallway to say 'bye to our friends. Out there, Taylor is speaking to some of the guys who are leaving. Ricky is there too. Carmen has noticed him, and goes over and kisses him.

"Ouch." He flinches. "Watch the nose."

His face and nose are red. Bobs comes out of the living room to see his guests off. He is followed by Marco and his Richard, who are leaving to join the exodus of clubbers.

"Hello, you must be Richard. Carmen has talked about you non-stop for the past year. It is great to finally meet you," Bobs says.

"Hi, I'm Carlo," Marco says, "and this is my friend Richard."

Richard hugs Ricky and tells him he has a great name.

I watch this whole exchange from afar. Bobs sees Taylor, who is waiting by the door, and says hello for the first time that night. Marco's Richard is talking non-stop about how amazing the apartment and the building are. Ricky looks zoned out and is staring toward the exit.

2

HE IS JUST TOO UNMISTAKABLE

Clapham used to be the gay Mecca south of the Thames and second only to Soho as the gay place to be in London, but times are changing and the scene is evolving. The area of East London has seen an overhaul, and now commands the attention of the young and trendiest things emerging on the scene: emaciated, arty types who would have once adjourned to Clapham the moment they came out. The technological advances with the Internet and global positioning systems that are readily available and give more access to men have put paid to the former necessity of cruising around a well-known outdoor spot such as Clapham Common to find gratification. The super-clubs, places open from dawn till dusk and then some, have always been in Vauxhall. But they are now seen, due to some great promotion, as widely acceptable places to go that cater to every taste, not as sleazy sex joints. The publicity makes Vauxhall the new gay place to be. All in all, these factors have led to a definite change in the Clapham scene

Sitting in Twilight on Clapham High Street, the former trendiest gay bar outside of Soho, I am contemplating these changes. Back in the good old days, people would come up to me and be like Joe, Joseph, Joseph Thompson—but not anymore.

It is about a week after Bobs's and Tim's party and I

am waiting for some friends. I consider myself a true Claphamite. I had gotten a part-time job working weekends at the art house cinema, Flicks, when I was twenty. It never felt like a job because there was always some party to be had, either with the rich customers or the like-minded co-workers who were a mixture of students like me or out-of-work actors, musicians, or playwrights. When I first started working there, I met two really close friends, Bobs and Nat. Every Saturday night the three of us worked as ushers. We were inseparable. When we had finished for the night, we would go to the in-house bar and drink the money we earned from the night. In addition to our salary we got cash in hand, usually in the form of Clapham cinema-goers being too lazy to get out of their seats and giving the usher money to get whatever refreshments they required. In a final act of snobbery and to impress their dates, they would tell us to keep the change. Or, when we had to clean out the seating areas after the showing, we would find money, mainly loose change or sometimes notes, among the leftover popcorn, spilt drinks, used condoms, dirty underwear (it was always the women who felt the need to leave their underpants behind, men apparently just continued to wear them regardless), and various other items.

After the Flicks bar, we usually had time for a quick few in the crammed Twilight, and then we would move on to the premier gay club down the road, The Common, where the drinking would continue with dancing and merriment until the club chucked us out. Bobs just drank and danced and spurned the advances of any admirers because he was already seeing the love of his life, Tim, a guy he'd met during his first week at university. Nat just drank and danced and spurned the advances of most admirers, and there were lots, as he did not like to hook up with guys in a club; he always wanted something more. Occasionally, however, he did slip. I just drank and danced and would have spurned the advances of any admirers if anyone had bothered to make a move. I could have had a few one-night stands, but I did not turn them down for the reasons Bobs or Nat did. In fact, now I regret turning down anyone who showed interest in me. My reason was because I was usually sexed out.

Making a fiver an hour with maybe an extra tenner from usher tips, I found that particular salary alone could not sustain me. Bobs did not have to work; he did it to be close to his family on the weekend without actually having to spend time with them. Nat just seemed to like working and took pride in doing a good job. But I needed the money; I was financially supporting myself through my university studies unlike my peers who all had wealthy families.

I had left my family home in Romford the moment I could. In between working out like a madman (probably to look as different from me, the effeminate twin, as possible) and being involved in no end of "minor" criminal activities in Essex, my twin seemed intent on making my life a misery. My mother had been no help. I had not seen her since she ran off with another man when I was ten. And I was sure my dad, egged on by my twin brother, would have kicked his "queer" son out the first chance he had.

When I first took the job at the cinema a middle-aged customer started flirting with me. I was not particularly interested, and politely let the man down. A few weeks later, the day after I'd had an argument on the phone with my twin and was feeling down, the flirting man came back. Bobs and Nat were both absent from work. The man was watching a film, some pretentious foreign language film. Halfway through, he came out for something. I needed a little companionship, so I started talking to him and flirted a little myself. Fifteen minutes later, I found myself in the toilets sucking the man off. Once the man had cum in my mouth, he zipped up his trousers, adjusted his clothes, took out his wallet, left three twenty notes for me, and left the cubicle. I would have protested, but had a mouth full of cum. The fleeting moment of intimacy we shared felt good and was more important to me than the money—the money was a welcome bonus.

I never saw that man again. There was always someone else, but not anyone I ever found attractive or with whom I would want a relationship. Usually it was middle-aged men who were married, bored, or just disinterested in the film they had come to see. These men included minor TV personalities: a chef, a children's show host, and a reality show contestant. They always sought me out. For some reason, just by looking at me, people know I am gay; something about me gives this away even before I move or speak. In the beginning I sucked the guys off, but it soon moved on to them fucking me. I never asked for money, but they automatically left something behind; the amounts varied from person to person. I never considered myself a prostitute because I never approached a person, never advertised my services, and never actually asked for any money. At my peak, a year after I gave my first paid blow-job, I could get through three men a night. A year after that, men stopped asking me as frequently, and the companionships started to dwindle. I did not really care because it had seen me financially through university. After I finished my degree in the history of art, I took a full-time position at the cinema and worked my way up to assistant manager. My income became sufficient for my needs, and I no longer required supplementation. Now I miss the fleeting moments in which I was desired by someone else.

That's another way the scene has changed, I think. Back in the good old days, only five years ago, I had plenty of suitors; admittedly, not men I found very attractive or sexy, but the offers were there. Now these men do not have to leave the comfort of their own homes. They can sit at their computer or go on their phones and find someone for sexual gratification, probably for free. Even Twilight has changed with the times; it has lots of TV screens and it is showing, on mute, re-runs of the previous night's Starz, a reality show in which wannabe pop stars try to dazzle the public with amazing singing voices and heart-breaking life stories to justify why they deserve to win. The screens also display sections where you can request songs and send messages via text that everyone in the bar can read. So, if you fancied a stranger, instead of going over to speak to them, you could let them know by sending a text message. While I am up for ways to help men get together, I think this is a waste of time. I quite like a guy in the bar at this moment, but what am I meant to text? "Man with dark hair in the blue t-shirt, skinny man also in a blue t-shirt would like to get to know you." Then suddenly, the man I want to get the message will see it, correctly identify me as the sender, come over, and it will be the start of a beautiful relationship. No! What is more likely is that the guy in the grayish top will see the message and go over to the guy I intended the message for, to ask if he had sent it. The other guy will laugh and say no but wish he had, and they will get civil partnered then and there.

I know I should not be so hard on myself, but after all the negativity I got from my dad and brother growing up, I can't help it. The only one who supported me was my aunt, who had worked in the theater as an administrator. She told me to just be myself and not to care about what anyone said. I try to tell myself that I am a type who is not to everyone's taste. Anyone who says they are not into effeminate/fems, camp, queen/queenie guys or wants someone who was straight/str8-acting/SA is not for me, and it is his loss. But I still should have a boyfriend by now and not just a string of endless one-night stands or companions I met at work. Whenever I try to initiate going on a date with someone with whom I have slept, I am met with a look of "would I really be seen out in public with you?" If I could throw a punch, I would hit those people, but I can't so I have to live with it.

As I go to get another drink, I wonder if I should get my friend one, as she should be here soon. I am waiting for Benita Sanders, aptly called Ben by everyone who meets her. A kindred spirit, the other assistant manager, and my roommate. I look at my watch and see there is only ten minutes left to go until we can meet up and indulge in a hair of the dog session before going home. Thinking about it, that Sunday shift is a real drag. She should definitely look at changing the schedule, but I can't see anyone wanting to give up their Sunday morning easily. The place is full of really obnoxious creatures who come into the bar, order coffee, and read the Sunday newspapers before going off to watch some foreign language film that some reviewer has bigged up. All the workers wonder why they can't be like normal people and just go out and get completely wasted on a Saturday night and then spend Sunday in bed and not annoy us with orders or skinny lattes, cappuccinos, or virgin Bloody Marys. But this is Clapham, and the poor man's Chelsea has a point to prove.

* * * *

My thoughts of escaping work leave when a better-than-average looking woman comes up to the bar and orders drinks. I do not register her drink order, as I am too busy checking her out. While anyone would instinctively know that I am gay by my appearance, I have a terrible gaydar myself and cannot tell a fellow lesbian straight away. I usually assume rightly that most of the ladies in this area are straight; after all, it is Clapham, not Stoke Newington. The woman is smiling back at me and I start to wonder if she is checking me out. Suddenly, it dawns on me that she has ordered drinks. I make an inquisitive expression to indicate, what was that order again? The woman repeats it. I turn around and bend down to get the reordered bottle of beer, thinking the woman is definitely a breeder, getting her a man a beer while he parks the Porsche outside.

I turn away from the fridge, still kneeling slightly, and look up over the top of my thick red-rimmed glasses to see the woman's blurred partner. I move my eyes down to look through the lenses and clearly see the six-two frame of the attractive woman's girlfriend…a woman with a hand on her shoulder. I slam the beer on the counter.

"What the fuck are you doing here?"

The tall woman opens her mouth to say something, but I do not want to hear it. I storm out of the bar and cinema. As I run through the back streets to get to Twilight, I can feel my eyes well up and the tears come. I continue to run and am glad that I'd had the instinct not to go via the high street because it is busier, and the locals do not need to see the fat dyke from the cinema wobble down the street. I slow down when I have put enough distance between myself and the bitch. I am tired and want what my lungs do not really need following that unprecedented bout of exercise, a cigarette. As I slow down to a walk and light one up, my life with the giant flashes before my eyes.

We had first met during freshman week at the University of Kent, where I had established myself as something of a champion drinker. I could easily out-drink all of the girls, many of whom were adjusting to drinking pints of beers or cider and could only take a couple of these before becoming drunk. With the guys, I could match them pint for pint. Everyone I met seemed to assume I was a lesbian. I was not sure if it was because I was large with short brown hair and a boyish dress sense, but I never really cared what people thought. On my first night in Canterbury, some random guy looked me up and down.

"You gay?"

"Yes."

"That's cool."

The guys all seemed to find the concept interesting, and I was soon integrated as one of them, drinking pints with them, checking out which girls were fit, and sharing a liking of gratuitously bloody video games and films. At the end of one night, when all my male friends had coupled off with two-pint drunken girls, I was left drinking alone when I would have happily hooked up with a drunk girl too. Some girls liked to make out with each other to get attention from guys and be bought a few free female-friendly drinks, but they never made out with me. It was all a bit of fun kissing a straight girl, but a lot of the girls did not want to kiss the lesbian and be branded one too. In fact, a lot of girls gave me a wide berth.

Even though my university life was only just starting, I was missing females with whom I could just hang around. I was having a cigarette and thinking about my sexual experience to date—kissing two girls—when I was joined by a tall, skinny, awkward girl who asked for a light. Once her cigarette was lit, the tall girl, another freshman, stayed and chatted to me. She introduced herself as Susan Jones. I noticed that Susan, or Suze, was not like the other girls in the student union. She wore no makeup and was not dressed like she was looking to get lucky with a fellow student. Actually, her clothes were quite boring. I wondered if Suze was like me or if she was just deeply religious or something. After her cigarette, Suze went to the bar and bought two beers; she returned and gave me one of the drinks. Then she confided in me that she admired me for being so open about my sexuality; she herself had not told anyone at the university that she had a girlfriend back home. I had three thoughts at that moment.

The first was that I could not exactly help but be open about my sexuality because everyone just knew I was lesbian; the second was that I had the potential to make a lesbian friend here. Finally, I thought about how much I wanted to go down on Suze.

My second thought actually became a reality, and the two of us did become friends; people starting referring to us as Little and Large. Four months after our initial meeting, my last thought came to fruition. We had hung out almost every day since meeting, and I had fallen in love with her, but nothing had happened between us because of Suze's girlfriend. When we went out to a gay club together and I kissed another woman, Suze said she was ill and I ended up taking her home. She admitted her feelings for me, and took my virginity.

After the first night we spent together, we decided we would start going out as a couple. We spent the first week in bed together and were both really happy. Suze told me that she had to end it with her girlfriend back home, and she did so via email because she did not want to be apart from me. The next four months we spent making up for the "wasted" four months when we were just friends. It was an intense relationship. I stopped spending time with my other friends and spent most of my time with my lover. I ended up missing some lectures and deadlines for some coursework. Toward the end of the academic year, Suze's father passed away. I became not only her rock but also supported and comforted Suze's mother and brother. This time came at the expense of my studies, and I failed the first year of my English and Philosophy degree. I was told to re-do the year. Suze managed to pass the year by taking summer classes, because of special circumstances, since her dad had died.

We decided to room together in our second year at the university when dorms were no longer available to us. Now, due to the change of circumstances, we decided to move in with Suze's mother and brother in Gravesend. I got a job at a large chain supermarket as a shelf stacker working the night shift. We took out a loan and bought a black Ford Fiesta to commute to the university. I really settled into the new life, living with my lesbian partner and her family, and working and studying. My repeated first year flew by, and I comfortably passed my classes. We did not really go out much, but I did not really care. The lack of a social life was made up for by the annual Jones family (the mother, the brother and his girlfriend, an uncle and his wife) summer vacation in a few RVs driving around the U.K. My second year went pretty much the same way and was topped off with same summer vacation. We were all happy in the routine.

As I entered the final year of my degree, I wanted to go out more because I wanted to start seeing my friends a bit more away from lectures. After all, it was the last year and we had more money because Suze had gotten a full time job after her graduation. The next six months continued just as the two previous years. I went to all my lectures, worked the night shift, and played happy families with Suze and her relatives. The only change was that Suze was not around as much as she had been. She was doing really well in her new job, and had been given lots of responsibility. To show her how proud I was of her and to actually see something of each other, I bought tickets to the Easter ball at the student union. Suze was not exactly over the moon about the surprise, but went along with it.

I was driving us to the party and talking about what we should do after my graduation. "We could try a vacation other than the U.K. road trip, maybe move out of Gravesend to somewhere more happening."

Suze interrupted me. "I have met someone else."

I was not sure how I managed to stay calm for the next thirty seconds or how I managed to get the car onto the shoulder. There was maybe a split second in which I considered ploughing it into the one in front, but I remained calm. Once the car was stationary, the calmness was gone.

* * * *

"What?" I ask a red-eyed Ben.

She tells me her news through tears. "I just saw my ex with what looked like her latest girlfriend," Ben sighs

"Suze?"

"Yes, Joe, she is my only ex."

"What happened?"

"She came into the cinema and was all touchy-touchy with another woman. I asked, 'What the fuck are you doing here?' She opened her mouth to say something, but I just stormed out of the bar and cinema. I didn't bother waiting for a response, saying bye, or going to the staff room to get my coat and bag. Can you go back and get them for me?"

"Sure. What did you do next?"

"Before I left I could swear that bitch had a smirk on her face. I couldn't look at her and didn't want her to see me cry. So I ran off through the back streets to get to here.

Good job, eh? I am sure the locals didn't want to see the fat dyke from the cinema wobble down the street if I had come via the high street."

"Ben."

"You know what I mean. Anyway, I slowed down when I had put enough distance between me and the bitch. I smoked three cigarettes on my way here."

I can see that she is upset, so I move next to her and give her a big hug. "Do you want to talk more about it?"

"No, not yet, I need to clear my head." Ben turns to the screen. "What happened on Starz last night?"

I know what she is doing so I play along. I tell her how my favorite, a Twink from Manchester with floppy blond hair and the tightest bubble butt I have ever seen sung his little heart out and was amazing. She understands my obsession with the Twink, and this makes her smile at last. I go on to describe how some anorexic Irish twig of a girl forgot her lines and did a "like totally cringelicious" performance and is definitely up for the chop. This amuses her more. From what she has seen of the show so far, she thinks that girl deserves to go, and I quote: "She comes across as stuck up and needs some fanny fun."

Nat joins us, giving us both a kiss on the cheek as he says hello, and then goes to the bar to get a round in. While he is at the bar an older gentleman starts talking to him. Nat is polite and talks to the guy as they both wait for their drinks.

As we are alone, I use the opportunity to get something off my chest. "I know you must be traumatized by seeing the Bone."

"Don't call her that."

"Well, you shouldn't have told me that Susan Jones had such a prominent clitoris. I am still traumatized by the fact. But anyway I need to show you something, as I don't know what to do with the information."

"So you want to pass the buck to me, great."

"This will take your mind off your problems."

"Go on then."

"Don't judge me, but on Sunday of last week, I was bored and hung over after Bobs's and Tim's party and everything, so I was having a bit of a cringe binge and I came across this."

The words fly out of my mouth; I am slightly embarrassed at admitting them. Ben knows that my cringe binge is usually watching porn. Even though she is a lesbian, she once drunkenly admitted to me that she preferred gay male porn over anything with a woman in it. It was not a sexual thing, it was because the guys always looked like they were having fun and really enjoying themselves, but the women in porn always look like they are faking it and just doing a job.

She reaches out her hand and accepts my phone. The site is Gay XTC and the video is already loaded, so all she has to do is hit play. I watch the blue reflection on her glasses flickering away; I have muted the sound but know the images will say enough. I watch her face for signs that show she understands the video. Suddenly, she grimaces, and knows what I know.

"Well, I won't be able to look that one in the eye again, he's a big boy."

She tries to make light of the situation. Even though this sex video of one of her friends is totally unrelated to her problem, it probably makes her question relationships and love.

"What should I do about the video? Should I tell? She is going to be devastated once this video gets out."

Ben is thinking, maybe about her and Suze. She tells me I should say something, as these things always have a way of coming out, especially on the scene, and it is better to know up front. She passes the phone back to me.

Nat rejoins us.

"So who was the silver fox?" My tone may be coming across as slightly jealous. I don't mean it to, it's just I have always been the older man's crumpet.

"Oh, he's Roderick from work, I've told you all about him before. He's just a friend."

"Yeah, sure, another of your long list of friends. Even though he's like a gazillion years older, why don't you give it a go?" I ask.

"Ladies, you might want to tone it down a bit, as the mighty Rod is looking over here." With that, Ben finishes her beer and decides she needs some alone time. She makes her excuses to leave. As she leaves, I give her a hug again and say we can talk later when I get home.

Nat starts to ask me a question, but I interrupt him.

"Look, I don't want to be the group gossip, but there is something I need to show you."

Nat raises his eyebrows in a "go on" sort of way.

"I am not doing this to be malicious," I continue. "I just think the information needs to be out there." I hand Nat the phone.

Nat watches the video. His realization comes a lot quicker than Ben's. He probably recognizes the location first, for anyone who has been in a bathroom at the Phoenix would not fail to recognize it again. Then the all-too-familiar sex act taking place becomes clear. Finally, the distinguished features of someone he knows all too well and a guy he might recall glimpsing once become clear. The color visibly drains from my friend's already pale complexion.

3

HE MAKES AN EXCUSE TO CONTACT YOU

That banging is horrific. At first, I think it is just in my head after another wild night out, but then realize it is someone at the door. I try to open my eyes, but they feel too heavy. I would happily go back to bed, but this caller seems persistent. Suddenly I remember what had happened earlier in the week, and hope it is not the same guy. The memory of that incident causes me to forget how tired I am, open both eyes, and squint over my shoulder. I see my makeshift curtains, sheets taped up over the windows, are still in place. That's good. As I am adjusting to being semi-awake, I glance over to my bedside cabinet where the light from my digital radio shows me objects scattered around; an open packet of condoms (yeah, it was a good night), a bunch of tissues (I need a wastebasket in here), a few used condoms (I really need a wastebasket in here), a tube of Slide (such a great name for lube), the remnants of a line of coke…I lick my finger, run it over what is left and rub it on my gums. There is a home-made foil wrap for my pills—it looks like there is only one left—and a little plastic bottle containing a bit of clear liquid—the GHB is low, as well as the pills..

The thumping at the front door continues, and my eyes finally make their way to the source of the light to seek out the time—8:35 p.m. I had better get up and face whatever music there is to face. Getting out of bed, I notice the guy next to me and place my hand on his big hairy chest and leave it there for a while. My new friend's heartbeat is fine. He's just a heavy sleeper, or really out of it. I start to get a bit aroused, thinking about screwing the guy. I cannot remember much of it, but by looking at the guy's physique and what is on my bedside cabinet, I realize it must have been a good night.

I get out of bed delicately so as not to disturb my new friend. I decide I will wake the Muscle Bear when I want to fuck again, but until then, I will let him sleep. I do not really want to find out about his gym routine, his opinion on the current Starz line-up, which clubs he likes, and blah. Plus, I have to deal with the STD, a little term I just thought up for the Stranger at The Door, a fitting name for an uninvited guest.

I open the top drawer of the cabinet and sweep the contents on top into it. I do not want the Muscle Bear to wake up and scarf the rest of the drugs. Then I proceed to put on some proper clothes; I do not want to get caught short again like earlier in the week. I am going commando and the grey jogging bottoms, even though they are baggy, do not hide the outline of my fully aroused member. I tuck myself into the waistband of the bottoms. I do not think the STD needs to see my cock, especially if it is that brick shithouse again, I want to show that I have paid attention. I grab my hoodie off the floor and leave the bedroom. I finish dressing on the way downstairs, and realize how I have lived in this hoodie this past week, especially whenever I left the house.

Earlier in the week, I had finished a screwing session

with a dancer who was very flexible and who demonstrated this by having sex in whatever position the two of us dreamt up. In terms of stamina, the guy managed to keep up with me, and I was using illegal pharmaceuticals to go all night and morning. The dancer had gone off to have a shower. I put on a pair of boxers and went to the kitchen to get him some food. I did not usually get guys I slept with food or encourage them to hang around, but thought the dancer had earned something.

That morning, there had been a loud whumping at the door; I was expecting the phone/broadband installer. I opened the door, and there before me was a guy who could only be described as a brick shithouse. His clothes told me he was not the service provider. The guy was pissed. I am not usually afraid of anyone or anything, but I felt a sense of trepidation. All at once I realized that I was practically nude.

"Man, I know you must have only just moved in, but put some fucking curtains up!" the shithouse boomed.

"Huh?"

"My eleven- and eight-year-olds don't need sex education in school anymore. They know it all now."

I looked blank.

"They saw you and your boyfriend at it all morning. My wife went into their bedroom to get them when they hadn't come down for breakfast and found them giggling, staring out of the window straight into your bedroom."

I looked past the shithouse and across the road into the house opposite, where a Stepford-wife-looking woman had lifted up the curtains of the kids' room and was looking at us.

I was not about to correct the shithouse by saying my sex partner was not my boyfriend or that it was not my fault the man's children were Peeping Toms. On further reflection, though, I had thought all the stuff those children saw could have been traumatic for young minds. "Oh shit, sorry."

"Man, I don't care what you get up to, just buy some fucking curtains," the shithouse continued ranting.

"Sorry, mate," I apologized again, understanding now why all the gays preferred the sanctuary of the Phoenix.

"And put some clothes on when you answer the door; this is a family street," the shithouse finished.

I watched as the shithouse walked away. The guy moved very rigidly, like a cyborg or something.

This morning, I am just puzzled by the pounding. "I'm coming," I shout at the door. I cannot understand why it would be the shithouse again. I'd put sheets up over the windows until I could find some blinds. I am not going to put up curtains, I am not a granny. For the past week I have been discreet and kept a low profile on the street with my comings and goings. I had, for all intents and purposes, stayed hidden under my hoodie. By way of an apology I'd sent the Stepford wife some flowers, chocolates, and a card. You know, "sorry for everything, hope we can be good neighbors"—signed Jason Vaughan, and all that. So everything should be okay, and the shithouse has nothing to complain about. I brace myself and open the door.

* * * *

Taylor stands at my door with a massive grin and two bottles of wine. I just stare at him, feeling pissed off.

"So, Ricky, aren't you going to invite me?" Taylor asks.

I do not say anything, just open the door wider and stand aside. As Taylor enters the apartment he tries to hug me hello, but I stand with my arms folded. I unwillingly extend my hand, and he shuffles the wine bottles under one arm and shakes it.

"I am visiting your neighbors and wanted to check in on my patient. Plus, I brought a bottle of wine by way of apology for the nose." Taylor beams. "And I want to pick up my jacket."

For some unknown reason this angers me. I do not care about the bloody nose nor did I think Taylor was a complete twat. In fact, it was quite the opposite. We get along well, so I cannot understand why he is riling me. Taylor asks me which wine Carmen would prefer. He will take the other one next door because they are making him dinner. I look at the wines. I prefer red, but Carmen only ever drinks white or rosé. I should have just picked the white, but because of the mood I am in I think I will just pick the most expensive one. I know about wines. Carmen's dad gave us a wine tasting experience one Christmas, mainly something for his daughter to enjoy, but he probably thought it would not hurt her heathen boyfriend to get some manufactured class. Both bottles look expensive based on the names and years, so I just pick the red. I then proceed to open the 2007 Vosne-Romanée, despite a lame attempt on Taylor's part saying to save it for Carmen. As we sit down and start drinking the wine, Taylor talks to me about photography. That gets me thinking back to two weeks ago, when we first met.

After the nosebleed stopped, the doctor had told me,

"We should just sit and wait for twenty minutes to make sure you do not feel faint and that the bleeding has stopped for good."

"Sure."

"This picture on the wall, is it by Carli Hermès? Looks like his style."

"You're joking, right? I took it. I'm really flattered and impressed that you know who Carli Hermès is. Let me show you some more of my pictures."

"Your work is so good. This gay football team I play for is looking for someone to take some promotional pictures for us. Should I link you up?"

"That would be amazing. So you support a team?"

"Eagles fan."

"I have been a Sky Blue fan all my life." We continued chatting for a few hours. Then we realized we'd better get to the party next door.

As Taylor talks now, I find myself becoming engaged. I realize I like this guy as a friend; we have lots in common. I recognize the reason for my earlier hostility—it was annoyance that Taylor had not bothered to check in on me before now, or suggest meeting up. The first night we met he had mentioned that as I was new to the area and did not know anyone else, he would be happy to show me around properly. Then, when Taylor finally does turn up now, it is only because he wants to get his fucking jacket and kill time before his meal next door is ready. I know I am being juvenile and could have contacted him myself because we did exchange phone numbers, but I felt a little bit weird doing that. After all, Taylor is gay. It is not a negative thing, but I know that gay men apparently like to shop, bitch about other people, go clubbing, and then sleep with as many other gay men as possible. I did not want to get in the way of Taylor being able to do those things by having to babysit me.

"Look, Ricky, is everything okay? You seem distracted."

"Yeah. I'm fine. Well, actually my nose still hurts," I lie. "Are you sure there's no permanent damage?" I need an excuse for my behavior and think this is the perfect out.

Taylor seems concerned and puts his hands on my face, examining my nose for any signs of damage. "It doesn't feel like there is anything broken, but if it persists, it would be best to have it properly checked out. When it kept on hurting, why didn't you call me?"

"I know you're busy. I didn't want to bother you."

"Don't be so silly. It would not have been any bother. Actually, I was sort of hoping you would contact me," Taylor replies.

"Yeah?"

Taylor smiles. "Well, some conversation about the state of the world and not what the 'girlfriend' on TV wore last night is always welcome. I would have called, but I didn't want to disturb you and Carmen after your big reunion."

This makes me feel better. I think maybe this guy wants a break from all things gay and wants a straight friend, which would be good for me. I like Taylor, and can definitely do with a local friend. I pour more wine and we talk about photography, football, work, politics, and house prices among other topics. Talking to Taylor is really easy. It isn't like talking to a straight male friend—somehow it is different. Before I know it, the bottle of red is finished.

"I would prefer to continue drinking with you than go to the blind-date dinner party next door."

"More drinks would be good, why don't we start on the white. As you're skipping the dinner anyway they won't miss your 2008 Puligny-Montrachet."

"Okay. I will text them an apology along the lines that an ongoing medical emergency has come up at work."

I proceed to open the bottle of white, and after pouring two large glasses there is a rap at my door.

* * * *

I am in the hallway with a bouquet of flowers. Marco accepts them with a kiss on the cheek and invites me in. I am one of the few people who actually knows where he lives. "I need to pick your brain."

"Always happy to help, Joe," Marco tells me. He settles me down on the sofa with a drink and asks how I am doing. I think some small talk is appropriate, before jumping into the mysterious issue.

I'd met Marco through Bobs and always found him to be kind and approachable. Marco keeps a very select few friends, and I feel slightly honored to be one of them. For that reason I have never tried to be anything more than friends with him even though every ounce of me really wants more. While I crave a relationship, I see what a player Marco is, moving from guy to guy, lying about his name and occupation, and never taking guys back to his own place. I want to be the one who makes him change. Even though we are friends, I feel too ashamed to reveal the secrets of my past to him. Only Bobs and Nat know some sketchy details and that is because they were present at the time—it was harder to lie to co-workers when I needed them to cover for me. While they never judged me, they do not know the full details of my exploits, such as the number of men there were, the type of men, and the fact that I was being paid.

"So, I met this guy at the Common last week and we met up for dinner last night," I lie. I do not want any pity, and hate my friends thinking I am a loser who cannot get laid. I watch Marco carefully to see if he realizes that I am lying, if he is happy for me, or even if he is a bit jealous, but Marco's expression gives nothing away. Instead, he asks all the questions that a friend would: What was the guy's name? Occupation? Where does he work? What does he look like? Are we going to meet up again? He omits asking any intimate questions at this stage. I know that that type of question might come later, so I start to recall some of my more enjoyable one-night stands in case I need to lie more. Then I decide to change the subject and ask Marco if he has seen that cutie he brought to Bobs's party again. I know the chances are slim, as that was nearly two weeks ago, but I think it will be a good distraction. I also think the guy was feminine in his manners like me, and I want to know if Marco would settle with a guy like that.

I get admonished for not going to the club with them that night. Apparently I could have saved Marco from a psycho. Then I hear the details of the rest of the night. Basically, in the taxi to the club, the guy had become very amorous. Marco had gone along with it because they were both very turned on from their earlier swimming pool antics. They'd got into a club in Vauxhall, one of the ones that stayed open all night, which has its own dark rooms, cubicles with glory holes, and an "outside" area inside called Scally Alley.

"Joe, are you sure you want to hear this? I know it's a far cry from the Common."

I just nod my head with a sly grin on my face. What else am I meant to do?

"Well, Richard, I think that was his name, was like a kid in a candy store. He dragged me off to a cubicle and started to go down on me. Then he stopped and wanted me to fuck him down Scally Alley with everyone watching, so we went there. He seemed to get annoyed with the other guys touching us as we made our way down the artificial alley. So, we went to the darkroom and he let me fuck him. Well, I basically just stood against the wall, and he did everything else. Then afterward, I went to find the other guys. Richard was just following me around. I had fucked him twice that evening. He'd had a good time, so I wasn't sure what he wanted. I even bought him drinks in the first bar where we met at the beginning of the night. I had brought him to the Phoenix even though I hate that place, so I was done, but he wouldn't leave me alone. I couldn't talk to anyone else and no other guys could speak to me without him scowling at them. He was a nightmare, very possessive. In the end, I had to tell him to fuck off, and he still tried to get my phone number. Seriously, men are more trouble than they are worth."

I smile. "Women are just as much trouble, my friend, which is why I need your advice." Marco is intrigued and arches an eyebrow to say, "Go on." He does not think that I ever could have any problems with the opposite sex. Women just love me, the effeminate gay guy, as they always know where they stand.

"The problem is with Ben. Her ex-girlfriend the Bone has come back into her life, and I am worried about her and what she will do. Since they met back up, she's become withdrawn and stopped speaking to her friends."

"What is so wrong with her?"

"Ben gave up all her friends and fundamentally her life to be with the Bone and support her family. The Bone made Ben move back into her family home after making her fail the first year of college. They bought a car together, which the whole Bone family used, and Ben had to work night shifts to pay for the car and pay rent and bills to Mrs. Bone. The Bone family took her on all these mundane family holidays and turned her life upside down. Then the Bone cheated on her, kicked her out of her home, and took the car away. The situation just kept getting worse for Ben. It was only after she had moved to Clapham and started working that she managed to get her life back on track, but she still has emotional scars from that relationship. And now the Bone is back to rip them all open again. I am worried that Ben might do something stupid. I don't really know what to advise her to do, apart from kicking the Bone in her lady garden."

"That's what I admire the most about you, the way you care so passionately about your friends. I hope the guy you went on the date with last night treated you right. You deserve happiness, and someone to look after you as well as you look after your friends."

Oh God, let it be you, I pray silently

The intercom bursts into life, which makes me jump a bit and spill some of the wine I am drinking. "Oh pish!" I start to clean up the spillage.

Marco moves over to see who buzzed.

* * * *

As I identify the familiar face and body through the peephole, a nauseous wave rolls across me. How have I been tracked down? The voice from the other side says, "Ben, I heard you come to the door and I can see your shadow under it. Can I come in and speak to you for a few minutes? I am sorry about my earlier behavior. You don't really want me to apologize out here in front of all your neighbors, do you? Ben, please."

The door opens, and Suze walks back into my life for the second time this week. I am not a violent person, but I really do want to hit the bitch. Instead, I tell her she has five minutes to say whatever she has come to say before I kick her out.

"Actually, how the fuck did you find out where I live?"

"I went back to the cinema hoping to see you, and when I did not, I asked around." Suze explains. "I asked five people before getting an address."

"I always knew you were a resourceful cow." I am mildly flattered that she went to so much trouble, but I feel violated and want a description of the colleague to have a go at them for disclosing such information. Somehow, and I am not certain how this happened, Suze has now managed to worm herself into the apartment and is sitting on Joe's "thinking sofa," a psychiatrist-type couch Joe bought, on which he likes to think. In reality, he usually falls asleep on it after watching too much late-night television. I have to cover him up with a spare duvet and leave him to sleep.

"I just wanted to apologize for everything that

57

happened between us. I am sorry that I hurt you. I was a total bitch. I think it was because we got stuck in a rut and the spark went out of our relationship. But I handled the situation badly. I still care for you as a person, so I want to try to be friends," Suze recites her rehearsed speech.

"You want to be fucking friends?" I whisper. The shock of the request leaves me unable to shout, which is what I want to do, but I am shaking and whispering is all I can do. When I manage to compose myself I want Suze to know the full extent of the damage she caused and why I am so pissed off. "On our first night out in ages, while I was driving, you decided to break the news that you are a cheating cow, and nearly caused me to crash the car. Afterwards, we talked on the side of the road for a few hours, and then you casually ripped out my heart by divulging the secrets of your affair. Then you dumped me, telling me it would be for the best if I moved out of your mother's house. That was all I could take. I got out of the car and walked away. You drove off in the car and that was the last time we saw each other until Flicks."

She is looking at me.

"But that was only the start of my misery." I continue the rest of the story, the part she doesn't know. "I had to walk for an hour to find a bus stop, and then when I did, I did not know where to go, so I waited at the bus stop letting the buses go by. Only after my cigarettes ran out did I decide to head to the university. When I got there, I had to try to seek out the few people I knew from my courses, but everyone was at the ball. I had no one to call because all my closest friends—well, people with whom I stayed in contact after you and I got together—had left the university because they had graduated on time. In the end, I had to go to the personal services center, but it was late at night so the building was not open. I spent the night sleeping rough on campus. The next day, I had to bite the bullet and call Martin. Your brother came, picked me up, and I moved in with him and his girlfriend temporarily. When I moved my stuff out of your mother's place and for the month I spent at the brother's place, you were always conveniently absent. You never made any attempt to contact me and see if I was okay."

I continue telling her the painful home truths. "I got through the month at Martin's okay because it was familiar, but once I got a place back at the halls, things started to take a turn for the worse. I tried to settle back into university life and started going out again. I even had two one-night stands, but after each one, I felt low. I realized one-night stands were not for me, and the second one was the last time I had sex. Feeling low spread into all aspects of my life; I could not concentrate on anything or study for my finals, which were rapidly approaching. I found it harder to wake up in the mornings, eat or drink properly, or even sit my exams. I failed the year and had to go to see a university doctor, who diagnosed me with depression. For the second time in my studies, I had to repeat my courses. When I entered my fifth year, I was older than the majority of the other third-year students in my class by two years. I did not have any friends left at the university, and I was on antidepressants. I had to go to regular counseling sessions. I was off sex, I did not trust women, and I felt my life had no meaning."

When I finish explaining what my life had been like and

why I did not want to be friends, I break down. Suze tries to comfort me by putting her arm around me. I push the arm off and tell her to leave.

"Ben, don't be like this, I'm sorry."

This is the last straw for me. I cannot control myself and swing my hand to slap Suze. I connect with Suze's face, but with just my fingertips. It is my first time hitting another person, but it can barely be described as a slap. After the half-slap, Suze grabs my wrist, pulls me toward her, and starts to kiss me passionately.

4

HE GIVES HIMSELF AWAY BY HIS BATHROOM BEHAVIOR

What starts as a light drizzle soon turns into a heavy downpour, which probably means an end to the Indian summer that London has been experiencing. This lack of sunshine and hot temperatures will definitely bring an end to the pounds of flesh, ripped muscles, defined stomachs, and short-shorts to which the Common has been host. Of course, there are always the few diehards who will not let the cold dampen their immodesty. Generally though, the all-day voyeurism of the male form has come to an end until the first glint of sunshine in the spring of next year. These exhibitions of skin will now move inside and be reserved for nighttime in the clubs.

I am witnessing the weather from Marco's terrace. After cleaning up the spilt drink, I had moved to the sheltered outside to get some fresh air. I see the brilliance of everything glowing as a bolt of lightning illuminates the sky, and surrounding area like the flash from a camera. In that brief moment of light I imagine the Common soaking up all the nourishing water instead of the usual fluids it has received over the long summer.

Marco makes his way back inside the apartment after collecting the goods from the teenage delivery boy in his building lobby. He never has any delivery people come to his front door; he never actually gives them his address. He tells them the building address and to wait in the lobby, then the concierge buzzes him down. It is an arrangement that works well for him and all the staff in the building, as he always takes care of them. Talk about paranoia.

I go back inside.

"You know the way to a man's heart is through his stomach."

Marco puts the Thai take-out he ordered down on the table, and pinches my stomach. "You don't have one, Joe. I feel the need to feed you before you waste away."

"Aren't you meant to dazzle me with your fantastic Italian culinary skills and not order take-out?" I say giddily, trying to recover from the touch and play it cool.

"Don't stereotype! Anyway, as I'm only half Italian, you would end up with fish and chips on a pizza."

"Fizza, lovely."

"Isn't the way to a man's heart being great in the kitchen and the bedroom? So after the Fizza, we would have to do the other thing." Marco beams.

I pray that he cannot hear my heart, which is beating really fast and loud.

"Should we go and take this food over to Ben then?" Marco asks.

Damn, I think—I forget that I had actually come over here for a reason, which is not about me and Marco. The moment Marco mentioned the bedroom, I was all for stripping off and going to show him that, while I can't cook, I am an expert in that room. Even though it is raining outside, the romantic in me thinks it will be nice to walk. "Come on then, let's go and Resbian."

"Joe, you know I don't speak gay."

"Rescue the lesbian. I just made that one up. Maybe I should trademark it and start my own business where I rescue lesbians from fucked-up exes, crimes against fashion, and moving in with someone they just met. I could even give half of the profits to a cat sanctuary, for all the cats not adopted after the lesbians stop their too-soon co-habiting ways."

* * * *

My hand is in Suze's pants and I am busy working a few fingers. In between gasping with pleasure, Suze is kissing me, her hand is up my t-shirt, and she is caressing my breasts. We roll off Joe's couch when we start rubbing against each other after the first kiss, and the burning desire means we do not bother going to the bedroom, but continue where we are. We proceed to remove all our clothes and I start to fuck Suze on the living room floor.

* * * *

I open the door to Tim, who is standing there looking distraught. He tells me that I have to come right away to save his disaster of a night. Tim glances down at the glass of wine in my hand. I might be slightly buzzed. Instead of making his excuses for interrupting me, he flounces into the apartment. I am taken aback by this, but should not really be surprised because in the two weeks I have known Tim I have learned that he has no interpersonal boundaries.

"Carmen is away visiting her folks," I say, hoping to stop Tim going further into the apartment and finding I have stolen his guest.

"Yes, Ricky, I know, she told me," Tim says, making his way into the living room. He surveys the room, sees no evidence of anyone else, and seems to get less testy with me. "Oh, darling, if you were bored you should have said so. You're always welcome at our place. There's no point in drinking all by yourself. You must come over to ours right away. We are having a small dinner party, and it's become a disaster because three of the guests have cancelled." He starts ushering me to my own front door. "Don't look so hurt, my dear, we were always going to have you over, we were just waiting to set a date with Carmen."

I am about to make another attempt not to go to the dinner party, saying that I have already eaten, but the first bottle of wine must have slowed my senses and Tim prattles on before I can get the line in. "Well, we were trying to set Taylor up with a colleague of Bobs's. The colleague is at our place now but Taylor cancelled, and then my friends Skinny and Skinnier were meant to be coming but they have had a little falling out, so we don't want this guy to think we lured him here to be untoward." At hearing the T-word, I realize Taylor has disappeared and wonder where he has gone. I decide the only way I will get out of going to the dinner party is to actually go and then make a quick exit.

"Tim, you know what? I'd love to come over. Give me five minutes to get ready," I tell him. Tim seems relieved. His shoulders drop and he exhales, then he snatches the open bottle of wine from the kitchen to add an extra incentive for me to go over. After getting a definite promise that I will be over in five, Tim leaves.

* * * *

"Sorry Tim is so highly strung tonight; it must be the

weather, and he's upset that his friends aren't going to be able to make it. He's not usually like this," I lie to my work colleague. I know Tim always gets panicked when we entertain, but I can't understand why, it is not like he has a job. What is so difficult about cooking some food, going to get some decent drinks, tidying up a bit (we already have a cleaner, so all he has to do is a bit of touching up), and just making sure everything runs smoothly? I know that Tim should be well-practiced, as we have hosted so many gatherings. It is expected of us, living where we do, but on each occasion I have to step in to micro-manage the situation, and for bigger parties, I have to get extra hands in to help. It was not always like this. In the beginning, Tim was so organized. I am not sure if he has become lazy, stupid with age, or just complacent. I do not want Tim to make a hissy scene in front of my special colleague. So, I make a mental note to look into this situation and have a talk with him later tonight. I smile as Tim comes back into the apartment, to put him at ease.

* * * *

I look for Taylor in my bedroom. It happens to be the first room I go to, and not a decision made by any sort of rational choice. Taylor is not in here. I move on to the bathroom. As I open the door, Taylor is standing there taking a piss. He is not one of those guys who takes his member out of the little slit in the boxers, he has pulled his pants and jeans down and lets it all hang. I am embarrassed walking in on him, but Taylor just turns to me with a smile and says that he never thought Tim would leave, and he was bursting to go after all that wine. There is no shame on Taylor's part, so I try to act cool and not leave the way I would have done if it was another friend. Taylor finishes peeing and shakes himself off. I am not actually sure where to look, as movement tends to draw one's eyes.

Taylor is obviously used to deception and hiding in toilets, because he'd brought the empty bottle of wine and his glass in with him. When I notice them, I comment on the good save. Taylor jokes that if he had been caught in the lie, he would probably be ostracized from their lives and would have to move to a different country, because no other gay in the area would speak to him once the GIT (gay hit) had been put out.

"Maybe being ostracized from the gay community would be a good thing, and I should go next door, confess all, and then there'd be no more of these stupid dinner parties."

"Yeah, do it."

"I'll miss all the sex though."

This new life is strange, yet familiar. This culture is similar to that of Cambridge—throwing dinner parties, caring about matching guests and everything, but I have never participated in them. Maybe my lack of interest is a throwback to my friends in the Midlands who never have dinner parties and if they did, wouldn't really care if the numbers were uneven. But I am in Carmen's world now and I should assimilate. Taylor is already one step ahead of me; he texts next door to say his work crisis is over and he is on his way. He hugs me in camaraderie and tells me to be strong. He will follow me over in about twenty minutes.

* * * *

Nat is at the gate with his back to the door when I call

his name.

"I just popped around to make sure you were still alive, Jas, as you haven't been answering your phone and no one has heard from you."

"You know me and what an enigma I am," I tell him. "Anyway, would anyone care if I'm not around?"

"Fuck you, you selfish pig," Nat shouts at me. With his free hand he playfully punches me on the bicep.

"So are you going to come in out of the rain and see my new digs?" I ask, rubbing my arm.

On the guided tour, I tell Nat all the furniture I plan to get. I then explain about the brick shithouse and how I was scared it was him at the door again.

"You know you should be more discreet. It wouldn't go amiss, and you don't want trouble from your neighbors. Speaking of your exhibitionism, I saw your sex tape from the bathroom in Bobs's and Tim's place."

"I guess all the guys know then, that's why the number of hits increased. What did you think?"

"I didn't come here to critique your performance. I just wanted to say that you need to be careful having videos of you like that on the Internet. What if a family member, potential employer, or future boyfriend saw that clip?"

"Look, it was just a bit of fun, and I actually never gave my permission for them to film or upload it, but it's done now and will be forgotten soon. At any rate, if my mom, dad, sister, or little niece start browsing Gay XTC then I have full respect for them for trying to understand me better. I work for myself, and if my Cow saw the video, I would probably get more lucrative deals. As for any future boyfriend, well, I don't do relationships. Anyway, since when did you become so prudish? Dude, when did you last get laid?"

Nat decides not to answer the question, "You know you look like shit. Maybe some food will help you. I brought you groceries as a housewarming gift."

"You are a great friend, sorry." The truth is, I am embarrassed by the video but didn't want to admit it aloud.

* * * *

I am introduced to Bobs's work colleague, Michael, but do not really listen to anything he has to say. Instead, I try to picture him with Taylor. Somehow, I cannot see it. The guy seems boring and not interested in the things which Taylor has shown enthusiasm for. In fact, from the vibe Mike is giving off, I take an instant dislike to him. Tim is being ultra-attentive, topping up everyone's drinks and announcing that we will eat as soon as Taylor arrives. I note even the mention of his supposed blind date turning up does not seem to rouse Mike.

I become conscious that I have not seen much of Bobs and only know the stuff that Carmen has told me about the man. I use this opportunity to try to get to know him better. Plus, I do not really want to talk to the dull fish, Mike. I gauge that Bobs is like Carmen to some extent; they are both extremely driven, pursuing their well-respected professional degrees even though they do not have to because they both have mountains of family wealth. The motivated quality in Carmen is attractive; in Bobs, it is mildly compulsive.

* * * *

"The table looks lovely, Tim," Taylor tells me once I have seated him next to Mike. He surveys the crisp white linen cloth, red and white wine glasses, a whole canteen of 18/10 stainless steel cutlery, flowers, and candles set upon it. The other guests join in with their approval.

"Well, I hope the food lives up to the expectations," I say expectantly.

"I am sure it will, honey."

As we tuck into the starter, a timbale of crab and avocado, Mike seems to come to life a bit more and starts bombarding the table with anecdotes. Taylor is playing the part of someone interested and is umming and ahhing in all the right places. Ricky is concentrating on the white wine I have poured and is not listening. Bobs is playing with his food. I hope he does not think that the avocado could have been a bit softer; the firmness has lent itself to the dish maintaining its shape. I am giggling along with the stories but thinking about the next course.

* * * *

As we are walking down the street to my place, Marco is holding the umbrella while I hold the take-out and dream we look like a couple. I notice the looks we get from other people at the bus shelter and outside bars where they huddle over a cigarette. The looks from straight men say to Marco, "Bro, why are you hanging out with that queen?" The looks from women say to him, "You are a ten, fuck me now." The looks from gay men say to me, "Yeah right, dream on." For someone so astute, Marco seems either oblivious to all these looks or he does not care. I hope it is the latter. With everything that was said and done earlier, especially the flirting, I think maybe now is the time to come clean and tell Marco all about my past so we can have a future. My heart starts to beat really fast again. I should have a cigarette to calm myself down, but I never smoke in front of him—that urge is filled by other desires.

"You know your darkroom-stalker story, well, it got me thinking to some of my past indiscretions," I say nervously.

"Joe, you know you don't have to tell me anything you don't want to, but whatever you did, nothing will change my opinion of you."

Damn you for being way too understanding, I think. *It is decision time for me—bite the bullet now or forever hold my peace.*

"Well, you know how a lady never tells, but I guess I owe you a story by now. Remember that guy I met last week in the Common I told you about? When we first met, we were both drunk, and it was a case of hands all over each other. We couldn't wait to go home together. Well, we went into one of the cubicles and had sex. Seriously, I felt like a newbie gay doing toilet-sex at my age. I think we were really loud because a bouncer started banging on the door, and we never got to finish. I had to pretend I was feeling ill and my friend was helping me. Then, we proceeded to get kicked out of the club, so I can't go back until they forget about it."

Marco laughs at the story, puts his arm around my shoulder, and says "I hope the guy was worth it. I know you love the Common. Look, we're here now, time to start 'Operation Resbian.' You know if you get caught in the toilet again and a bouncer is banging on the door you can always call me to 'gayscue' you."

"You made your first gayism; there's hope for you yet." I try to make light of the situation, because with him touching me I feel ecstatic but cannot let him know how I feel. I cannot handle rejection from him. Everyone else is fine, but not him.

* * * *

I disappear from the kitchen where Nat has decided to make me dinner, and sneak back into the bedroom. The Muscle Bear is still asleep, which is good. I think a little pick-me-up is in order until I can go back to sleep. I open my top drawer and grab the little bottle and go to the toilet where I neck the last remains of the GHB. I don't have an appetite, but I don't have the heart to tell Nat that, because the food smells so nice. I will pretend to eat something. Nat has cooked us some big fat steaks and homemade chips served with bagged salad.

"This looks awesome."

We are about to eat when the door opens and the Muscle Bear enters the kitchen. "I thought I smelled food," he says gruffly, taking a seat.

I push my plate over to the interloper and catch a look of disgust on Nat's face. I should have told Nat I had company, but it had not seemed relevant at the time. Then my train of thought goes to pieces. I cannot help myself, and spout out drug-fueled verbal diarrhea. I'm vaguely aware that Nat has to take a call and then has to leave suddenly for an emergency. The Muscle Bear finishes off both dinners. The next thing I am aware of is the pleasure of the drug mixed with the pleasure of the Muscle Bear fucking me on the kitchen table.

* * * *

Taylor is regaling us with one of his worst doctor moment stories. He was in the Common recently and was at the bar chatting with a girl from work when this guy started cruising him, saddling up close to them. Later on that night Taylor was dancing with the group of girls from work—they were out celebrating one woman's engagement—when Taylor went to the bathroom. Ricky makes a face at this story; maybe we are subjecting him to too much gay.

"So anyway, this guy followed me into the toilets, and before I knew it, we were in a cubicle together. I went along with it because he was cute and I was drunk. He said he heard me say I was a doctor, so I thought he had a medic fantasy he was about to fulfill. There was no kissing or foreplay or anything, he just dropped his pants. Now I am all for seeing a nice erect penis, but this one was flaccid, red, and oozing. He'd had a Prince Albert done, and it was infected."

"Well, that's turned me off my pork." Bobs smiles, puts down his knife and fork, and stops eating the main course—pork belly with celeriac purée, cider and calvados jus. The story isn't that bad; he could have finished the meal I made.

"So what happened next?" Mike pipes up.

"Looking at it just sobered me up. I wasn't about to touch it, but I advised him to go and see his regular doctor. And that is my worst doctor story because I was totally unprepared for it and thought something else was going to happen," Taylor finishes.

"What about when you nearly killed me with the door and gave me medical attention afterward?" Ricky adds.

* * * *

"I have food," I shout into the apartment as I open the

door. Ben is sitting on my thinking chair, a place she never sits, wearing a lot less clothing than she normally does and looking really flushed. The moment I see her I know that something is up. When I see the remainder of her clothes chucked around the room, it starts to dawn on me. I hear a noise from the bathroom. "We came here to cheer you up, but I can see that you are okay after all. Marco, let's go back to your place to eat, and leave Ben with her friend."

Marco heads for the door. I am very happy for Ben and jump up and down on the spot and do a little clap. Before I head for the door, I go over to kiss her on the cheek. As I turn to leave, a giant emerges.

"Sorry for disturbing you gals, we are just going," I say and make for the door thinking, *Christ, she likes them tall.* The words seems to trigger something in my head. Before I get to the door, I spin around to have a closer look at the giant, "the Bone." I'd seen pictures of her on Ben's computer on many a drunken night in. I had tried to make Ben delete them all, and she definitely culled a lot, but kept some back. This is my first time having the displeasure of meeting the Bone face-to-face. I lunge at the evil-ex, because of all the pain she has caused my best friend. Marco holds me back. I'm not sure what I would do if I reach her—she would probably swat me away like a fly.

"Joe," Ben snaps, as she is starting to put more clothes on.

"Arghhh, get that thing out of my apartment."

"It's our apartment, we both pay the rent. I have never been this rude to any of your guests before, so how dare you speak to one of my friends like that?"

"Look, Joe, we can come back later," Marco says,

trying to diffuse the situation.

"None of my friends ever ripped out my heart, ate it in front of my face while the last dregs of blood spewed out the hole in my chest, and then punched me in the face with the uneaten portion just for good measure."

"What about him next to you?" Ben screams back at me.

"You fucking bitch," I shriek and lob the bag of Thai food at her; it misses the intended target and hits Suze.

Ben and I look around simultaneously, see the mess, realize what we have both said, and start to cry.

* * * *

Everyone finishes off their baked vanilla cheesecake with blueberry compote. The night is coming to an end. Bobs takes Ricky aside to get his advice on a picture while I clear the table, leaving Mike and Taylor alone, but I listen.

"This was fun," Taylor says, and Mike agrees. They swap numbers and agree to meet up sometime. As they say goodbye, they kiss each other lightly on the lips.

Bobs escorts Mike out because they have some work to discuss for a big meeting coming up. Ricky proceeds to drain his glass and get more wasted, but I have caught him up in that department by knocking them back after the main course was served. I am asking for feedback—well, reassurance—on the dinner. Ricky slurs that it was really nice and goes to top up his drink, but the bottle is empty. This prompts me to jump up and get the after-dinner brandy; I'd forgotten to get it when all the guests were present. While getting the bottle, I shout to him, asking if Taylor likes Mike.

Ricky adds, "Oooh, Taylor's new boyfriend," and bursts out laughing.

I return with the bottle and starting laughing too. "Taylor, would you like a nightcap?"

"It's all right for housewives to get drunk on a Thursday night, but I have patients to see tomorrow."

When Bobs returns, I pose the question again, which Taylor again avoids answering by saying he has to go because he has an early start tomorrow.

Taylor asks Ricky if he can collect the jacket he left behind on nosebleed night, so he leaves too.

* * * *

"How come we keep ending up in the bathroom together?" I joke as we collect his jacket from where Taylor had hidden it earlier that night. "You know, women go to the bathroom together, that's like us now." I wave my hand between myself and Taylor. "Maybe I should show you my Prince Albert."

"I don't believe you have a Prince Albert," Taylor says in disbelief. I move my hands to my belt and slowly undo it, then open my top jeans button, all the time looking Taylor in the eye. I start to undo the rest of the buttons when the left side of my jeans start glowing and emitting a noise.

I answer the phone to say my good night to Carmen. Taylor picks up his jacket, back-slap hugs me goodbye, and motions that he will call me.

* * * *

"I think the evening went really well considering two of our friends didn't even show up."

"You mean your friends did not turn up. Do you think

Mike and Taylor liked each other?" Bobs asks, but he does not wait for an answer. Instead, he smiles and says, "Come to bed. I want to show you my appreciation for all your effort tonight."

"I'm a bit tired. You can show me in the morning or on the weekend. Plus, I still have some tidying up to do."

Bobs just continues to smile at me, takes my hand, and leads me to the bedroom. After minimal kissing and cuddling, Bobs is fucking me doggy style. I am loving it, screaming my head off in ecstasy, and begging for it harder. As Bobs is fucking me, he suddenly withdraws his cock, causing me to gasp. A wetness appears on my back. I turn over, thinking my lover is done after feeling his hot juices on my back, but Bobs cums all over my face. The cum covers my eyes, nose, and ears.

"What was that?" I ask as cum dribbles down onto my mouth.

"A Houdini, you know we always talked about doing it in the past," Bobs replies.

I cannot remember having that conversation but do not want to bring it up now, because I am drunk and could be wrong. Bobs kisses the top of my head, a part with no cum on it, and tells me, "You can finish the cleaning now." He gets under the covers and goes to sleep.

I silently get up and go to the main bathroom, not the en suite. I sit on the toilet, wiping the now-cold cum off my face, which has started to mix with hot tears.

5

HE SMELLS

'Twas the twelfth day of Christmas,
And the fairy gave the gays
Twelve sets of balls drumming,
Eleven man-whores piping,
Ten jocks a-leaping,
Nine disco bunnies dancing,
Eight wank circlers a-milking,
Seven femmes a-trimming,
Six geezers a-chaving,
Five cock rings,
Four muscle bears,
Three fumbling men,
Two twinky loves,
And a confused straight man.

As Miss Luscious Bush finishes her song, the bar erupts into applause. She announces there will be a short break before she continues with more festive stories and songs.

"I can't believe it's nearly Christmas. I mean, where did the year go?" Rod passes me a drink. I cannot believe I am in a bar in north London, as I do not tend to venture past central London when going out, listening to a drag queen—I do not really like cabaret—with the old guy from my work (I do not like him in that way).

When Rod first approached me in Twilight over three months ago he said that he never knew I was gay, and we had chatted a bit about work. The conversation ended with him asking me out. I declined. That was the night Joe showed me the clip of Jas being noshed off by some random guy he'd brought to Bobs's party, then fucking that guy while some other guy filmed it. That night, in the privacy of my own bedroom, I watched the video over and over again, and before I went to bed, masturbated several times until I started feeling slightly raw and had no more semen left. The next day at work I was feeling tired and mildly depressed when Rod popped over to my desk to say that there were no hard feelings, and that he hoped that we could be friends. I agreed it would be nice if we could be buddies, which opened the door for me to receive casual chatty emails from Rod.

I spent the beginning of that week trying to contact Jas, but was unsuccessful. Eventually, I visited Jas later in the week and saw that he was too hung up on sleeping around, going out nearly every night, and doing drugs. Jas did not care about the things I did, like wanting to be in a relationship, but then Jas was younger. Maybe I had unrealistic expectations of a gay man in his early twenties. I'd tried to speak about all these issues with Joe and Bobs, but neither had been available. Joe was dealing with house hunting, and his old roommate Ben, whom he was fighting with, was also unavailable to talk. However, I would not have spoken to her about this matter because she did not get the nuances of gay men as well as an actual gay man can. Bobs was ultra-busy at work since his promotion and had not been sociable at all. Bobs had never been a club-whore, since he'd started seeing Tim at a very young age. They preferred to stay in and do things like a married couple. To a certain extent, I am jealous of what this dream couple have together, as that is what I want. I had considered going around to speak to Tim, but that would feel weird without Bobs around. I have known Tim for seven years, since Bobs and he first got together, and while Tim seemed not to be cold, he definitely kept some sort of distance between himself and Bobs's friends.

After I walked away from Jas's place, I had found myself talking over my feelings with Rod. This gentleman had a maturity about him which I find reassuring, and he seemed to know something about unrequited love. It was our initial lunch together that I appreciated the most because that stopped me from going to "that dark place" which I had visited before in my life. After seeing I was not going to be with Jas, and not having any friends with whom I could talk, I felt myself being drawn back to the darkness, but Rod saved me by just being there and listening. Our lunches became a regular activity. On top of the daily emails and weekly lunches, after a while, going out for a few post-work drinks with other colleagues was introduced to our developing relationship.

* * * *

I am meeting up with Skinny and Skinnier to have a Christmas lunch with friends. They are still together; their fight was not as big as Bobs had said. Skinny and Skinnier are always fighting; even the straights have their problems. Bobs and I normally celebrate our Christmas before the actual day, as I go back to Newcastle to spend the holiday with my mother and stepfather while Bobs plans to stay in

London and have the real Christmas day in the company of his parents, "Lord and Lady" Ashton. I think of them as Lord and Lady, even though they are just rich, because they are the epitome of snobs. They do not mind that Bobs is gay. In fact, gin-swilling Lady Ashton has even said she preferred having a gay son. However, they do not like the "country bumpkin" their golden boy has picked up. I'd tried to wrangle an invite many a year even though it would have been a terrible way for me to spend Christmas. I just want to be with my partner, but Bobs has never challenged his parents to get me the invite. Of course, Bobs could join my family up north where he is always welcome, but he would not dream of leaving the Lord and Lady on a "family" occasion. Our relationship is not perfect, but no one's is.

Before the lunch with the "manorexic" couple, I had done a bit of Christmas shopping with Carmen. She was alone for the day, as Ricky was on a job. I got the impression she wanted to off-load on someone. She told me the first night Ricky officially moved into Nightingale Hall was just how she imagined it. He had wanted her. He had been attentive and gave her an amazingly thoughtful gift. Then, after the first night, he had become disengaged and moody, and she'd worried that he regretted moving in. She had tried to speak to him about it, but he said he was fine and was just settling in. At this point, I felt the need to ask her if they were at it like rabbits. Carmen admitted the truth to me. She said that since the first night, it was practically non-existent, then after about two weeks, he had reverted to his normal self.

"So what changed?"

She explained that he might have been slightly depressed living at her place with no steady income and no real friends with whom he could go out. Then he and Taylor became friends, and they started hanging out.

I raised my eyebrows. "Oh yeah."

Carmen giggled and told me it was not like that. "They go to football matches together, watch sports on TV, play computer games, drink beer, you know, guy stuff."

The guy stuff Bobs and I do is totally different. "So having a friend got him out of his slump then?" As I asked the question, I started looking forward to seeing Skinny and Skinnier.

"Plus, his work has started to take off, which is what made the real difference. I know you won't tell anyone—I got him his first few jobs because I asked my father to see if any of his friends needed a photographer. I have nothing to do with today's job, but I have been secretly supportive by giving him that initial push and letting the world see how great he is."

As we sit down to Christmas lunch and wait for the rest of the party to join us, Carmen mentions the stranger from earlier. "That guy. I was gobsmacked."

"Me too, he was beautiful. It wasn't just us; as he passed by, he left a trail of eyes following him. Nearly everyone in the shop was lost in his smoldering good looks. He was the quintessence of tall, dark, and handsome."

"He winked at you."

"At us."

"He was too good-looking to be straight, plus with your guns everyone looks at you."

"Are you kidding, sista'? It was definitely at you. When he walked by I couldn't smell him."

"Eh?"

"You know, I couldn't sniff him out, and I did try."

"Tim, you have lost me. You can smell if someone is gay?"

"Yes, quite literally. Gay men, when out and about, always wear too much aftershave, deodorant, or perfumed soap, unlike a straight man, who wears any sort of olfactory delight in a minuscule way, if any. Test it out on our lunch guinea pigs."

I proclaim my hypothesis when my friends join us. As Carmen greet the guys, she takes a whiff, and, sure enough, can distinctively smell pleasant odors. She bursts out laughing and congratulates me on my flawless generalization of every gay man. The guys nod in agreement but then start adding the caveats.

"Well, the problem is this generation's metrosexual men, who like to confuse us all by dressing too well, smelling too good, and breaking all the rules we set for straight guys to tell them apart from us. You would not believe the amount of guys I have approached thinking they were one of us only to be told..." Skinny sees the look of shock on his partner's face. "Not that I was a complete slag or anything. Love you, darling."

Skinnier does not mind, but wants to wade into the debate. "You also have the opposite problem of the next generation of gay guys who want to be less effeminate and prefer just to smell of sweat and natural scents, and don't even get me started on the geographical thing. Certain countries and certain regions all have their own rules."

Before he gets the chance to elaborate on this political minefield and further clarify the situation to Carmen, the waiter comes to take our order.

I start. "I'll have the Christmas dinner with all the trimmings."

After everyone else orders, all different meals, Skinny asks, "How could you eat a turkey dinner now when you have to eat the big one in a week's time?"

Carmen agrees. "At all the Christmas parties and events I avoid anything remotely similar to what would be served on Christmas Day."

I think it better not mention that I am due to have another Christmas meal tonight with Bobs, and that I am actually using this one to make sure I perfect everything for tonight. I'm trying to memorize precisely the presentation, taste, and even the smell of the food, as for lunch I had wanted a trial Christmas dinner that I could replicate for myself and Bobs. I believe that I will manage to successfully duplicate and improve on the dining experience.

* * * *

The past few months have been busy for me. I have sufficient work to get by, and can afford to pay the rent, albeit low for where I am living. I'd insisted Carmen take the money mainly to shut her father up. The work had started off as mainly corporate events, and from those came fancy parties. Now I am "sort of" doing my second wedding—"sort of" because I am not the main photographer. A friend of Taylor's wants a second photographer to take pictures of her friends in a more natural way, not the official, more formal way. I would have probably turned something like this down so as not to play second fiddle—most photographers only take a job if they are the only professional on site—but I thought I could spend the day goofing around with Taylor, and Taylor had practically begged me to take the job because he would be the only single person there and wanted another person around with whom he could hang out.

This wedding is pretty routine, and I am bored by the time the ceremony finishes. While weddings are the bread and butter of a photographer, once I am more established, I think I will stop doing them. Luckily, I do not have to wear my "must be nice and professional" hat, as I don't have to ask people to smile and pose. Nor do I have to interact with the guests, as I am meant to catch them in natural acts and get lots of scenery shots. As I continue my photographic duties, I seek out Taylor because he is someone I know here. Taylor tells me that this is the wedding of a friend of his from work, and while he liked his colleagues, he tended not to hang out with them on social occasions unless it was a special event and he feels obliged. I note that this is true because earlier I'd caught some animosity between Taylor and some other doctor with whom he worked.

That's why he likes hanging out with me, because we get along so well. Taylor is good for my work and my morale. He'd had me take pictures of the gay football team on which he played. I like varying my work, and the action shots I took for the team's website are a good example of my work. Plus, the subjects are livelier than blue-rinse grandmothers at weddings.

Sweeping the camera around, I see Taylor with the

bride. They are too far off for me to capture the moment, so I move on.

* * * *

"You're such a good friend. It's an unusual gift, but thanks, Taylor" the bride tells me.

I give her a congratulatory hug and whisper in her ear. "No worries, babes, but remember our arrangement. If Ricky should ask you, you wanted a second wedding photographer and checked out the pictures on his website after I recommended him. He must not know that I am not paying for this."

* * * *

At the work Christmas party two weeks ago, Rod had been quite drunk and more suggestive than usual. It got to the stage where he was actually slobbering on me, and I had to use all my willpower not to be very rude. Eventually, to stop him, I had to remind him that I did not want to be out at work. Then Rod had asked me outright if we could just go out together, not with others from work nor for a rushed lunch. I'd remembered what it felt like to like someone and not have those feelings returned, and how kind Rod had been when I had been so down. I knew the man liked me, but for my part, there was nothing sexual going on and no feelings beyond friendship. So, I decided to let him down gently. I could not be mean and just say no, so I ended up agreeing to this date as friends. I added that qualifier on acceptance.

This evening I am having a good time and enjoying Rod's company. After all, we are sort of friends, and when he is not trying to take the friendship further, we get along really well. I just hope I am not giving mixed signals.

On my round, I get myself soft drinks; I do not want to get too drunk and allow Rod to try to take advantage. I know it is mean to think of Rod as a lecherous old man, and I honestly do not see him as that, but I know that is how others will see us. I come back from the toilet thinking the smoking ban is a bad thing in a place this dingy, as the odor of smoke used to hide the smell of a skanky gay bar—shit, sweat, and sex.

My thoughts are interrupted as Rod accosts me. "I am having such a good time. Can we go out again?" I don't have the heart to say no; I can smell the desperation on Rod. "Sure, but just as friends." I realize this will keep happening, since Rod is nothing if not relentless. I need to diplomatically stop this pursuit somehow. An idea comes to me, which is not wholly a lie. "Look Rod, there is something I need to tell you. Even though we are just friends, I get the feeling that you may want to take things further, but I have a very low sex drive and am just not into it that much. So if things were to ever proceed further between us, which I am not saying they will, but if they were, I think that you should know it would never be sexual."

I look at a totally baffled Rod, who seems surprised at this curveball. I have accomplished my goal without hurting his feelings, planting a seed which will hopefully grow and ensure that Rod and I remain nothing more than friends. For my part, it is not a blatant lie. I don't like random hook-up sex or one-night stands, and I am not a very sexual person with someone I am not in love with.

* * * *

"Aren't you enjoying your food?" Bobs asks me. I

guess I am playing with the food. I am on my second Christmas dinner of the day. I lie that I am really enjoying it and start to eat with more gusto.

"You should be enjoying it, it's really good," Bobs says appreciatively.

As we are finishing the meal, I seriously consider going to the bathroom to purge myself, as I feel so full. I am not worried about gaining weight as I have ramped up my gym routine with Christmas coming, because I do not want to get fat so that Bobs will find me unattractive. Eventually I swallow it all and am happy that Bobs likes it.

Bobs starts getting amorous, kissing my neck, stroking my arms; however, being stuffed, the last thing I feel like is sex. Luckily for me, Bobs leads me to the tree in the living room, not into the bedroom.

"Lets exchange gifts. So this first present, you don't need it but I thought it would be fun for you."

I open the card and a voucher for cookery lessons fall out, I am surprised but happy. It is a practical gift, and as Bobs said. "It will be fun learning from an expert. Here is the first of the presents I got for you." I think back to the list that he had given me a month ago. I wonder if he will be surprised by the items I chose from said list. It should not really be a surprise, though; Bobs gives me my money, so he knows which of the items I can afford for him.

The second present I receive is a large rectangular box. I like the look of this one; it is more fun to unwrap a gift than to receive an envelope. Bobs is beaming away as he watches me unwrap the rather large dildo. The surprise I felt when I opened the first gift is nothing compared to the surprise I feel now.

"I thought you were ready to upgrade from Gilbert," Bobs adds.

"Thanks, sweetness, but this looks way too big." I am flabbergasted, I am not really a fan of using our current dildo, Gilbert.

"It will be fun. I'm getting hard thinking about it," Bobs responds, tearing into his second present.

I open my last present, which is another card with two tickets to Amsterdam over New Year's Eve. Before I can say anything Bobs tells me proudly, "I know I have been working really hard lately, so I thought it would be nice if we went away and had some 'us time.'"

I like the idea, but I had been looking forward to going to Skinny and Skinnier's New Year's Eve house party. "What about the New Year's Eve party at Sam and Mitch's?"

"Oh, I thought you would prefer us to go away together as a couple." He sounds hurt.

"Yes, of course, maybe we can take Gilbert II with us," I quickly respond, and give Bobs his last present. This one will be a surprise for him, as I had saved up from the housekeeping money I receive to get him an off-beat present. As Bobs opens the gift, his face lights up. It is something he likes but would not have thought about asking for.

"I love you so much," he tells me, and starts to undress me. I am about to say that I am not really in the mood but I stop when I see how excited my lover is; I want to please him. During thelovemaking, Bobs withdraws from me and for some weird reason starts lubing me up more.

"You have an excellent ass. It is so toned and firm."

Then, he reaches for Gilbert II and starts to play with it around my ass.

I realize where this is going and really do not want to be stretched further tonight. "I thought we were going to save that for Amsterdam."

Bobs unscrews the top of a little black bottle, and the smell of the poppers hits me straight away. Even though I hate the odor, I know it might help with Gilbert II, and Bobs seems determined to use it tonight. As Bobs puts the bottle under my nostrils, I have no choice but to inhale a big slug of vapor and liquid. Then a sharp pain shoots up my anus and through to my midsection as Gilbert II makes his entrance.

* * * *

The wedding is drawing to a close, and Ricky is a little merry. I have been providing him with drinks after telling him that the bride will not mind. He says he had taken lots of pictures earlier, some abstract shots which he hopes the happy couple would like. Then we spent the rest of the day hanging out together. Now he is off again taking his last few pictures of the night, which include one woman crying after another woman leapt in front of her to snatch the bouquet from under her nose.

"She obviously wanted it more," I hear her friend consoling her. They are oblivious to Ricky snapping away.

As I watch him, I think of a conversation we had earlier in the day. He had asked me if I was happy for the couple. Instead of the automatic "yes" response ninety percent of the population would have given, I said "Not really." Surprised, he looked at me.

"I think the couple are getting married too young, they

are twenty-four and twenty-five and need to see more of the world and of other people, and have time as single people. Plus, in my opinion no one ends up with their first love," I had elaborated. Ricky seems to like my bluntness; maybe that is why we have become such good friends over the past few months. "So are you and Carmen going to get married?"

"I have never really considered it. We are both only twenty-two and I still have to earn her family's respect; well, her father's at least."

Playing devil's advocate, I say, "Now that you are living together she might want things to change."

He looks panicked by the thought. "It is definitely not something that would be happening in the next four to five years, unless she got pregnant." He laughs nervously.

"So does your boyfriend do profile pictures?" Gavin, a nurse from work, interrupts us.

I do not correct him about the boyfriend label. "What do you mean?"

The nurse lifts up his shirt to reveal his tanned six-pack. This is an unexpected pleasant surprise, as I do not find the guy's face attractive, so I'd presumed the body would be just as rough. But he ruins the look by going overboard with a fake tan—can't these guys just try to be natural? Anyway, it does not matter if I am attracted to Nursey or not—I have a rule that I do not shit where I work (apart from that one little indiscretion, but that was for totally different reasons). This introspection is interrupted by the nurse again.

"Anyway, since I got dumped five months ago, I have been working out like crazy. Now that I am hot, I want proper profile pictures of me so that bitch can see what he is missing and everyone else can share in my hotness and see what I have available."

What Gavin is asking dawns on me: I glance at Ricky and start to wonder if this is the opportunity I have been waiting for. I pat the man's six-pack. "I'll see what I can do."

Gavin dances off as the last song of the night comes on. The situation, as I smell it, is that Ricky is a straight man, but from our conversations I know he has never really experimented and is quite limited in his experiences. There is a possibility that he might be ever so curious, and I definitely want to be the one with whom he explores his curiosity. If he is going to experiment, I realize that he will need a gentle push to awaken those feelings.

6

HE HAS AT LEAST ONE OBSESSION

What is taking the guy in front so long? It isn't difficult; he doesn't have to make any decisions. He should have done his thinking before he got to the front of the queue.

At last. The random gets served and moves off.

"Happy New Year, Ben," the familiar face greets me.

Ten days after January 1st and people are still saying that—jeez. "Yeah, and you. I'll have the..."

"So where is your little friend?"

"He's at home waiting for his dinner." I smile back. "So we'll have the family bucket."

Once I have collected the food and am on my way home, part of me wishes Joe was there. I would not have minded sharing my fried chicken and chips with him. It is not like he would have eaten much of it anyway. Back when we used to live together and frequented this take-out restaurant, he would just eat a maximum of two pieces and half a portion of chips and leave the rest for me. In those days, we used to share a smaller sized bucket, but even with the smaller bucket, Joe used to tell me not to eat all of it because I would give myself a heart attack. At times like this I miss his nagging. I tried to speak to him a few times at work when we were changing over shifts, but he had just been polite and not very responsive, and he always made sure we were never alone.

When I get to the apartment, I do not bother taking my

jacket off. Instead, I put down the bag with the drink and sides and dive into the first piece of chicken. As I tear through the batter with my teeth, the hot flesh from the chicken hits my tongue. A momentary sense of pleasure hits me and all my pain is washed away.

The pain started in the days after my reconciliation with Suze, which had come at the cost of my friendship with Joe. At the time, I did not care about him; I lost all sense because I was deliriously happy. The morning after that night of passion, however, reality started to kick in. Suze had managed to avoid answering all the questions I had: What happens next? Where is this going? What about the woman at the cinema? No alarms bells in my head went off, or maybe I chose to ignore them, and we continued seeing each other for weeks. I became reclusive at work and obsessive in my rekindled romance with my ex. Joe moved out. Deep down I knew it was too good to be true. Then, just when I was starting to allow myself to feel the happiness I felt back in my university days, Suze dropped the unsurprising bombshell that she was still seeing that woman she had been with at the cinema. She did not want to cheat on her anymore, so she had decided to end it with me.

My only comfort now comes from my oldest ally, food. By reacquainting myself with this old love, I had gained nearly fourteen pounds in a few months. When I do not order it online but face-to-face, I rotate the shops and pretend the food is for a group of friends. I continue devouring the pieces of fried chicken and feel some mild indigestion. I do not care. Maybe it is good to feel some discomfort, so I remember all the pain I have endured.

* * * *

The meeting room in my office erupts into a round of applause, partly because the drinks have started flowing and it is the end of the day, but mainly because of the big win. I sit there taking in the admiration. I feel that familiar high—the rush I get from praise. My heart starts beating faster as the sense of control and power washes over my body; the sensation makes me feel truly awesome. As the head architect comes over to congratulate me on my presentation, a summary of the winning pitch my team did earlier in the week, the high continues. I had landed a major new client for the firm with one of my designs. I am not senior enough to get all the recognition, but in the end it was my design. This win today will definitely show that I deserved my promotion. I am mapping my advancement in the company in my head, along with how proud my family will be, when a familiar voice interrupts me.

Mike places his hand on my shoulder. "Congratulations on the win for the company, Bobs."

Under normal conditions this would have had excited me a lot more than it currently does, which makes me think I should probably take a beta-blocker more often when I am alone with him. I cannot stand the idea of losing control in front of work colleagues, or anyone in fact. When I'd heard that we won the contract and I would have to give the office presentation, I took some of the drug, which I had obtained to calm my anxiety and to make sure I did not sweat profusely during the pitch. Giving a presentation and showing signs of weakness, especially such a visible sign as sweating, is not something I will allow to happen.

The temporary calmness around Mike that the beta-blocker provides me is a good thing. I want nothing more than to rip his clothes off and fuck him senseless. When I fantasize about it, I even imagine Mike being active with me, something that I am not into and never allow Tim to do. I had tried to contain the situation and remove the temptation by setting Mike up with Taylor. I knew I would be jealous seeing Mike with someone else, but I knew Taylor would have been a good match. Taylor is not one to easily fall in love, and they would not have acted very coupley in front of me if they did end up together. Nevertheless, Taylor managed to inadvertently pay me back, not by getting Mike loved up but by writing a stockpile of prescriptions for me.

After the champagne is finished Mike tells me some of them are going out for a few drinks. He insists I come, as I am such an integral part of the team. I agree. I should go home and celebrate with Tim, but looking at Mike's face, I cannot say no. I feel okay about it, as the drug has given me back my control.

* * * *

This model seems a lot more confident than the previous one. I watch him take off his dressing gown to reveal only a pair of tiny, brightly colored briefs with a large waistband and a logo. Looking at this man, I realize that I no longer feel uncomfortable around all the male flesh as I had on the first shoot. When Taylor first introduced me to the notion of photographing guys in various states of undress so that they could use the pictures to get more men, I'd had my doubts. After I thought about it, I had decided my passion for photography won out over any weirdness I felt about taking risqué pictures of men. Taylor had helped me to see that I was a professional, and this was my career. What did it matter if I had to take some pictures of guys? If it were women I might enjoy the job more, but it was paid work and I could establish my name. Besides, you never know with whom you would network when taking pictures of half of Clapham. I also thought that Carmen would not have a problem with me taking pictures of guys, as she would have done if it were women in their bras and panties. Nevertheless, I decided not to tell her about this little sideline activity.

I position my eye next to the viewfinder and look at the guy. I zoom in to the man's feet, then take in all the details of the man's whole body. Ideas of which angles I should use and the positions that will make him look the most flattering come into my head. Not that I am gay or would feel comfortable discussing it with another man, but I can now tell if another guy is good-looking. This guy has the best body out of the three guys I have photographed so far; it looks more natural and not overly pumped up. As I scan the man's legs, I notice the calf muscles and thighs and how they are in proportion to the rest of his body. I rush past the purple briefs and the package that is not so hidden inside. His upper torso has a nice V-shape to it and he has a muscular chest, which is complimented by the not-too-defined muscles of his flat stomach. I have the correct lens on the camera, so I adjust the f-stop and start to take a series of pictures. I make minor adjustments to the metering, setting the correct ISO speed, and start to direct my subject on which ways to turn. My subject seems to be getting more relaxed as the photography session continues. He tells me I put him at ease with my way of directing and providing encouragement. An hour later when the shoot is over and I am packing away my equipment, I realize that even though the money is good for the hours I put into shooting and touching them up, I do it mainly because of my passion for photography.

* * * *

The barman places a VOC in front of my fuck. The guy stirs the drink with the straw and subtly glances at his watch. I am now late for our rendezvous by ten minutes. Technically I am not late, as I have been here the whole time, but I am just watching the guy, observing. It is what I do. It is natural to me. I had suggested we meet later on that night, so it would have been more obvious that it was for a quick drink then back to his place for sex, but it seems he is trying to steer this drunken one-night stand into something more. He drains his drink and orders another. Maybe he needs some liquid courage. I decide to head over; I take a detour to make it look like I am just entering the bar. Near the door I am intercepted by some other guy I had fucked before.

After a brief chat I sit down with my original "date." I look at his drink and ask what it is. [LIE 1: I hang out with enough gay males to know a vodka, orange, and cranberry when I see it.] I order myself a bottle of Italian beer, telling my date it is my favorite. [LIE 2: I am thinking I should just play to the stereotype.] I tell my date he looks nice and the guy-liner he is wearing makes him look hot. [LIE 3.]

"So, Carlo." [LIE 4.] The date motions toward the door and asks, "Is he a friend of yours?"

I tell him the guy is someone I just met [LIE 5]. I tell the date I stopped his unwanted advances by pretending to speak just Italian. [LIE 6: I told the guy that I would call him later.] My date seems to relax at this news and starts to make small talk. I am only half-listening and thinking I should probably switch from my Italian aliases to some English ones for the new year. "Randoms" are getting too familiar with my personas. I can pass for either English or Italian but always find the Italian lie is easier to sell if packaged correctly, because people look at my tan and my black hair and prefer to believe I am not English. I tell my date I have an early start in the morning. [LIE 7: I do not really want to stay out drinking with this guy when we could just cut to the chase.] I place my hand on the guy's inner thigh, suggesting we go back to his place after these drinks. The guy wants to stay out, get something to eat, and show me off, but he buys into the series of lies because he wants to believe them and because I am too well-practiced in the art. He agrees to go. When he finishes his VOC he makes a last-ditch attempt to try the relationship thing by suggesting we go back to my place; that way, we would have spent a night at each other's. I tell him that I have relatives staying over [LIE 8], and I only left them home alone because I wanted to see him so much [LIE 9], so it would not be practical.

* * * *

Lying on my front in just my pants, I have nothing else to do but stare at the panels on the walls. Each group of designs is a variation on a theme. Some look tacky, while some look like they are designed with real passion and skill. I select the ones I would pick from each group if I had to, and where they would go.

"So are you ready?"

"Yes, you know I am an old pro at this," I reply. "Anyway, thanks again for seeing me so late. I just had a desire to get it done today."

"For you I would be happy to keep the studio open all night."

Okay, this is a bit awkward. My feet are nervously tapping the bed. "It must be because I spend way too much money here."

"Something like that, Nathan. I like to etch my art on you as on a canvas; my gifts suit you. I still remember the first time I penetrated your dermis all those years ago."

I got my first tattoo when I was nineteen, to camouflage the two centimeter-long scars on my right shoulder that I had given myself in my early teens. These self-inflicted souvenirs were from the darkest time in my life, that period when I was unable to deal with my sexuality and was abused for it. When the darkness had completely gone, I did not want anyone to see the scars so I had an Egyptian eye tattooed to hide them. After the first tattoo, I was hooked. I do not know why people said they hurt. I like the initial burning sensation, then numbness when I get inked. In the following years, I got more and more tattoos and ended up with a half-sleeve on my right shoulder and bicep, which included an eye, an eagle, some flowers, and various classical elements all beautifully blended into one. When my upper arm was finished, I got a large black tribal design added to my left outer thigh, that crept up my abdominal oblique and extended above my pants. Just above the ankle on my right leg, I got a band that went all the way around. This is my favorite one to date because it hurt the most and is a pattern I came up with myself. Today, I am getting a cross on my lower back, not for any religious reason but because I like the look. I am looking forward to it because I heard this area is supposed to be especially sensitive. As the needle starts pricking my skin, I want to shout out "harder" but I do not. I continue to stare at the designs on the wall while the hotness works away on my lower back. I pick out a sun that I like and start to visualize what it would look like on my upper back in between my shoulder blades.

* * * *

I care about the well-being of each and every one of my patients, but some of them tug at my heart strings more than others. Earlier today I got a visit from a twenty-one-year-old regular. This particular patient, who happens to be very cute, was diagnosed with HIV a couple of years ago, forcing him to become a lot more mature than his years. He had been so eager to lose his virginity, and he thought the older guy he met in the club would take care of the practical aspects. Through the elation of making out with the guy, the alcohol, going back to his place, and the sexual acts, he did not even realize he was being barebacked. Even after the event, he never dreamed he was at risk of catching anything, because surely the guy would have been more careful. This was what he told me when he first became my patient. Months later, when he was about to embark on a serious relationship with a new guy he met, the guy insisted that they both be tested before they did anything unprotected. When he was diagnosed with HIV, the guy he was dating split—but that was the least of his worries.

I am concerned about the pain he is suffering in his hands and feet. This neuropathy could be a complication of the HIV or a side effect of the medication he is taking. I conduct a series of neurological examinations to try to find the cause. I feel the guy is handling his situation well, playing the hand that life dealt him. It is this aspect of human nature that intrigues me. Contemplating this patient, the game of life, and how I would play things differently if I had HIV, I decide to go get a coffee.

I see Gavin at the coffee machine. "Hello, I didn't realize you were working tonight."

"You know what it is like, no rest for the wicked. Speaking of which, it was wicked of you not to tell me your photographer was straight."

Game on. This is just the light-hearted diversion I need after seeing that HIV patient. "Did he take bad pictures because he was not one of us?"

"No, darling, but you know what I mean."

I know exactly what he means but I respond with the blankest expression I can muster. "Well, it would have been nice to know beforehand is all."

Gavin does not rise to the bait because he is too stupid to know he is being baited.

I decide it is best to change tack and make it all about the nurse. "So have your new pictures sparked up your love life?" Talking about himself means Gavin is likely to babble on and reveal something that I can use against him.

Gavin smiles, probably remembering all the recent activity his new profile has gotten him. "I seem to be attracting all these cute guys now that I have a six-pack.

It's great." He is about to say something else, but stops himself and hurries away. "Anyway, I had better get going; let's do drinks soon."

I walk back to my examination room and wonder if I should continue to toy with Gavin. After all, I feel Gavin seems to be holding back on me. Messing with people is fun, but then again I am a busy boy and have the major project to concentrate on.

* * * *

The guy picks up the metal effortlessly. He is bench-pressing the weight with such ease that I cannot help but stare. The pumped-up gym guy is wearing a tank top that shows off his upper body, athletic arms, brawny back, and chiseled chest. I am not sexually attracted to the guy; I prefer guys with a similar natural build to Bobs, but I can appreciate the level of dedication the guy puts into his body. I share his devotedness. I have already been to the gym once today, but since Bobs is going to be home late due to after-work drinks, I thought I would go to the gym again. My first session was spent at the Phoenix gym. This morning's workout involved mainly cardiovascular exercises—my own little triathlon of twenty-five laps in the swimming pool, a 20K ride on the exercise bike, and a 5K run on the treadmill. I do this mini-triathlon every few weeks to burn off fat because I know the only way to let my definition show is by keeping the weight off. I had not planned to go to the gym again today, but after Bobs called, I wanted to do something that would feel good. I wanted some company, so I came to the mainstream not-gay chain just off the high street.

I am not here to do a full workout, as I do not have the

energy. Instead, I enjoy watching other guys exercise to see if I can get any tips or ideas while I do various positions on the power plate. This is the least strenuous part of my session, so I only occasionally bother doing it. The bench press guy finishes his particular weight set and sits up. He glances around and then looks in my direction. I quickly look around. The gym is practically deserted at this time of night, and no one else is in my vicinity. The guy gets up and heads over. He introduces himself as a personal trainer who works at the other gym in Clapham, the gay one, and wants to know if I have a trainer or do I want a free session with him. Ten minutes later, we are in the gym's juice bar, vigorously shaking our protein powder shakes, discussing weights, exercises, diet, and lifestyle.

* * * *

"You are one of my best," the Cow says. "Jas, I hope you are you going to continue in this chosen career. You have a knack for selling."

"Thank you," I tell the Cow. This is the nickname I have given my dealer, as he provides the white stuff (cocaine) the way a cow provides the white stuff (milk) to the masses. Plus, what we do by selling drugs is quite a cowish activity. All in all, as dealers go, the Cow is a good one. I have used other dealers in the past, but the Cow never puts pressure on me to sell more, or sell anything beyond that than which I ask. He is competitively priced and seems to have unlimited access to anything. My relationship with the Cow is a good one, probably because I always pay up front so I am never in debt. Our comfortable arrangement might quickly turn very nasty if I owe the Cow money, so I never intend to allow that to happen.

I make a mental note to try to find out what the Cow does to someone who does not pay up. So far, I have stayed out of the Cow's business, because to discover this information I might have to find out who the Cow's dealer is and that will mean knowing too much about the chain. Besides, being involved in the top end means being in too deep, and in this game that is always dangerous.

"I was wondering if you can get steroids."

The Cow flashes a grin and shows off his gold crown. "Of course, I see that besides being a great salesman, you are an entrepreneur."

Nice. The idea had come to me while I was last speaking to Tim. I was wondering if his gains were fully natural. Even though his were, there is still a market for steroids because the less ethical guys out there want quick results and will be up for it.

"So, to celebrate our newfound extension, do you want to do a couple of lines? On me, of course."

"Sure."

Not one to turn down a free score, I watch as the Cow cuts up a couple of lines each. I wish he would do it quicker because once the offer is made, I am really craving it. My heart is beating in anticipation of the glorious accelerant when the Cow hands me a rolled-up twenty. I take one of the lines up my left nostril in a heartbeat. The near-instant rush is exhilarating. I hand the note back to the Cow. After the Cow finishes taking in both his lines, he hands it back to me. I shove the tube up my right nostril, press down on my left one, place the free end of the note at one end of the line, and start to inhale.

* * * *

As the day draws to an end, I am lying on the bed in my new accommodation, the spare room of the house Jas is renting. I have been feeling mildly depressed ever since my fight with Ben and I moved out of our place. I am more desperate than ever to find a boyfriend. In the past month my desperation has resulted in my trawling through various websites looking for guys to "date." In my world dating equals meeting some guy for a quick drink and then going for sex. In my search for love, I find this acceptable behavior, because you have to try before you buy. Besides, even if it is just an ONS or one-night stand, I do feel love on the nights I am with a man. Currently, as I am in a new gay-affluent area, I am using a program designed for mobile phones. I upload a picture of my stomach, which is flat and smooth and seems to appeal to lots of guys, and a couple of lines about myself. Then, based on my location, nearby guys will see this information and start a conversation, which usually ends up in me sending more pictures—my ass, as I am a bottom, and then my face. Which is where I tend to lose the interest of most guys.

It annoys me that they can smell my effeminate nature from my face picture, but I do not want to go with a guy who only likes "straight-acting" men or a "muscle bottom," the new "in thing" on the scene. We would not be a good match, and it is better to get this out of the way early. Despite all these issues I have been getting my fair share of attention, usually from older men. The multiple ONSs make me feel loved, and I am certain the perfect boyfriend is the next ONS around the corner. A gorgeous black man called Anthony has been chatting with me tonight, and I am starting to think he could be the one. I find out the guy is around my age, and has a good job. He even sends a picture of his cock, which I think is too big, but I will somehow cope. The guy pays me lots of compliments, saying how much he likes my tight ass and my cute face. I send my location to Ant and tell him to come over. He says he will, but only if it is discreet, no-strings fun because he is bisexual and has a girlfriend.

Story of my life, the very song my "special friends" from the cinema used to sing. I tell the guy to come over. Being the eternal optimist when it comes to my own love life, I always believe that just maybe they will change their mind and decide to give me a chance once the deed is done.

Half an hour later, when the guy has turned up on my doorstep, I think he is better-looking in person than the pictures, and this really could be the one—I will do whatever it takes to make a relationship with this latest love.

7

HE LOOKS, YOU LOOK

I have done well. The man is absolutely beautiful, at least from behind, as that is all that can be seen of him. He conjures up a sense of longing in his admirers and evokes a sense of jealousy in his haters. His photograph elicits the emotions people in the sixteenth century would have felt when the statue of David was first revealed. As the public walks around Ricky's exhibition I had arranged in my cinema, people stop at this picture and make comments:

"When God created us in his image, he demonstrated his affinity for his gay sons by making us more aesthetically pleasing than our straight counterparts, so we could survive the other trials we have to face."

"You don't even know if he is gay."

"He might have that amazing body, but he could be totally ugly"

"Gay or straight, what does it matter, he is perfect."

"Micro-penis."

"He is obviously 'gugly.' You know, one of those gays so ugly they work out non-stop to achieve an incredible body, so people only look at the body and not the hideous face."

"Don't be so mean. It's art; from behind he is mysterious, and we have to talk about the picture more."

"We should ask the artist."

"He's astoundingly talented."

"What does the red symbolize? Is it blood? It's ghastly."

"It is the wounds of his life flowing out of him."

"So what does it mean?"

"Is it something to do with Valentine's Day? After all, that's today."

"Why didn't he use rose petals or something else for the red then? Why blood?"

The picture is truly a work of art in that it stirred passion and debate in those who have seen it, and this is only its first public viewing. I take a break from playing host and having to network and am staring at Carmen in the distance. She sees me looking and smiles back. I have not spent much time with her recently, as my work has really taken off. Now I have my first art exhibition, it has been all go. When the opportunity to display some of my work was first presented to me I jumped at the chance, but never thought my Dick C piece would steal the show.

Just before Christmas, Taylor had properly introduced me to Joe. Joe explained that they had monthly mini-exhibitions in the cinema bar mainly for local up-and-coming artists to showcase some of their work—paintings, posters, pictures, whatever. He organized these because he was "the only one at the cinema with taste" and he had some arty degree that he wanted to use now and again. These mini-exhibitions were usually booked out a year in advance, but the woman doing the February slot had had some accident and would not be able to do it. Usually he would just move everyone up a month, but March had an Easter theme going that would be unsuitable for February.

Taylor had recommended me, and Joe filled in the details. The exhibit would need ten to fifteen photographs blown up to the appropriate size, framed, and priced. The work had to be original, but it could be from wherever as long as I had taken the pictures myself. I realized this was a great opportunity to show my work to the masses and be able to charge exorbitant prices. Before I had even agreed, I'd thought of at least twenty pictures with commercial appeal that would fit nicely into the program, and gratefully accepted the offer.

Soon after I agreed to do the exhibition, my best friend Taylor got me more work. Some guys wanted to improve their chances of finding other men on the Internet by using professional photographs. I soon found myself taking pictures of a very flirtatious nurse, who toned it down when I told him I was straight and lived with my girlfriend. The nurse told me he felt safer having his pictures taken by a straight guy, because he felt reassured they would not be used unprofessionally (wank material for the photographer, or posted on racy websites). The nurse recommended me to a friend. I added my signature to each photo so guys looking at them would know who the artist was and where to go to if they wanted some pictures done. I did not want to use my real name to cloud the perception of my other, more straight-laced work, so Dick C, which seemed to appeal more to this clientele, was born. Before I knew it, guys were visiting the Dick C photography website and booking me up.

The first job with the nurse had been pretty run of the mill, taking pictures of him dressed up looking dapper in a suit, then removing the jacket, tie, shirt, trousers, until I was taking pictures of him in his underpants. The second client, another nurse, was quite nervous, and I had to coax him to relax to get better shots. With this guy, there were not as many flesh shots, but he seemed to have a thing for dressing up in various uniforms. On my third job, I snapped this guy who was quite happily posing in his purple underpants and getting suggestive by tugging them down to reveal his butt cheeks and his trimmed pubic area. I realized if I continued down this route, it would get to the stage where guys wanted to do nude pictures. I had never considered this before, because often when women pose it is more likely to be the photographer suggesting they remove their clothes. From what I was learning about gay guys and how they were using the pictures, I knew they would soon want nude shots.

Dick C the photographer continued working. Maybe it was my relaxed attitude and non-predatory behavior that had prompted number four to ask if I would take full frontal naked shots. When I'd raised my eyebrows at the request, the guy offered me more money. The pictures included cock shots, both flaccid and erect, and a picture of him from behind on all fours spreading his ass cheeks. Number five looked immaculate, and actually wanted the pictures to build up a portfolio to try to become a model/actor. He also wanted some naked shots but more artistic and subtle, from a side angle with his leg raised a bit so all that was visible was his trimmed pubes but no cock and definitely not his insides. I, however, got an eyeful.

I told the guy I would waive my extra fee for taking nude pictures if I could use one for an exhibition I had coming up. The guy agreed as long as his face was blurred out; he was not sure he wanted to be credited with being in risqué pictures in case it hurt his professional chances. So, I spent the rest of the day with the guy taking more pictures. I knew since the guy wanted to be a model, he would be up for having more daring shots done. I popped out to the store to look for some props to get some alternative shots while the guy took a break. As I left, the guy started doing push-ups to get his body pumped for the next session. He was still at it when I returned with a pot of red paint.

The guy had been up for it. I thought his eagerness and looks meant he really had model potential. We spread a shower curtain on the floor and experimented with painting stripes on his chest and his groin area. I thought since I could not use his face, it might be better to take the picture from behind. I poured the paint down the model's back and watched it drip down his spine and pool at the small of his lower back, then stream down his gluteus maximus. If any paint got on his right leg I wiped it off, so my model would only have it running down his left leg. When I was taking the pictures I had known they would be something special.

That night when I was reviewing the pictures one of them jumped out at me, and I knew I had to use it in the exhibition. I changed the picture to black and white, leaving only the color from the red paint. Then I went through the rest of the pictures that I was going to exhibit and changed them all to black and white, leaving only one color in each one. That would be the theme for the exhibition. That night, I called Joe to have a look at the pictures and give his opinion of the set as an exhibition.

The next day when Joe came around and saw the pictures, he loved them. He said the man's picture with the red was the strongest of the collection.

"Glorious," he said.

Joe advised me that if I really wanted to make it big, especially in Clapham, I should try to be somewhat of an enigma and not tell people if I was gay or straight, if I had a partner, where I lived, etc. He'd tried to find out who the guy was, but I kept that a closely guarded secret.

With a week to go to the exhibition, I took Carmen out for dinner in the West End to get a break from Clapham. We had not been spending that much time together since my career started to take off, and while she had not openly said anything, she had started to come across as resentful. With my opening night falling on Valentine's Day, I knew I had some crawling to do. Plus, I was worried about how she would take the new changes to my career, of which she was soon to learn. Even though I had nothing to be ashamed of, I did not want to tell her I was taking pictures of naked guys, so I tried to sugar-coat it. I ended up telling her I was no longer doing wedding photography. Instead, I was helping models create their portfolios, which meant that I got more artistic usable shots that I could use.

Thinking back to it, I probably should have phrased it better, because the moment she heard "models" she assumed skinny twig-women who would pay for the photographs and my expertise on their backs. At first I hadn't noticed the alteration in her expression, so I continued to tell her about the other change—that it might be better to keep our relationship quiet for the time being for the sake of my career. She looked liked she did not understand. I spelled out that at the exhibition we would have to pretend we were not a couple. Carmen stood up sharply, threw her napkin onto the table, and stormed off to the bathroom. I was totally bewildered by her overreaction; it was not like we wouldn't celebrate Valentine's Day later that night. Besides, the exhibition was a manufactured event, so why was she so bothered? I ordered some drinks. The drinks arrived at the table before Carmen. I had a gulp of whiskey and coke, and thought I would finish it before I went looking for her. I was halfway through the drink when a red-eyed Carmen reappeared.

I knew better than to get defensive, so I moved my chair next to hers and held her hand. "What's wrong?"

"I am upset that I never get to see much of you because you are spending all your time with pretty young women. And why do we have to pretend not to be together? Also, as I'm being frank, you always seem too tired for sex."

"The models are all men. And think rationally, any up-and-coming figure who is going to be in the public eye, even a local art exhibition, should keep details about their private life just that, private." I was not happy with her lack of trust in me and some of the other stuff she said, but I let it go.

I was with her because she was not clingy and needy like my first girlfriend. She had never before shown this insecure side. She seemed to settle down after I explained, and became more like the Carmen I knew, but the dinner caused a number of questions to fly around in my head: Had we made a mistake moving in together? Did she only like me when she was doing better than me? She apparently did not trust me around other women—what was that all about? Did she take my photography seriously?

She relaxed a lot more as she ate and drank, and things between us returned to normal. We agreed that at the exhibition we would not be coupley, but I would not go out of my way to reject her. That night, even though I did not really feel like it, we made love because I was hurt about her saying I was too tired for sex. She knew I did not have a big sex drive, she never complained before, so why was she throwing this in my face now?

* * * *

I move away from the picture and all the things people are saying and go looking for the man of the moment. Some of his new fans are crowded around him, asking him all sorts of questions. I interrupt him and take him aside. "We need to talk some business."

"Joe, I thought you told me to network," Ricky cheekily responds.

"You don't need to, the work is speaking for itself." I beam. "*Bloody Adonis* could sell out tonight if we start taking orders. Are you sure you want to limit the print run to just fifty copies per photograph?"

"*Bloody Adonis*? I'll have to work out some better name. Anyway, are you serious? You are saying you could sell fifty copies of that picture at four hundred a pop tonight."

"I counted at least twenty people showing a definite interest. Remember, this is Clapham—people like to spend. We should have set the price higher."

Ricky ignores me. "What about the other pictures?"

"Use the LWTL theory."

114

"Joe, you are going to have to explain that one to me. I don't speak gay."

"It's not a gay thing, it's a theory of life. Don't you straight people know anything? 'Look Where They Look.' If you want to know what someone is thinking or if someone fancies someone, look where they are looking. If we glance over at Tim, we see he is looking off into the distance, so we follow his gaze and we find Bobs. Ah, love's young dream, those two! We use that same principle here and look where the majority of the guests are looking; by following their gazes we see it's at *Bloody Adonis*."

"Well, I think that is more reason to limit the numbers for every picture. We priced *Bloody Adonis* higher than the others because we expected it to do better. If *Bloody Adonis* sells out, disappointed buyers might want a piece of this hot, young, good-looking artist and buy his other pictures. As an artist, I don't want to flood lots of the same picture onto the market. Part of the reason we can get away with a higher price for this one is because people know they are buying a limited edition." Ricky calls it right.

"Okay, sweetie." I am glad that he is not quite the innocent idiot I had originally pegged him for. I give him a quick congratulatory peck on the cheek and leave him to continue to mingle. Ricky joins the group under *Bloody Adonis* and starts chatting to them. I decide I will do a quick LWTL myself to see where everyone is at. I have already ascertained that Tim is looking longingly at his boyfriend. I look at Bobs and follow his gaze; he is checking out some arty guy. I see Jas looking toward the bathroom, Nat is looking at Jas; Taylor is looking at *Bloody Adonis*. I look at Ben, who is looking at me. When she sees me catch her glance, she moves off. I do not see Marco at this event.

After Ben dropped me in it, the night I brought Marco round to help her, I'd had to lie to Marco. So, I told him that when we first met I'd had a crush on him, and Ben was just teasing me about it. I had to laugh it off by saying I am a hopeless romantic, which Marco knows, and that I fall "in love" with everyone—it was not serious, just me being foolish. Marco seemed to buy my lie, but it definitely strained our relationship, and Marco went cold on me. Ben betrayed me by revealing that secret; she and I were meant to be best friends, general outcasts who stuck together. She blurted out my most intimate thoughts to the one person who was never meant to know them, and it was that Judas kiss that hurt the most.

* * * *

I quickly make a detour, as Joe is giving me a death stare. I am at that awkward stage in which I just have to speak to the nearest person at hand. I find myself talking to Carmen. Previously, we had only ever made small talk, as I think she is a stuck up rich girl and usually give her a wide berth. Carmen, who has had a few already, starts telling me all about pretending she is not with Ricky, as she had been ordered to do that night.

"So it's Valentine's Day, and I can't go and speak to my boyfriend or hang out with him or tell him how great his pictures are," she slurs at me and continues her rant. "I'm sure he's got something going on with one of his models, that's what happens between photographers and models. That's the real reason he doesn't want people to know he has a girlfriend, isn't it, Ben?"

So the spoiled little rich girl has the same insecurities as the rest of us. That makes me feel better about myself. "I'm sure it's not true. What did he say when you asked him about it?"

"He blew me off with some random excuse. We have not properly talked about it."

"Okay, well, look at it this way. If he doesn't want it to get back to his bit on the side that he has a girlfriend, then that hypothetical woman must be here, so which modelesque women has he been hanging out with?" I am trying to make Carmen see, as I feel sorry for the woman, that she is being silly. I myself don't see any particularly gorgeous women who could be models.

"I don't know. Maybe he is being more subtle than that."

"You could always look where he looks, to see what he is up to." I have to explain the LWTL theory to Carmen who is looking blankly at me.

Carmen looks at Ricky, and sees that he is enjoying the attention he is getting from the crowd who is appreciating his work. When he looks up from his conversations, it is always at his pictures. She is being foolish. She says she will go over to him as just another woman in the crowd and let him know how great his work is. She thanks me for the counsel. I have a better idea. I give her the key to the manager's office and tell her to wait for him in there; I will tell him to meet her so they can have some alone time.

"Thank you, Ben. You know, you are a good sort."

* * * *

I think I have misjudged the lesbian. Ben is really kind, I think as I gratefully take the key. I make my way out of the bar and look into the room, hoping to catch Ricky's eye to get him to follow me without the need for third-party intervention. I cannot establish eye contact because he is looking at something else. I follow his glance and feel sick.

* * * *

I can't help but smile at the real-life Bloody Adonis. I do not want to go over to him just in case anyone in the room manages to work out it is him in the picture. I do not want to give away the mystery or break the trust the guy has placed in me, but the model nods for me to join him away from the other people. As I am moving away from the group I am in I am intercepted by Ben, who tells me to go the manager's office. I tell her I will go once I have spoken to someone.

"Congratulations, Ricky on such a great exhibition," the model says as he hugs me. "That picture of me looks better in the flesh than the digital version you showed me."

I look at the tall blond woman standing next to the guy.

"Oh, don't worry about Lucy, she's a friend of mine who is looking for a photographer to take some portfolio pictures for her. I said you might be able to help her out."

"Yeah, sure. Lucy, get my details from our star of the night here and we can sort something out. Look, a lot of people have asked me who the model in the picture is. What do you want me to tell them?"

"Unless it's an agency or industry expert, you don't have to tell anyone. I am happy to retain the mystery, as you put it the other day."

"That's great. I will speak to you soon about doing some other pictures before you become a professional model and will no longer pose for me."

We embrace goodbye, and I make my way to the manager's office to see what Joe, as I assume it is Joe, wants now. As I open the door, I am pleasantly surprised to see Carmen, alone. I go over to kiss her, but she is acting strangely and does not respond to my kiss.

"Are you enjoying the exhibition? It looks better now they are printed out than when I first showed them to you on the computer, no?"

"Who was that blond woman that you were speaking to?" she hisses at me.

I am taken aback by her accusatory tone and respond angrily. "What woman?"

"That tall blond one you were looking at just now."

"You're sounding crazy. Didn't we sort this out already? There is no other woman."

"Since we moved in together, things have been off. It feels like we saw each other more when we didn't live together. You're always so busy with work now..."

"What, so you don't want me to have a job and make money? You know tonight is the biggest night of my career so far. You are supposed to support me, not act like a deranged bunny boiler. Oh, so here comes the waterworks now because I told it like it is."

"Support you! Support you! I have done nothing but support you. If it wasn't for me you wouldn't have a career." Carmen stops crying and blushes, she has said enough to stir my interest.

"What does that mean? Support would mean helping me de-stress, not giving me additional headaches and accusing me of lying and cheating."

"I started you off by getting Daddy to set you up with work. You owe it all to me, and you repay me by sleeping with another woman."

"What the fuck?" I am shocked. I made my career happen. If anything, Taylor has helped me and supported me more than Carmen. "I am going to say this just one more time. I have not cheated on you. I don't know where you got that idea from, but it is not true. Now stop being demented. I am going to go back to my public. I'll see you at home."

Carmen leaves. I am fuming. I take a moment to compose myself and let the anger subside before going back out to the crowd. Just then, the door opens and Taylor walks in.

"I just wanted to congratulate you on such a successful night. I think you are going to become really big."

"You know what, you have the right idea about not bothering with women. They are more hassle than they are worth." I can't help it, and end up thumping my fists on the desk.

Taylor moves next to me and asks what is wrong. I tell him what happened with Carmen.

"You know what?" I finish. "If anything, I owe you the most for helping me to jump-start my career. I need to thank you properly."

"You know, Richard, just helping you was thanks enough. I did it because we are friends." He moves closer. "Actually, there is a way you can thank me."

8

HE HAS THE HANDS

Excuse me. Some people have no manners.

"That was rude."

"I wonder what her problem was?"

"Typical Claphamite."

I don't hear my date, as I am too busy staring at the woman who just barged into me. I watch her stalk fuming out of the cinema. What gets to me even more is the man I notice watching her. He is someone I hate with a passion, a guy who tried to ruin my life a couple of years ago. The doctor has not noticed me, is deliberately ignoring me, or is too busy watching the woman leave, I am not sure which. I nod toward my nemesis. "Did you know he would be here?"

"I never really thought about it, but it's no surprise that he should be here. What is it between the two of you? But we all have skeletons in our closets," Gavin reassures me. We watch as the doctor moves away from his present location and heads through a door marked "Staff Only."

* * * *

I am starting to get lightheaded from all the free drinks at the exhibition. They make me feel good, so instead of speaking to the usual suspects or looking around for Bobs, I start to mingle with others. Some random muscle guy starts speaking to me. I guess like attracts like, but the guy's words just flow over me because I am not really paying any attention. I can't help but notice the guy's hand holding what looks like an orange juice. This guy looks, through his clothes, to be as well-stacked as I am, but he has the tiniest little hands I have ever seen on an adult male of his size. His fingernails are quite shiny and look manicured, so I categorize him as gay. I wonder if I have found a new breed of gay man, a muscle-queen perhaps, a "musceen." I will have to check the word with Joe, who is always in the know. The musceen thought makes me laugh. The guy must believe I am responding to his conversation and thinks his luck is in, so he moves closer to me. This makes me pay attention.

The guy asks me out in a roundabout way, I guess assuming that since I am at this exhibition on Valentine's Day I must be single. I take a closer look at the guy. He is okay, but I never understood the gay man's obsession of dating someone who looks similar, at least body wise, to himself. Are we all so narcissistic we have to fundamentally do ourselves?

The musceen is still waiting for a response, so I tell him that my boyfriend is here, and we are out supporting our friends who put the exhibition together. The musceen looks disappointed, tut-tuts at having wasted ten minutes of his time chatting up someone who is not available, tells me I should have said so from the beginning, and moves off. I think I should go and find Bobs to visually corroborate my story in case the guy seeks me out again. I grab another glass of wine as the tray goes by, and look for my other half. Bobs is chatting away to a slender guy who looks right at home here.

He looks like a typical arty Claphamite, with his

checkered shirt, geeky gloss-black glasses, quiffed dark brown hair, and enough stubble to make him interesting-looking but not enough to only attract bears. I feel a pang of jealously when I see how animated Bobs is with the guy, and that art-asshole is all over my man. I down the drink, get another, and go over to them.

* * * *

I don't want to come off as a bitter old fool with lots of baggage, even though I am only in my thirties, and I feel I owe Gavin the truth about my history with Taylor, especially if we are going to see each other more steadily. So, I decide to tell him.

"When we first met, there was an immediate attraction between us, but I knew nothing would happen because I was living with my then-boyfriend and Taylor was actively dating different men. We shared a good professional relationship and quickly became close friends. But as our friendship grew, so did the sexual tension. One day after work, Taylor came to me with a problem. I was his superior. Apparently, a patient had asked him out. Taylor told me that the patient was really good-looking, had a great body, which he got to see from his examination, and that the guy was constantly flirting with him. Taylor confessed that if they had met in a club, he would have been all over the guy, but he had to remain professional because they met as patient-doctor. The patient asked him out directly and he said no, so he wanted to tell someone as a witness, for legal reasons. A week later, the patient made an excuse to come back and see him under the guise of needing a follow-up that was not required. Again, he asked Taylor out, saying that he was changing doctors so there would be no problem going out with him. When the patient departed he left a letter behind. Taylor showed me the letter, which corroborated his story."

"So why did the patient have it so bad for him? I just don't see it myself," Gavin interrupts.

"Dunno. It was not just the patient who developed feelings for Taylor. After that incident which Taylor shared, I respected Taylor more for doing everything by the book, which meant that the tension between us was near to exploding. One night after work drinks, we decided to share a taxi home. When we arrived at Taylor's place, he did not get out of the car, and I did not want him too. Before we knew it, our knees were touching and the spark between us was too much. I 'accidentally' put my hand on Taylor's leg, and the next thing I knew, we were kissing. It was amazing. I would have followed him inside then and there, but Taylor played me well. He reminded me about my boyfriend and said he didn't want to get involved with an attached guy. This made me want him more. The next time we saw each other at work, I could not control myself, and we ended up kissing again. I said I would end it with my boyfriend, but it would take a little while, because my boyfriend relied on me to provide the financial stability and lifestyle to which we were accustomed."

Gavin looks at me unhappily. Taylor might cause me to lose another guy.

"The potential for a promotion came up for Taylor. It was between him and another doctor; the other doctor had more experience, but Taylor was better with the patients. The decision lay with me and some of the more senior doctors. Taylor played it cool, saying that he did not want to compromise me, and I should just make the best decision for the clinic. I prepared him for the interview during our 'working late' sex sessions. After the selection process, it was two votes for Taylor—one was mine—and two votes for the other guy. The most senior doctor had the deciding vote, and he would have gone for the other guy because he had the most experience. I put forward the case, ignoring the irony, about how well Taylor had handled the difficult case of the patient coming on to him. This swung the vote toward Taylor, and he got the promotion. After getting the promotion Taylor dumped me, saying that he felt bad about how we started, and because of our working relationship it might be better to just be friends. I was gutted and ended up breaking up with my boyfriend in an attempt to take things further with Taylor, but to no avail. It was a very messy affair because my boyfriend complained to my family and colleagues that I had been cheating on him with another doctor. Afterward, the doctor who did not get the job complained about my relationship with Taylor. I got in trouble for fraternizing with a junior member of staff for whom I was responsible, and I had to leave. I knew that I was in the wrong for cheating and for trying to start another relationship, but I had just gone with my heart. Once I got over being dumped and had the chance to deliberate, I had the feeling that I had been played. That is why I hate Taylor so much and do not trust him."

"I understand a broken heart, and don't think you're being foolish—there is something about Taylor. He comes across smug, and there is just something about him that I don't trust."

* * * *

Tim cuts in front of me, stumbles a little, and kisses me hello. This is embarrassing, I take him by the arms, sort of spin him around to the guy. "This is Tim, my boyfriend I was telling you about."

"Hello, I am Ged."

Tim looks at him like he only just realizes he is there and hugs him hello, probably more to support himself from falling over rather than to be friendly.

"Ged works at the library where I do a lot of my research," I add. Tim hiccups while trying to say something about architecture while I just look at Ged in an apologetic way, before taking Tim by the shoulders and leading him off.

* * * *

The crowd has died down somewhat. I decide to go over and look at the picture everyone is talking about to see what all the fuss is. Then I will cautiously make my way to the office to see if it is free yet. I have not seen either Carmen or Ricky emerge, so I guess they have made up. I hope they are not at it in my office, but I don't realistically think they would be since they are a straight couple. I would have been more concerned if I had sent a gay couple in, but then again I have more sense than to give away a golden ticket to such a couple who would have used the empty room to have sex.

"So what do you think of it?" I look at the hand pointing at the picture. The woman has neat, unpolished, short nails. That is supposed to be the number one tell for spotting a male or female gay, but I have a shit ability to deduce whether a woman is in my club or not, and the number of times I am wrong about women (secretaries, those into sports, musicians) based on their nails makes me think nothing more of this initial contact.

"I don't quite get it myself," the woman continues.

I look at the photograph. I can see the gay men will like it because of the sheer physical beauty of the man in it. They will all want to either be ploughing the guy and his rock hard ass from behind or they will be fantasizing that his man part reflects the rest of his muscular body and want it inside them. For the latter reason, women are probably infatuated with the picture too. The only people who will not really get it are straight men and gay women. I turn to look at the critic. The self-expressive connoisseur is gorgeous. She is not pretty in an obvious way, but to me she is. She has a natural strawberry tint to her hair, which is wavy and short to her chin. She has pale blue eyes which are accentuated by the slight crow's feet next to them, so I place her in her late thirties. She is wearing dark jeans and a black t-shirt which has a gold pattern on it that I can't make out, topped off with a bespoke black leather jacket. I want to rip all her clothes off and get intimate with her. Ever since the whore dumped me for the second time, I have been really desperate for it. The reawakening of my sexual appetite is the only good thing to come out of being dumped again.

"Me neither. Maybe it would have worked better with a woman," I respond.

"That might look like it was her time of month and no one would want to see that," the woman replies and smiles.

I laugh at this, and agree. "So, do you like any of the

other pieces?"

"Well, I have an eye on something and there's a picture of one of the landscapes that I like."

"If you are serious about buying a piece I can take your details and let you know when they are available. I could even see about getting you a discount. I'm Benita, one of the managers of the cinema," I promote myself in my introduction.

The other woman puts out her hand to shake mine. "I'm Alison, and I am definitely interested in the items I have seen here." She hands me one of her business cards. "Maybe I should take your number too, in case I have any further questions."

* * * *

The apartment is pitch black. Usually if one of us is out, the other one would leave the hallway light on, but I know she is in because I asked the doorman. I guess Carmen is still pissed off that I admonished her earlier in the evening, but really I am the one who should be annoyed. It is my night, and she should have championed me better. But it is done now. I rub my finger over my lips as I think about the events of the night. I go to the kitchen to get a drink; I really crave something dark and I don't care if it is whiskey, scotch, bourbon, or brandy. There is an expensive bottle of brandy, one she keeps around for when her dad visits. I am half-tempted to pour it all down the sink to spite them. Just knowing it is meant for "Daddy" puts me off drinking it, not out of a fear of upsetting the man but because I don't want to be like him in any way. If liking the same drink labels me in that category, I have to pass on it. I check for alternatives in the fridge. The moment the door is open, I am greeted by a bottle of champagne with a large red bow on it. I think that Carmen must have gotten it earlier in the day and meant for us to share it tonight after the exhibition and party. That would have been nice, but why did she have to go so schizo earlier?

What the fuck was her comment about her getting "Daddy" to get me work all about? That man always has to interfere, and she always has to go running to him. If my exhibition is as well received as Joe seems to think, I will make some real money and my reputation will soar. I will be able to get my own place and her dad can go and fuck off. But following the events of tonight, I am not sure if I want her to come with me. I pour a large brandy, but mix it with a little coke just to differentiate myself from her father. I know Mr. Howard would never do that, and would complain about it if he saw me do it. I go into the living room and sit down on the single sofa, keep the lights off, and sip my drink. Lots has happened tonight and to say I am confused is an understatement. I take another sip of the diluted brandy and run my tongue over my lips. With my free hand, I rub my trousers over my crotch. I decide what I'm going to do. I gulp the rest of the drink and go back to the kitchen, grab two champagne flutes, take the champagne out of the fridge, and head towards the bedroom.

I gently open the bedroom door, so as not to wake her up in case she is sleeping. I slip inside the room and close the door behind me.

"Carmen?" I whisper. She does not reply. I say her name again, this time more intimately, and move around to my side of the bed. I place the bottle and glasses on the floor and sit down on the bed. I rub the small of her back over the covers. Even though the covers are between us, I use the hand that is not cold from holding the champagne.

"Car." I move her hair out of the way to expose her neck and start kissing it. She stirs and turns over. Before she can say anything, my tongue is in her mouth and she responds. After we finish this make-up kiss, I move away to open the bottle and pour us a drink. I put a finger to my lips to indicate we should not talk. We clink the glasses as a toast, have a sip each, and set the glasses down.

* * * *

"I am sorry about Tim, he doesn't get out much," I joke, but it is true.

"Stop apologizing, it's not your fault. We all have a few too many now and again," Ged counters. "Are you sure he will get home okay?"

The question makes me wonder if I should have walked Tim the ten minutes home instead of dumping him in a taxi. When we'd gone outside and the cold February air hit him, he seemed to wake up out of his alcohol-induced slumber. I paid the taxi driver, so Tim would be fine. I hope he went to bed, not to sleep off his inevitable hangover, but so he will not notice that a good few hours have passed and I haven't returned. When I put him in the taxi Tim had asked if I was not coming home too. I said I would follow shortly, but first I wanted to speak to Ricky about commissioning him to take some pictures of buildings, and I wanted to do it before he got too booked up after becoming famous. In truth, I'd wanted to spend more time with Ged, because I enjoy his company. Tim is lucky to have me because I have never cheated on him despite all the opportunities I have had to do so. Well, there was my one indiscretion, but that really does not count.

Once, when I sprained my back and was in some pain, Taylor had suggested that instead of taking run of the mill painkillers, I should go for a sports massage. Taylor recommended a guy, saying it would be more effective than a woman as she would not be strong enough to do it properly—it was not just a spa treatment. The guy had been an expert with his hands. I relaxed, and the pain was soon gone. After the official back massage, the guy offered to do the rest of my body because he could tell I was stressed. I was not sure if it was all the oil, the fact that the guy had fixed me, or that he was so manly, but I was super turned on, especially when the guy worked his magic on my thighs. When I turned over I tried to hide my erection, but the masseur told me not to worry about it, it was a natural reaction. He finished the job, and once done, he asked me if I wanted him to take care of the one area that he had not done. I could not have said no if my life depended on it, so the guy jerked me off. I had looked at the guy's hands as they worked their way along my shaft. It was pure magic. The jerk-off was so perfectly done that when I shot my load, I splurted further than I had ever done before. I had made up for the guilt I felt by taking Tim to Croatia on a spontaneous holiday, a place Tim had always wanted to go. That indiscretion did not count because I'd paid for the massage, I didn't kiss the guy or anything, and would never see him again.

Now, here I am keying in the code (a good thing they

never changed it) to the projection room to show Ged what it looks like and explain how a cinema works. Ged had asked to see the projection room once I told him I used to work at the cinema, and he seems fascinated. The room is not well lit. Everything is shut off because no films are running at this time of night. I take him by the hand to lead him around. I like the feel of his large hands, especially those long fingers. I cannot feel anything sharp at the end of them, which turns me on because all I can think of is what it will be like to have them pleasuring me.

* * * *

I start to kiss Carmen's face and neck as she undoes the buttons on my shirt. I move my hands to her shoulders and grab the two straps to her nightie and pull them down. I pull the whole thing down her body as I continue to kiss her, this time kissing newly exposed parts. Now she is fully naked. I start to caress her breasts, and kiss the areas that get her going. She whips my belt off and starts to liberate my manhood. I finish the task for her by removing my boxers and trousers. Now that we are both naked, I push her back unto the bed and continue to massage her breasts. With my tongue I work my way between her legs. As I start lapping at her, she is groaning in pleasure. She swivels underneath me and shimmies down the bed to suck my cock, as I continue to go down on her. In the 69 position, she takes me in her mouth.

"You're so precummy."

I continue to eat her out and work my fingers into the equation. We continue to pleasure each other. Suddenly, I get harder and bigger, and then fill her mouth with cum. This takes her by surprise, not because it was quite quick, but because she has never been able to get me off with just sucking. Normally either of us, mainly I, would have to strum Little Ricky while she sucked for this to happen.

She takes up her champagne glass and spits in it. I continue performing my act on her. This continues for a while, then I am back at her mouth with mine. I am hard again.

"Are you going to ride your fast car, baby?" she coos.

"I am going to fuck you like a Dirty Van."

This is a sort of role-play exchange we had established early on in our relationship, when we had been more sexual. She spreads her legs as wide as she can, wraps them around me, arches her body upwards. One arm is around my neck. With her free hand she guides me inside her. My first thrust is deep—I decide to fill her with all of me—she gasps in pleasure and begs to be ridden like the Dirty Van she is.

I am pumping away at her, achieving a good rhythm. I put my thoughts, present earlier when I unexpectedly came in her mouth, out of my head. She is wriggling and panting with every prod, loving each moment. She starts to breathe faster. My earlier fantasies re-enter my head and I try to push them aside. Lucy, the incredible looking half-English, half-German model friend of Bloody Adonis, comes to the front of my mind. Carmen starts shouting for my sex more as she is about to climax. Usually she would then be satisfied, and I would withdraw from her and finish myself off over her belly. We both find this good because the pill makes her ill, and I have the level of control required to do it; plus, although I never would admit it, it is the only way I can finish.

As the thoughts race through my head, I am super turned on. She starts to climax, and thrashes around in joy. I continue to pump away at her. I can feel myself on the brink of no return. I continue going as I need to prove to her and, most importantly, to myself how much I love her. She rakes her long fingernails across my back leaving her mark as she orgasms, and I fill her with my cum, groaning in pleasure.

"That was the best ever," Carmen declares. She moves her head into the nook between my arm and chest and we position ourselves for sleep. "I am sorry for being a complete crazy bitch, it's just I thought you were losing interest in me, and I couldn't handle that. Anyway, it is in the past. I love you. Tell me all about your exhibition."

"I love you too, and I will tomorrow, but I am exhausted now. Can we just sleep?"

"Sure, after that session, I am tired too. Happy Valentine's Day." With that, she kisses me lightly on the lips and goes to sleep.

"Happy Valentine's Day too, baby," I murmur back to her. I listen to her breathing pattern change as she falls asleep. Sleep is the last thing on my mind. I am still disturbed at what had occurred. I do not want to think about it, but cannot help but analyze what had happened. When she was sucking me off, I had started to fantasize about some of the guys I had photographed and what it might be like if they were sucking me off, and before I knew it, I had cum. When I was having sex with her, I'd tried to think about the extremely stunning female model to whom I had been introduced. It had done nothing for me, but when I thought about Taylor I could not control myself. And that kiss with Taylor in the office was mind blowing. Thinking of where that kiss could have led had turned me on so much, made me finish off with a woman for the first time. With my free hand, I trace the outline of my mouth and wonder what it all means, but my mind wanders back to that moment when Taylor kissed me so passionately, and I find my cock starting to stir again.

9

HE BEHAVES A CERTAIN WAY IN THE CHANGING ROOM

Twenty-two knights and warriors position themselves strategically around the green battlefield. The combatants look closely at where their allies stand, but consider the enemy's placement more intently as they try to ascertain any weaknesses that can be exploited.

The warriors place themselves into a classic attack formation, and I consider our defensive line. To our opponents it will appear to be flawed—there is a part of the defense that lacks strength, and they will plan to use that to their advantage. We knights are being more cunning than usual. We decide to opt out of being obvious and try something that will look like a random approach. It is really anything but random, our deliberate opening is to draw the enemy in and close ranks around them before they notice the maneuver. Using the element of surprise, we will take the upper hand. The only down side is that for this to work, we have to let our opponents deep into our lines, but we understand the risk and want to try something new against this reputed behemoth.

Certain individuals, while focused on the bigger goal, have their own unique mission—unsanctioned by me—to carry out, whether it is to seek and destroy a former confederate (an ex), gather intelligence on a new faction (a new hook-up), or perform their role so brilliantly that there will be a handsome reward (all-night drinks and partying). All the soldiers stand here, the anticipation slowly building up. Each wants to act out his role to the best of his ability, to be integral in leading his side to victory, and to capture some of the glory and spoils for himself. All we need is the sound of the war cry so that this battle can commence.

The whistle sounds, the Brighton Warriors secondary striker taps the football to the striker, who runs forward with it before passing it backwards and heading for the opening that we, the South London Knights (SLK), have not filled. He is supported by the right winger. The secondary striker passes the ball to the attacking midfielder, who plays around with it by crossing the ball to and fro to the other midfielders before advancing on the winger and striker. Out of nowhere, the center backs and wingback are on the striker. The Warriors are trying to take advantage of the hole in our defense, not knowing that it is a deliberate trap.

I look on. I have a lot of hope for one of the center backs, a straight photographer who one of the gay players had brought along a few months earlier. When the photographer first joined, he was eager, and this translated into being skillful on the pitch, so when it came to giving him a permanent position on the team for the league matches I thought it would be a no-brainer and that the rest of the team would support my decision. Of course, life is never that easy. Some of the team moaned about my decision to have another straight player on what was meant to be a gay-friendly team, and this latest player, Ricky put the number of straight guys on the permanent team to three. Maybe I do have to be more selective and give priority to gay players because this is a team meant to encourage gay guys to play more sports. Nevertheless, gay guys have hardly been banging down the changing room door demanding a place on the team. I decide I will talk to my captain counterpart on the Warriors team, who is very fit, after the match and see how he handles the situation.

Something is wrong with my up-and-coming star, though. His initial spark of talent is gone, replaced with aggression. I know the guy missed the last match and practice session due to having some big work event. He had even invited me to go, but I'd declined because it was not really my thing. Being invited had not impaired my judgment to let the guy play today, but am I being too lenient on him? Usually I will not play someone who has not been at practice, but the photographer has always been in shape. What is wrong with him? I look on and anticipate my number thirteen will calm down once his nerves go away. This hope is dashed when the center back obviously fouls a Warrior. This act seems really out of character for him, even though deep down I actually know very little about him. From what I had seen previously he is a good-humored, likeable guy who does not drop the ball and would not deliberately foul someone. I watch Taylor jog over to where a situation is developing to check on the fallen Warrior. I decide to not join them, and continue to watch from the opponent's half. Taylor and the fouler are friends; Taylor brought him onto the team, so he can talk to him. The referee rightly penalizes number thirteen and gives the Warriors a free kick. It is a small consolation that we did not concede the penalty because the foul happened near the box. I hope Taylor restores some order by diffusing his friend's aggression, but when he goes to speak to him, the guy shrinks away.

* * * *

The vibrations are causing everything to shake. I am dead embarrassed standing here wobbling away. I look down at Tim and wonder why he is making me go through this. Does it really help in any way? He is on his side, facing me, supporting himself with just one of his big arms tensed on the power plate. I watch him do a plank. I feel like an idiot standing on a power plate hoping it will magically vibrate all my fat away. It does not look like Tim is shaking, so maybe the same is true for me, in which case everyone in the gym probably doesn't have a view of me as a big fat lump of jelly wobbling about. Tim changes position and does another plank, supporting himself on his other arm. My machine kicks into life again, so I hold on to the sides and just stand here, glad that he is not making me do what he is doing. When Tim finishes, he stands up and waits for me. Upon completion, I ask him if it works if I just stand there. He explains that everyone has to start somewhere, and it is a good way to wake up all my body parts.

"Anyway, Ben, I thought you would like things vibrating you."

My face flushes red, not from the exercise. "Oh, ha ha. Nothing can compare to the feel of a real woman. When I use toys, they are always the non-battery operated types, and I am the wearer." I decide to change the topic of conversation. "So what is next, oh Mighty Sensei?"

"We need to do some cardiovascular exercises to get

your heart rate going and start to burn off some pounds. Usually, I would suggest going for a run...er...jog on the treadmill, but since you said you don't want to run until you've lost some weight, we are going swimming."

A couple of days after Valentine's Day, Alison had called me and suggested we grab coffee. I accepted. Then the usual fears of what to wear, will we get along, and what about post-coffee if we do get along, crept into my mind. I had been consumed by that last thought—I had put on a lot of weight and was not exactly a small girl to begin with. I'd tried to tell myself that this did not matter to Alison because she knew what I looked like, flirted with me, and asked me out anyway. But it was different being naked. After the Suze affair part two my confidence took a knock, and I comfort-ate my problems away. So, after accepting the date and giving the situation some thought, I decided to reach out to one of the gays who was obsessed with the body beautiful. I emailed Tim to ask his advice about some weight loss exercises. He'd offered to be a bit more hands-on and go with me to the gym, show me some exercises, and help tailor a plan to suit my needs. I didn't really want to accept it because the thought of this muscle-bound guy training me was not appealing, but he seemed so keen to help, to the point of insistence, that I went along with it. He told me that on the night of the exhibition Jas had asked for a similar favor, so he was really not putting himself out.

Two days after his initial suggestion and two days before my coffee with Alison, I found myself at the Phoenix gym with Tim (I had the day off because I had worked the evening before). It was Thursday during the daytime, so the place was empty—that is how he had sold me on the idea. I'd picked my gay well. He knew how to use all the machines, he knew what each one worked out, he knew extra exercises and dietary advice, but mostly he seemed really happy to help. He told me the best way to lose weight was to go running, which I did not feel comfortable doing. He asked me what cardiovascular exercises I liked, which were not many, but we reached a compromise on swimming. He told me that next time we would go to the proper gym that had more equipment, and he would start me off on a power plate. He'd had to explain what this was, and the potential benefits. I tried to get out of going to the public gym by saying that I was not a member, but he offered me a free guest pass. After my coffee with Alison, which turned into a walk, lunch, and a couple of drinks, I knew more was in the cards, but I had ended that date at that point with a lame excuse. However, I promised to meet up soon, and sealed it with a kiss to let her know that I was interested. Thus began my frantic dieting and gym-going.

* * * *

"Ben, I will meet you in the pool because I want to do some weights beforehand and find pet project number two." Really, I want to give her the chance to get into the water by herself without me watching. Once she is in the pool, she is fine, but I know that she is intimidated right now. I go over to the bench and am about to start working out my chest when two women approach me.

"Excuse me, but we were wondering what your availability is like and how much you charge."

"We saw how good you were with that other woman,

and we are looking for a new personal trainer."

I laugh and am flattered. "She's just a friend that I am helping out, but I can give you some pointers."

Half an hour later, the session ends and I agree to join them for some thank-you drinks the following evening. I make sure to pick Twilight when they suggest drinks, so they will know I am gay and not have any untoward expectations.

* * * *

"The other night, I had a really great steak for dinner."

"Was it just steak, or did you have anything else?"

"No, just steak."

"That sounds good, man. The other day at work, I was eating a large can of tuna, and one girl seemed shocked I was having it by itself. She asked if I wanted mayo with it. I don't understand what it had to do with her. I like tuna by itself. I mean obviously if I didn't, I wouldn't be eating it. Why do people always have to put pressure on you?"

Bingo, I have found the perfect pair. The Cow would be proud.

Spending the day skulking around the changing room has paid off. Tim got me into the gym for free, which was good, but based on today's success I will definitely consider getting my own membership. When I first approached Tim, it was to see if he used a little chemical help and what his feelings were on the matter. Tim had proved to be too straight-laced that way but was keen to help me "train." Tim had started me on some random weight machine because I told him I wanted to tone up my shoulders. When Tim moved off to help Ben, I sloped back to the changing room to get down to my real business. I had a shower, and then wrapped myself in a towel to listen and observe the other people in the changing room.

I am fascinated by how homoerotic the whole thing is among the straight guys. There are lots of compliments— "Great arms!" "How do you get your back so big?" There are guys touching other guys' biceps—I note that it does not seem restricted to the biceps. There is a general atmosphere of guys weighing themselves and walking around nude for the sake of it. I now understand why gay guys like going to the gym so much.

My greatest skill is reading what people want—that is my profession. I just need to do a few tests with these guys to make sure they will be suitable clients. "Sorry to interrupt you guys, but you both have such a great upper body." I hope I do not burst out laughing. When the straight guys say it to each other it sounds so natural, but hearing my own words sounds like a come-on. "I was wondering if you could give a skinny guy like me some tips."

The guys simultaneously look at me, assessing themselves to be bigger and therefore stronger than I. I'm actually quite lean, but my skin color gives my body a definition that is not actually there. My disarming gestures make the guys see me as non threatening, someone with whom they can talk. I listen and nod in the right places while they talk about the various workouts I can do.

"So what sort of food should I be eating—carbs or proteins?" I change the talk to diet because I know from their earlier conversation they are both quite passionate about the role of food in the emancipation of their muscles. "And what about supplements, do those shakes everyone has do any good?" Then I casually drop the idea of additional supplements, reinforce the message with a selling point, and then move on without waiting for an answer. "What about other supplements? I heard some of the other guys in here talking about steroids. It would be good to get bigger faster because I have a date with this really hot woman who only dates real muscle houses." I then show them a picture of some random clothed porn star I had earlier screen-grabbed on my phone. "So are pills or injections better for you?"

"What do you mean?" asks the tuna guy.

I explain that I bought a pill and an injectable steroid from a guy, but am not sure which one to take.

"You don't want to start messing with those. They are no good for you in the long run."

"They fuck you up."

"The side effects are bad, man."

"I might pass on the drugs." Then comes the most delicate part—positioning the sale. I have managed to establish trust with the guys by asking for advice. Now I will ask for another favor, taking the drugs off my hands, without implying they take steroids themselves. "You guys couldn't help me out one more time and take them off my hands? Maybe you know a friend who uses them?" "I will even sell them to you for less than I paid. I just can't afford to lose all that money."

"Sorry, dude, we are not interested," says the steak guy.

"Oh well, no fuss. I'll just look for the guy I got them from and ask him for my money back." I walk away, listening to their whispered tones.

"Won't taking steroids for a little while help you to get a bit bigger and then you just stop taking them?" Tuna Man asks Steak Man. At that point, they witness another guy enter the changing room and talk to me. My two potential customers watch as the other guy chats with me and then strips off and heads toward the shower. They look at his rock-hard chest and firm buttocks.

I change into my swimming trunks and make my way to the pool. I pass the showers and see Tim having a quick washdown before doing lengths in the pool with Ben, as he just had told me.

As I am about to enter the pool area, Steak Man whispers that he will help me out. He has a friend who will be interested, but he did not want to say anything in front of the other guy. I nod, thinking it's always "a friend," and make arrangements to sell both the pill, oxymetholone, and the vial of nandrolone, to the guy outside the gym an hour later, with instructions on how to use them. The fact he is buying both types tell me that he is a novice at this, but I do not mark my prices up further. I leave them competitively priced—any mark-ups come once my customers have developed a need for the drugs. I walk past the pool where Ben is really going for it. Tim hasn't joined her yet, so I can easily sneak pass, I make my way to the sauna and slip in.

* * * *

I finish washing the sweat off and make my way back to my locker to change into my swimming trunks. I am toweling myself dry, just enough so that I will not leave a huge puddle where I walk, when I notice a guy enter the changing room. The guy walks around the entire changing room looking for a free spot. The place is fairly empty, but he picks the same bench as me, only slightly further down. I find him very attractive, so I slow down the pace of my drying off. His features are very exotic. Not being an expert, I place him from somewhere like Malaysia. The guy removes the top half of his clothes and is facing me while he undoes his belt and pulls down his trousers. I am looking at his smooth skin and start to get aroused. I haven't had sex for most of February. Ever since my appalling behavior at the exhibition, Bobs has been very cold towards me. I quickly turn around so the guy will not notice my cock starting to get hard.

I start to fumble around in my locker looking for my swimming trunks; in my haste, I drop them on the floor. I quickly bend over to pick them up and realize that I could have inadvertently thrust my ass in the guy's face. I turn around to see where he is. Luckily my honor is still intact, because the guy has not moved. Now, however, he is fully naked and hard, and he is staring at me. He looks down at his cock and then into my eyes. I keep looking him up and down, drawn to his small but perfectly formed penis. I feel myself getting more and more aroused. The guy moves his hand down to his groin and continues to watch me. Suddenly, some noise from elsewhere in the changing room breaks me out of the gaze. I pick up my trunks and pull them on, tucking in my erection as best I can, wrap my towel over myself and beat a hasty retreat. As I move past the guy, I notice disappointment in his eyes.

* * * *

Despite the defeat, nearly all the South London Knights are being jovial, and the changing room is full of laughter and banter. The Knights and the Brighton Warriors start to take off their uniforms and discuss where they are going to go tonight. I turn my back on the room, the captain and Taylor. I do not listen to any conversations, I just hear the noise. I am not sure what I should do. Previously I would have joined in the conversation, showered, changed, maybe gone for a few drinks, but something has changed. I have changed. For a start, I do not know where to look. I am scared of what might happen if I turn around and see a naked guy. What if someone catches me looking? I know I am being stupid. Most of these guys are gay. They are surrounded by other guys and they do not walk around with boners, so I remove that thought from my head. I am not one of them anyway. I hear the showers starting to go on, which is good because there will be fewer people in the room now. I do not bother to turn around. I start to undress, but feel very self-conscious. I pull down my left sock, take out the shin pad, and remove the sock. A weird thought enters my head—have I always taken off my left sock first or do I normally start with the right one? A hand is on my shoulder; I slowly turn around.

It is the captain. Part of me is relieved that it is not Taylor, but a bigger part is disappointed. I know I basically blanked Taylor on the pitch earlier after I had fouled some poor Warrior. I know I was uncommunicative when he attempted to contact me after the event, but I still wanted it to have been him.

"Are you okay?" the SLK captain asks, and gives reasons why he does not think I am okay. "Missing practice, fouling players, no motivation."

I hear some of it, I do not reply; I remain deadpan. I scan the room and realize it is just us; everyone else must be in the showers. Even Taylor is not waiting in the wings to talk to me afterward. Still covered in mud, I look at the captain and want to ask him when he first knew he was gay, but decide against it. "Sorry, boss, lots on the mind. Relationship issues."

"Well, we've all been there before. Come out for a few drinks, drown your sorrows, and worry about them tomorrow. But try to sort them out before the next practice session."

I smile back at his kindness. The captain continues, "Anyway, you owe that guy you fouled an apology, and you owe me for not kicking you off the team. You can buy us a few drinks."

The players start to return from the showers. Among them is Taylor, who briefly looks at me. I take out my other shin pad and take my other sock off and grab my towel. I make my way to the shower and decide I will finish undressing away from everyone else. I hope the water will not only wash away the dirt and sweat but also will clean my mind and give me clarity. Should I go home to my girlfriend and just forget about what was probably just a drunken fumble, or should I get drunk with the guys and see what happens next?

10

HE HAS LOTS OF FEMALE FRIENDS

The artificial light from the surroundings catches the surface, and a golden luminance resonates around it. I look on, not so much in awe as in admiration; each individual piece seems to play its own unique role while managing to work together to complete the whole. Erica notices me staring and takes this to mean that I like her. Perhaps to get flirty, she starts laughing at her own joke. As she gently shakes from the laughter, her hair sways modestly. I watch as the focal point of my attention moves. I am not a trichophiliac, but I do like looking at women's hair. Watching her, I want to touch it and feel whether it is as soft as I imagine it to be. I start thinking about whether I should try dating a guy with long hair. Then she goes quiet; she has asked some question and is waiting for a response. I do not know how to reply.

"Sorry, what did you say? I missed the last bit because I was thinking of getting us another drink."

"Nat, I suggested we go and get something to eat, but if you want another drink that's cool."

I do not really want to eat dinner with the not-so-new intern from my work, but I am happy to continue to drink with her. I go to the bar and order another bottle of rosé.

* * * *

The three women sit at a table in Twilight checking out all the gay guys. They tell me they are out to have fun as a group of friends and are happy to be in a place where they will not be hit on by guys looking to score with women. They are enjoying observing the talent for the night. Later, when the go-go men dance around the poles, they will have a chance to objectify men, turning the table on the traditional gender inequality.

When I first join them, I felt they objectified me. I had walked into the bar, and one of the women spotted me and waved to beckon me over. "You're right, he's lovely. It's such a shame he's gay," said Phoebe, the woman who was not at the gym with the other two the day before, like I wasn't even standing there.

Helen said, "Well, if he were straight he probably wouldn't have such a great body. Do you know many straight guys with bodies like that?"

As I settle down with my second bottle of beer I do not mind their banter. The trio of women toast me and thank me again for helping them out the day before.

"Phoebe, Tim showed us how to use the equipment and do all these extra exercises, and there was no perving on his part."

"That is just what I am looking for. I need a personal trainer because I plan to get fit this year."

"Judging by how sore I feel today, I know that I worked areas that have never been worked before and it must have done me some good. I think we have found our guy," Helen chimes in.

"You told us yesterday you are not a personal trainer, but since you are always in the gym, we were wondering if you would consider helping us. Of course, we would pay you the going rate. We have some friends who would also be interested," says Claire.

* * * *

Anxious barely cuts it regarding my third date with Al, as I now called her. Not because I feel uncomfortable around her—quite the opposite. I am very relaxed, because we get along well, so well that I have been invited to meet some of Al's friends at a house party. If this date goes well I am fully prepared to let tonight be the night where we take our relationship to the full physical level. I really want to do that, but find it a bit nerve wracking. Despite the imbalance—her age and success—this relationship has a different dynamic than that with Suze. I know it is wrong to compare, but cannot help it. Suze was so parasitic. The dependency was not good for either of us. This one is healthier; Al already wants me to meet her friends. I think I am more mature now and have closure; well, at least the cold hard reality shock I needed from being dumped by my ex again. I stand outside the tube station having a cigarette, and I start to feel more confident because of the way the dates with Al are going and because of the amount of weight I have already lost. But since my life is going well, I also have a sense of apprehension that something bad will happen soon. This makes me scared.

* * * *

Looking around the Flicks bar, all the memories from my time working here come flooding back. Part of me wishes I could return to those happier times. I start to contemplate what I will have to do to get back to happiness, but that is too complicated. So I distract myself by looking at all the red dots on the picture information. How the fuck did Ricky, my quite dull neighbor, manage to sell so many pictures so quickly? I don't think they are that good.

Joe appears, having changed out of his uniform, the black t-shirt with the cinema logo on it, and kisses me hello. "Bobs, where do you want to go?"

"I sometimes miss working here," I tell him, "Can we stay here? If you don't mind shitting on your own doorstep."

Joe looks around the bar and sees that it is relatively quiet, so he nods and joins me. I knew he would agree, so I slide over the drink I already have waiting for him. Joe brings me up to speed on the latest Flicks gossip; most of the people I know have left, but I do not mind listening to the stories. It is relaxing being in the company of my second-oldest friend. In some ways, I am closer to Joe than Marco because of our complicated history. Maybe this is the friend I can open up to and clear my head with. Joe beats me to it though, and announces he has something he needs to tell me.

* * * *

As we finish the second bottle of wine, I am quite giddy. It is apparent that Erica is in the same state or worse. Maybe we should have just gone for dinner.

"Let's go to another bar, somewhere with music where we can go dancing," she exclaims. "You do like to dance, don't you, Nat?"

If only she knew the answer to her question: yes I love to dance, preferably surrounded by lots of topless men gyrating next me. I do feel like having another drink but I do not know where else to go; the only places I can suggest will shock her. I start to analyze the situation.

What is it with me getting into these situations with people from work? The end of her internship placement is coming up. She had asked my advice about whether she should stay on, if they valued her enough so she could stay on, and what competitor companies she could move to if necessary. I somehow agreed to help her over drinks. Before I knew it, I had agreed to meeting up today— Saturday. She gets up and starts swaying by her chair. At first, I am not sure if she cannot walk because she is drunk, but I soon realize she is—sort of—dancing.

Then she starts to move closer to me. I know what will happen next: she will get a bit touchy-feely and then come in for the kill. I quickly get up and go to the bar to get us some water and pre-empt her advances. I think the only way I can fully stop her is to tell her the truth. She claims to value our friendship, so maybe she will not betray me at work and out me. Even so, I am sure that some colleagues suspect that I am gay, and some probably have just assumed I am because of my friendship with Rod. Also, I do not know if Rod has told anyone. Back at the table with the water, I decide to out myself in natural conversation so as not to embarrass her.

"The barman is quite cute. I think he was flirting with me. Maybe I should give him my number. What do you think?" I watch her pupils grow larger as the news sinks in.

* * * *

"It's been seven years. I'm in my early thirties, not that I look it. My biological clock is ticking, and he still hasn't proposed," Phoebe moans.

Claire greets this by rolling her eyes. Phoebe looks at me, to whom she has directed the moan. I am usually very diplomatic in these situations, but I am really letting my hair down with the girls and am on my way to getting hammered. Plus, I need to vent my own frustrations. I end up telling her my real opinion.

"Seriously, if the guy doesn't know after three years, what is the point of going on? That's more than enough time for him to make up his mind. After seven years, that's just a joke. He's simply too comfortable. Rock the boat and ask him yourself; otherwise, move on, because you aren't going to get it from that guy," I eulogize.

A mortified Phoebe looks like her favorite pet has just been run over. She is about to say something, but I continue. "When he has wasted the best years of your life, he will dump you for a younger girl and will have her pregnant within the year, and they will be married before the kid pops out. But you know there is always a sexual act you can do to get the proposal from a straight guy— guaranteed." I down my beer and go to get another round of drinks.

"I love Tim. He speaks the truth." Claire says as I head off.

I return with the drinks, a lot quicker than if any of the women had gone to get them.

"So what is the act? I can't swallow, the taste makes me feel sick," Phoebe says.

I smile at her and reply with a sly grin on my face. "Just shove your finger up his butt when he's doing you or you're blowing him, and he'll come so hard that he'll agree to anything."

Helen, looking slightly embarrassed, moves the conversation on to long-term gay relationships and how come I am not married, as I had been with my partner for just as long as Phoebe.

"Well, it's up to me to ask him," I say. "He asked me once when we had been going out maybe eighteen months. We were walking across the Millennium Bridge when he asked. I said no because back then it wasn't legal, so I didn't think there was any point to saying yes. Then when civil partnerships did eventually become legal, I joked that he should re-ask me, but he said he asked once before and will not ask again; if I want to get married, I need to ask him."

"So why don't you?" Phoebe inquires. But before I can reply, the bar erupts in applause. The crowd welcomes the dancers.

* * * *

As house parties go, this one is really good. It is a housewarming in a gated property in Covent Garden that Al's friends have just bought. Stella is an investment banker and her partner Judy owns a shop selling homemade bath bombs, candles, face masks, and general items that smell like a princess has thrown up. Joe once dragged me into a major chain selling similar items. All the sales staff were women who looked like they had been drinking from the company's "Save the Planet" water cooler and all seemed to wear minimal makeup, if any. They were in homemade clothing, had too many piercings and tattoos on show, and spent their free time protesting at Westminster. Must be a lesbian thing. I keep that thought to myself, as I don't think the present company would appreciate it. It is sad that I can't share my appraisal of the situation with Joe. He would have found it as funny as I do.

I am pissed at him. Why is he being so queenie and not trying to make amends? I guess he has moved on, and it looks like I have too—with an older girlfriend who has friends the same age as herself, who are doing well and have Covent Garden apartments. Al has stayed by my side since we arrived at the party, but she does not have to; I am comfortable with the new women I meet because all the guests are being really nice to me. I have never really had a big group of lesbian friends, but now I have started to find my way. I am chatting to a diving buddy of Al's. This woman seems to know her well, so I try to find out if there is any basis for my earlier feelings of apprehension. I subtly ask about any ex-girlfriends, pretending to know all about them, but am totally unprepared for what I hear.

* * * *

"Are you sure he won't mind us going in and cramping his style?"

"What style, Joe? He doesn't have any," Bobs replies.

"There will be no sex for you if he hears that."

I push open the doors to Twilight. We see Tim with his new friends, but leave him to it. We find a discreet corner and continue our discussion of, as Bobs puts it, my newfound ability to play with fire. I have been sleeping with a closeted man for just under two months. The guy, Anthony, lives with his girlfriend. We do not date but meet up for sex at my place or in his car.

Bobs asks if I want a relationship with Anthony. I try to smooth out the situation saying that I am happy with the way things are going, and Anthony and I will be together when he is able to accept that he is gay. I have reason to hope that the time is coming really soon.

Earlier that night, Ant had asked me if I was going out this evening and if he could meet up with me. When I responded that I was already in a gay bar with a friend, Ant had been unperturbed by the situation and wanted to come along. This is a first in our dynamic; things are definitely looking up.

* * * *

I do not really enjoy kissing on the mouth, so I go back to caressing Erica's breasts and licking them, which I like more, maybe because I have never done it before. We keep changing positions, and I find myself on top in the missionary. I am continually slipping out of her; I do not know if I am doing it right. Am I trying to thrust too far and coming back too much, or is it because it is different than fucking a guy, who tends to be a lot tighter? From her moaning and movement, I assume she is having a good time, and that pleases me. Back in the bar when I came out to her, she was initially shocked, but then there was a sense of relief because it explained why I did not just jump her. Then she acted cool with the information rather than being embarrassed and running off, asking questions about who I liked at work. She'd asked about Rod, whom she knew was gay, and if the two of us were more than friends. I in turn named the best-looking guys who were straight and single, and said they all seemed interested in her. Before she even let the dust settle on her crush on me, she said she was interested in another guy. By the time we left the bar at closing we had drunk more, and I was worried about my young friend getting home okay. I offered up my place, she accepted, and we had found ourselves sharing my bed and talking. She admired my tattoos, then surprised me by asking if I had ever been with a woman. When I said no but was tempted to, she did not need any further encouragement. She removed her underwear, climbed astride me and pulled down my boxers. Before Erica lowered herself on to me she'd asked, "Nat, what are we doing?" I knew she wanted it more than I did, and went on to satisfy my curiosity about being with a woman.

* * * *

"All the guys in here have already mentally undressed you. Why not just give them and us a treat?" Claire encourages in a joking way.

Helen is thrilled. "Oh, come on, Tim, you have a much better body than the go-go boys here, come on. Off. Off. Off."

Phoebe moves behind me, grabs the bottom of my t-shirt and starts to tease it up suggestively by alternately yanking either side up and down. I am about to say why I can't, but I decide against it. I take my t-shirt off and jump up onto the empty podium. The three women cheer me on, so I start really going for it, spurred on by my three new friends, as the European summer hit of last year fills the room.

* * * *

Outside on the small but immaculate roof terrace of the apartment, I am having another cigarette. I do not feel like going back inside and being sociable. Then I feel a hand on my shoulder.

"There you are. I've been looking for you."

I turn around and look at Al. Damn, she looks hot. She wraps her arms around me, kisses me, and tells me she really likes me. She sees this as having potential, but first she has to tell me something.

"Don't worry, I know that you have a girlfriend already," I reply coolly.

"I was going to tell you, I wouldn't introduce you to all my friends if I was going to lie to you. I have a sort of girlfriend."

I put out my cigarette and am about to leave, but Al holds my hand and quickly blurts out lots of information before I have a chance to walk away.

"I have a girlfriend but she is twenty years older than me and she was my first serious relationship. The girlfriend was married to a man when we first met, and she still lives with her husband in Canada. 'Lesbian bed death' set into our relationship about ten years ago, and now we only see each other maybe three times a year. I regard the girlfriend as just a friend, not a girlfriend, and I will properly end the relationship with her for you."

* * * *

I notice Bobs's attention is elsewhere, and follow his eyes to see him watching Tim gyrating away on the podium.

"Aren't you lucky with the mega buff boyfriend? You can't even take your eyes off him."

Bobs looks back at me. "I'm going to get some more drinks. Do me a favor and go see if Ginger Rogers over there wants anything. Thanks." He goes off to the bar.

* * * *

The men in the bar are urging me to dance on, and I love being the center of attention for once. As the next song comes on, I momentarily come out of my trance and look down from the podium to the guys standing next to it. I recognize Joe waving up at me and am about to pull him up to join me, when I realize that means Bobs is here. I quickly pull my t-shirt back over my head and cover up. I hear Claire in the background booing me.

"Where is Bobs?"

"At the bar. He sent me over to see if you want a drink. Go back to your dancing and your friends. We don't want to intrude."

"It's okay. I'll go help Bobs with the drinks. I need to get some water; you wait here," I tell him. Joe nods, then takes a call and motions me off in the direction of Bobs, who is ordering drinks from the barman.

As I approach Bobs, I hope that maybe he has not seen me. I am just about to announce myself to my boyfriend when he speaks. "Your t-shirt is inside out."

"Bobs…"

"That was quite the little performance you were putting on there."

"Look, Bob-by honey, I am sorry I got carried away. My friends were egging me on. It's not like I was dancing with other guys."

"That makes it all right to betray my trust and cheat on me? You know you aren't allowed to dance with your top off unless we are out together. How do you think I feel?"

"I'm so sorry. It was only this time. It's not like I go out much without you anyway. You know you can trust me."

* * * *

The excitement about Ant wanting to meet up in gay public has me slightly delirious. Perhaps tonight is going to be my night. I responded to the earlier text message when Ant asked me what I was wearing. Now that beautiful name, which gives me chill bumps, flashes across the face of my phone. I keep saying hello, but I cannot hear a response. It is too crowded and noisy in Twilight. I start to make my way to the door. Suddenly, a woman with a phone in her hand barges into me. I apologize, but she does not move out of my way and doesn't seem sorry for "accidentally" bumping into me.

"Joe, is it?" she asks.

I nod, hoping that I have not forgotten one of my many female friends—the number seems to multiple every time I go to a club.

"I'm Anthony's girlfriend. I've seen your messages to him. At first I thought he was cheating on me, but then when I realized you're a guy…" she emphasizes the word "guy" as she looks me up and down. "He told me how you've been stalking him since he went to watch a film at that cinema down the road. Look, I know he's hot and all, but you have issues texting that shit to a dude you've only seen once in your life. If you don't stop, I'm going to go to the police and they are going to lock you up in some funny farm. Comprendez?"

* * * *

Bobs turns around and gives me a peck on the cheek. "It's fine, I forgive you, but you really hurt me. Seeing you putting yourself out there to all these men makes me feel sick. After tonight, don't see those women again. They are a bad influence. Anyway, go over there and give them this bottle of champagne I bought for you all—it can be a nice goodbye."

"But they have asked me to be their personal trainer. They said they would even pay me."

"Don't be so stupid. Now go on, before the champagne gets flat. I'll bring the rest of the glasses. Why are you looking at me like that? You know I love you."

"Do you? In that case, let's get married—civil partnered—or whatever scrap society has thrown to us. You always said I had to ask you, so I am asking you now."

He doesn't respond. Something is happening in the bar. We look to where a group of people is surrounding two people. It reminds me of school, when a fight is taking place and everyone stands around to watch it until the teacher comes and breaks it up. As the bouncer wades into the middle of the group, I see a woman throw a drink in Joe's face. At this point the music is turned down.

"Stay the fuck away from my man!" she screams as she is escorted out of the bar.

11

HE CAN KEEP A SECRET

Lunchtime always flies by, but today time seems to have stopped, or slowed down to a rate so incredibly stagnant that it might as well have stopped completely. I keep checking the piece of plastic and looking at the stopwatch on my phone—ten seconds have elapsed. I'm hiding out in a toilet stall at work, trying to avoid my co-workers. I need this alone time so much that I have my legs up so my shoes cannot be seen on the floor if anyone looks under the gap. Someone will only know a person is in here if they try the door and find it locked. I hear a couple of other women come into the bathroom, so I try to be even quieter. I can hear myself breathing and think it is really loud, but the other two women are talking quite audibly, so I am probably safe. I look back at my phone; only twenty seconds have passed since I started the timer. I turn my attention back to the piece of plastic, the thing that can very well change my life forever. Suddenly, my phone starts ringing loudly. This startles me and I drop the piece of plastic. I manage to reject the call and put the phone on silent. I keep my feet off the ground and look down at the dropped item; the part I need is not visible. I maneuver myself to reach down and pick it up. When I flip it over and see it, I get off the toilet, drop to my knees, lift up the lid, and proceed to throw up.

"Are you okay in there?"

I control my voice as best as I can, and lie that I am.

* * * *

It all seems a bit too cloak and dagger; the mysterious invite has put me on edge. However, my curiosity gets the better of me, so I accept and agree to play along with the rules. I will go to the Phoenix and enter the building via the underground car park courtesy of the code I was just given. From there, I will phone my host, who will enable the service elevator, which I will take to the appropriate floor. Then it will just be a case of "being discreet" as instructed, getting from the elevator to the apartment of the object of my desire. This carefully laid-out plan is obviously designed so I will not be seen entering the building and will not come into contact with anyone from main reception. It is a bit over the top considering I used to hang out at the Phoenix with my friend, walk in the front door, speak to people I see regularly, and even pop in to say hello to the neighbors. Being caught sneaking around leads to rumors, which no one wants.

In the Phoenix, my feeling of apprehension comes back. Is tonight finally the night when the kiss from Valentine's Day is going to be discussed? It is not the way I had expected it to happen, but maybe it is a good thing to talk it through. I walk straight into the apartment, as per the instructions. I enter the living room, and my host is sitting on the sofa. It looks like that is the place where everything is about to unravel.

"Have a seat." I must have been staring for too long. "Would you like some tea?"

I would have preferred something with a kick. "Sure."

This is way too polite; maybe the tea will be thrown in

my face, then I will be called a homo and beaten with the nearest object to hand. I accept the hot drink and look into my host's eyes, trying to get a sense of why I am here and where this is going. I do enjoy playing games with people but this situation has come out of the blue, and the curve ball has thrown me off. Nevertheless, the hunter part of me is intrigued, so I go along with it to see what it is like to be the prey, or in the worst-case scenario, the possum.

"Thank you for coming, Taylor."

"Sure, no problem. To be honest, I was surprised to hear from you, especially with all these strange instructions you gave me."

"Sorry about that. I'm going through some issues and needed to talk to someone privately. You know, I haven't seen you around much recently."

"I've been busy," I say. This meeting is very calm and not the attack I had expected. But I remain guarded, not wanting to give anything away. "You wanted to talk?"

There is some hesitation before, "well, it is a medical issue."

I can't see the eyes; they are looking down at the cushions on the sofa. For a fleeting moment, I think maybe it is about death. How easy that will make everything.

"I got myself into a situation, and I am not sure what to do about it."

I watch as the tears stream down. The empathetic doctor part of me prompts me to comfort my host with an embrace. I knew after I was invited to the Phoenix that the night would end in tears. I'd thought it would be because of Valentine's Day, but it looks like that is no longer the case.

"I'm here. Tell me when you are ready," I say reassuringly.

"I'm pregnant," Carmen manages to get out through her sobs. "I just found out a couple of days ago. I took a test at work. It was positive, and I don't know what to do."

I watch her closely. Any concern I had that Ricky had told her about our kissing session is erased. This is all about her.

"I thought you, being a doctor, would have heard this story a million times and would be able to advise me what to do."

"I guess this was unplanned?"

She nods. My next question is whether the baby was Ricky's, but I ask more tactfully, "Have you told the father yet?"

"No. We have been having lots of problems recently, and I don't know how Richard will take the news. That's another reason why I asked you over. You're his best friend in London. How do you think he'll take the news?"

So the baby is Ricky's. I get slightly turned on thinking about the virility of the guy who is the current object of my affection. I think about sex with Ricky, where I am the submissive one, lying there while he just fills me up. Carmen is looking at me. I draw my hand down my face from my cheek to my chin, briefly covering my mouth to look like I am thinking about the problem at hand and not my own personal desires.

Perhaps I am taking too long to respond, or maybe Carmen needs to validate asking me to see her under such conditions. "I feel bad about asking you to lie to Ricky, but

I really need to speak to someone. I never bothered signing up with a local doctor when I moved to London. Please, you won't say anything to anyone until I have my head sorted out? I mean doctor-patient confidentiality and all?"

It does not work like that. You cannot spill information to a random medic who is not your doctor and who was not even under the impression that he was having a medical discussion, and expect confidentiality. Despite feeling annoyed that she had tried to trap me like that, I let it go.

"Don't worry. I won't tell Ricky you are pregnant." I fully intend to keep my word. Besides, I have barely seen the guy since we made out on Valentine's Day. I owe her for trying to force my hand. Since our relationship has apparently progressed to a professional one, I ask, "Is it Ricky's?" I am careful not to refer to the fetus as a baby or child. I am surprised that she hesitates, but maybe she is shocked that I am questioning her honor. She looks at me with her bloodshot eyes and nods. I am not so sure; she seems secretive.

I decide not to go for an outstanding bedside manner award; after all, she is not my patient. "I guess you want a doctor, because you want to explore all your options, which are keep it and raise it, give it away, or get rid of it."

"I could never carry a child and then give it away. I have not thought much about the other two options. The timing is just bad. I mean, both of our careers are starting to take off, and we aren't even married."

To me, it sounds like she knows exactly what she wants to do. Under normal circumstances, I would suggest that she discuss the situation with her partner and make a decision together, but I do not want to. I know any clinic I send her to would provide the appropriate counseling, so I do not have to get more involved than she has already made me. Part of me is pissed off with her at how casually she seems to have made her decision, considering the amount of gay guys I know who want children.

Carmen continues justifying herself. "As you know, we have been having a few problems, so it is not the right environment to bring a baby into."

I did not know that they are having problems. Ricky never mentions her or the relationship—it has become sort of an unspoken rule not to mention things at home. This extends to Ricky never asking me about boyfriends. I have not seen or heard from Ricky since the last Knights match, which was about three weeks earlier. I take out my phone and start searching it, asking Carmen if she knows how far along she is.

"Six weeks. According to my math, it was the opening night of his art exhibition."

I give her the number of a clinic where she can get the help she seeks.

* * * *

Currently I feel vulnerable. I am sitting in a cafe waiting for my acquaintance to turn up. I never ask anyone for a favor—I never had to, but now I need help and have opened myself up. I order another double espresso as the waiter goes by. The guy looks very familiar. I wonder if we have slept together, but then I remember we only made out in a club. Safe in that knowledge, my mind switches back to the favor at hand. It is not a big ask, and I can use other means to achieve the purpose, but because it is a health thing I think it is better to do it by the book. If I have to pay the piper at a later date, I am resigned to doing so. What is tricky is that I know the guy on some level and everyone seems to get along well with him, but I do not personally know him well enough to predict his actions. Anyway, this gives me the opportunity to check in on the good doctor, who has been ingratiating himself quite comfortably into my group. I watch Taylor walk in, and get up to greet him. He arrives at my table.

"Hi, Marco."

We don't how to greet each other. In the end we opt for a handshake, foregoing a kiss on the cheek, a hug, or an affectionate pat. This is the first time we have met without anyone else from the group being present.

After Taylor has ordered a drink and a light bite to eat, I pass him a piece of paper. Taylor opens it, reads it, takes out a blank piece of paper and pen, and starts writing.

"Thanks for doing this," I say. "I am amazed that my dad came over here and forgot his medicines."

"No worries, Marco, I'm happy to help, and it is nice for just us to have lunch and catch up. When you messaged me with the Italian names, I looked up the English equivalents and have prescribed them. I must warn you, this is a private prescription so you will have to pay for it." He signs the prescription and hands it to me. He seems to be deep in thought, and then bursts out, "I have an issue that you might be able to help me with. Really, I need some advice, and you're a man of the world, so you might be able to help. Needless to say, what I am about to tell you has to stay just between us."

"Of course," I say, knowing the importance of keeping secrets and feeling relieved because my payback is now and not something I will have to do in the future. "I will give you my honest opinion if that's what you want."

"I have fallen for a guy in a relationship." He looks at me. My expression does not change, but it would have been the same whatever he said. This was hardly shocking or revolutionary news. "The complicated bit is the partner of the guy is a woman, and I am not sure if the guy is actually gay."

"Ah, the forbidden not-so-fruity fruit. When you say fallen, what do you mean? We can all appreciate a good-looking straight man, lust after him, and knock one out thinking about him. Usually it's just a fantasy, unless you achieve the Holy Grail and manage to sleep with one. But then, to me, once they put out, I no longer think of them as straight and a lot of the initial attraction goes." I look at Taylor as if to say, "over to you."

"We used to hang out every day and we did lots of things together, initially as friends. This went on for months, but there was always an undertone that something more had to happen. Then we ended up kissing. I could tell he enjoyed it because he got excited, but after that, he just went cold and has ignored me ever since."

I guess Taylor wants clarification that he has been encouraged, and that he is not acting like a teenager with a crush. "Well, it's unusual that he stopped after a kiss. If he were a straight man just fancying a bit of man action, he would have at least gone for some type of cock play. Maybe he is playing games with his girlfriend, but it sounds to me like he is confused."

"I know, and it is fucking with my head. I would have pursued him, but I found out yesterday that his girlfriend is pregnant. If there is a child involved, I would never go there. But she might not keep it, and if she does, it might not even be his."

"In my honest opinion, I would just walk away from the mess. I know that is probably not what you want to hear, but it could be easier to just remove yourself from these people and find somebody else. You never struck me as the type of guy who is looking for a relationship, so you need to ask yourself what exactly you want from the guy. Do you just want him because you can't have him?"

"I needed a sounding board and the opportunity to say the words aloud. I'm going to think about it. Thanks for your advice. So, do you have any plans for activities with your dad?"

* * * *

I have finished a session in the gym and am doing lengths in the pool. I enjoy swimming more than the monotony of working out in the gym, mainly because it gives me the chance to think more. Recently, I have a new reason to get more physically fit and stay in shape. As I swim I think about the upcoming rendezvous. Meeting at the Phoenix is not ideal, but it is the best I can do at the moment due to how thinly I have been spreading myself. Tim is out visiting Skinny and Skinnier, so meeting upstairs is an option, but I think it is safer to meet down in the leisure center of the building, given the request that was made of me: "Are you free to meet up so we can have a little private chat? I have some things to discuss."

Marco's message got me riled. Sometimes it is better

not to discuss things, especially about incidents from the past which are best left dead and buried. I flip around when I reach the side of the pool and do another length. As I approach the other end, I look up and see a pair of black trousers containing those all-too-familiar legs waiting for me. I reach that side and haul myself out; the other guy moves back so as not to get wet.

"I will forgo embracing you. I don't want to get wet." He blows me a kiss. "So where did you have in mind to talk?"

"I thought we could go into the sauna if it's empty," I reply with a large grin. "You will have to get naked and sweaty instead of wet."

As we sit here in the sauna, each with a towel loosely wrapped around the waist, we make a bit of small talk. I can tell my friend has something on his mind, and hope it is not that thing we had agreed never to talk about. But I often think about it, so I have to assume my old friend does too. Maybe he can no longer keep quiet.

"I have been thinking of finally coming out to my father," Marco says. "You know what he is like, so I want your advice. I know how it went with your dad. I thought you might have some tips on how to make the outing as painless for him and me as possible."

A sense of relief overcomes me; the unspeakable will remain just that. My best friend wants to break the number one secret every gay person lives with, that "little" thing they know about themselves but no one else does—that thing they fought so hard to keep a secret for fear of being bullied, treated like an outcast, taunted and beaten, made to feel unnatural or some sort of freak, and being tarred as an abomination of society. This is a secret of such importance that it could define a person or break them. Luckily for Marco, he is out to his friends and has our support, but he has never come out to his Italian father.

"Well my friend, you know how I feel. I do not believe we should have to lie on this matter, so tell him and set yourself free."

"Yeah, I know it has been a long time coming and I have been a coward about it, but I just don't want to disappoint him."

I move closer to Marco, to physically support him with my presence without actually touching him. It is far too hot in the sauna for that. "You have come out in the best possible way, you accepted yourself, and you made sure that what you feel is who you are. You made friends you know will support you. So now you just have to go that next step and tell family."

Marco smiles back weakly, knowing that I am right. It is not like he is a teenager trying to fight back feelings for a member of the same sex, unsure of what they meant. He is an adult. He is sure of himself. The time has come to do the right thing.

"Don Lanzetta loves you; all parents love their children. He might not be happy with it at first because he will worry that your life won't be easy, and the Italian in him will worry about what other people will say, but he will come around."

"Yes, I know. I remember when you came out to Lord Ashton. I thought he would disown you or send you to one of those camps in the States where they 'cure' you with religious spiel or brainwashing crap."

"Exactly! But look how he changed. They all mellow in time. I strongly believe his realization that he had a gay son has made him more tolerant of gay people. The more people we can educate and the more people who tell their parents about their sexuality when it is safe to do so, the more we will make the world a better place."

Marco pretends to be sick at my "let's change the world" speech, then laughs and concedes that I am right. If we can change the mind of one person at a time, the world can change. Maybe in the future gay people will not need to worry about keeping their orientation a secret.

* * * *

The picture in the recipe looks nothing like the thing I pull out of the oven. I start to flick through the book, looking for a simple sauce to make the dish more aesthetically pleasing. I look at the digital display on the stove and wonder if there is enough time to run out and get a ready-made sauce. There isn't. I start to root through the cupboards, looking for something to help me out. That is the bad thing about living with Jas—he does not cook, so he doesn't keep much food. Maybe I am unconsciously drawn to this in roommates, because Ben was barely able to boil water. I am not one to talk, though; I rarely cook either. Maybe it is because I didn't have a mother to show me how when I was growing up, and out of respect for her, I will not let anyone else teach me. But today I decide to go all out for my special guest who has invited himself over, rather than ordering in.

Twenty minutes later, my guest sits down to a plate of food with no sauce.

"This looks really good, Joe," he remarks.

I giggle, telling Bobs that he does not have to humor me.

"It's good to see you happy after what happened in Twilight all those weeks ago. I thought you would be down."

"Look, thanks for all your help and advice with that," I say. "Everything you said was right, I just needed to hear it. Ant's out of my life along with his crazy-ass girlfriend, and if he was any sort of decent man, he would never have dropped me into it and told lies when she found our messages. Coward and Crazy are welcome to each other."

"This is actually really good. It doesn't look like anything special, but it tastes good." He plays with his food. "I invited myself over because I really need to talk to someone," he quickly adds.

"You know you are welcome here any time. You don't need an invite. I should have had a party when I moved in, but I never got around to it after meeting the Coward. But I am here for you, and you can tell me anything," I say reassuringly.

"This is a top-level secret that no one else can ever know." Bobs looks at me. I nod, playing along. "I've slept with someone who isn't Tim."

When I realize what he has said, I clap my hand over my mouth. Then I remove it and the words, "Fuck no. Oh my gay. Shit no. Who? Fuck," just come out.

"Only two fucks and a shit? I guess you aren't that surprised after all." His face is red, and both hands are cradling the wine glass but he isn't drinking.

"Robert, I can't believe what you just told me. You guys were my role models, my hope that we gays could do long-term relationships. I'm shocked at the news." I feel empty; if even Romeo and Julian can't stay together, what hope is there for the rest of us?

Bobs starts to cry.

"I'm not judging you," I quickly add after regaining some composure.

"There was this guy at work I liked, but I managed to stay faithful. I was working on a big project that needed lots of research, so I ended up spending evenings in the library and met a guy who worked there. He started helping me, we spent more and more time together, but nothing happened. Then we bumped into each other outside the library, and we both realized we had feelings for one another," Bobs explains through his sniffling. "I never meant for it to happen, I wasn't looking for anyone else. But I was not strong enough to resist, and our relationship became physical. It was so easy compared to being with Tim; there was none of the drama that he seems to bring to every situation. Plus, it got me thinking about the fact that I haven't really been with many guys. I can count the number on one hand, which is a rare thing for any guy, let alone a gay guy my age. Maybe I settled too early."

I hug Bobs while he sits and cries some more. I wait a while before speaking. "So what do you want to do? Do you want to break up with Tim and start a relationship with this librarian? Do you want to be single? Or do you want to sleep around a bit?"

"I think I am really falling for this guy Ged. But..."

I cut him off. "How does he feel about you? I guess he knows about Tim, and if that is the case maybe he's happily playing along with you because he knows it won't get serious."

"He has said he loves me and tells me we should be the couple going out."

"Can you trust him? I mean you're a catch, living where you do, and with your family wealth, you need to be careful."

"I know, but he isn't like that. The other day, I was reminded of when I first came out and how my dad had reacted by saying gay men just sleep around and don't love each other. He told me men just like sex wherever they can find it and that I should still go ahead and marry a woman."

My heart starts beating faster. This hurts, but I do not interrupt him.

"I proved him wrong by staying with one guy and making a go of it, and he is proud of me now. He actually tells me so, but if I end things with Tim, what will he think?"

"You cannot stay together for the sake of your father if you don't love Tim any more. Look, maybe you're going through the seven-year itch stage. Why not try to spice things up? Take the relationship back to when you first met. Maybe you just need to talk to Tim and see where his head is at."

"He suggested that we get civil partnered."

"And I guess by the look on your face that you don't want to?" I start to wonder if I will ever have that, but I know right now is not about me. "Look, whatever you do, your friends will help get you through it." I hug Bobs again. I try to remain neutral by saying stuff I believe someone levelheaded like Marco would say, instead of screaming, "Marry your long-term boyfriend, you fool!"

"After the initial confession, we do not really discuss the matter in much more depth. We speak for another three hours before Bobs finally leaves. It seems like Bobs just wanted to get it off his chest. The rest of the time we reminisced about old times, with Bobs occasionally interjecting a pro or con concerning Tim compared to Ged and then crying more, which had set me off.

I pour myself the last of the red wine and sit here thinking. I am glad Bobs shared his secret, and I hope that I have helped him. I wish I could be a better friend and share my secrets too. But does Bobs really need to know about all the men I blew off and slept with at the cinema? Or about the one guy who seemed to get off on being very abusive, who paid me extremely well but was really rough with me? That he was so cruel he'd made me consider quitting my job at the cinema and extra activities? That the guy was never a regular of mine, and I had hoped I never saw him again? But I did eventually see him again, in a picture. He was the reason I'd said I felt sick and left Bobs's twenty-first birthday party almost as soon as I arrived. I had seen that man's face blown up on a canvas print with Bobs and his mother on vacation, and I knew I could not handle seeing Bobs's father in person again. As I sip the wine, I know it is definitely kinder to keep some secrets buried.

12

HE TOUCHES YOU

My arm has started to go to sleep, and I am tempted to pull it out from underneath "the one," but I do not want to disturb him. He looks so gorgeous lying there sleeping. I do not have the heart to risk waking him up, so leave my arm where it is. My free arm is gently resting on the guy's torso. Like me, he is naked apart from a pair of boxers. However, I am tenting mine. I have been since I realized we would be getting into bed together, but the guy is not as excited as I am and continues his deep slumber.

An unusual night brought us together. I had not been out for a while, since my night with Erica, and felt the need to go clubbing. I did not call anyone; I just got ready and went by myself. At the club, "the one" saw me and bounded over, acting really happy to see me. He was very touchy-feely and extremely chatty. Usually when I spotted "the one" at a club, he was super busy and always surrounded by people, so we had never spent much time together in that environment. Most often it was a polite hello and a quick dance in close proximity. I had not seen the guy in ages, as I had been purposely avoiding him, but now the anger that made me react in that way had gone. Back at the club, it had not taken me long to realize why the guy was so happy—he was high. This was usually the point at which I walk away, but my last sexual encounter had been out of the ordinary. For that reason, I did not act in my usual way; I stayed with the guy. The next thing I knew, I was being dragged onto the dance floor and we were dancing together. Just as I was about to make a move and kiss the guy, I was dragged off to a quiet corner of the club. That was even better for what I had in mind.

* * * *

Watching a little boy carrying a toy truck stomp up and down and generally be a public nuisance would usually have really irked me. But given recent events, I find him to be adorable and want to pick him up and give him the attention he is craving. I do not have much experience around children, but I guess he is about four years old. I wonder if I had a child, what his or her four-year-old self would look like. I must have been staring too hard because the boy comes up to me, hands me the truck, and runs away. He peers at me from behind the plastic seat where he is hiding. I roll the truck along the floor to him. He comes out of his hiding place and picks it up. His mother tells him to leave the nice lady alone, and takes him off to the arrival concourse while another group of passengers streams out of the doors. Not until this moment do I realize how hard I have been hit by going to that abortion clinic. I had never thought about having kids, maybe because of the obvious hurdles, but seeing that toddler and the smile he gave me starts to make me feel broody. Then I feel a sense of immense guilt like I have never felt before. For that reason, I resent Carmen. Since Valentine's night, the two of us had become friends. When we were having a coffee two weeks ago, Carmen told me she was pregnant. No one knew besides her doctor, who had referred her to a place. Carmen asked if I would go with her as a friend to help her. Out of some sense of female loyalty, I had agreed. Luckily, I did not literally have to hold Carmen's hand, because she did not want company in the room. For this, I had been glad. My thoughts are interrupted by Al standing over me, joking.

"When you meet someone at an airport, you are actually meant to look for said returning traveler."

* * * *

My cock and balls are being groped. Usually, I like being woken up in this way, but today it just does not feel right. "Tim, stop. I'm not in the mood, I'm too tired."

Tim tries to goad me into being intimate by pressing his naked ass into my groin, but he gets no further. I am just not excited by his attempts.

"Haven't I already told you, no?"

"We barely have sex anymore. What's the problem?"

"It's work. I'm busy and tired. But the big project will be over soon. I've spoken to my bosses, and I won't be working every weekend and so many evenings anymore."

Basically, all the time I used to spend on my now-ended affair with Ged will be Tim's. I have decided to make things work with Tim; nevertheless, part of me cannot help but resent him.

"I know how important your career is to you, and I appreciate that. I understand that things will go back to normal when you are no longer so tired, and I'm sorry for pressuring you; it's only because I miss and love you so much," Tim says and gives me a light peck on the cheek. He explains the "fun" day he has planned for us.

I am not really listening. "That sounds like fun."

He seems pleased, and goes off to have a shower. The

thought of joining him sends a shiver down my spine.

* * * *

On entering the apartment, the place seems foreign. Over the past weeks I have been spending less and less time here, mainly because I was traveling so much and working on new projects. The previous week I spent in Manchester. On my return journey, I'd decided to visit my friends and family from home. I had less baggage coming back to London than when I left, because I had left the bulk of my camera equipment at my parental home. Spending time, albeit only a couple of days, with the people with whom I am closest, was the respite I needed. It gave me the chance to think about everything, and about what I should do next. When I was talking to my oldest friend about women, Carmen had come off pretty sane and normal.

My friend had started seeing a new girl, and after the second date they ended up in bed together. They were about to get down to it when she told him she had a secret—she wore a wig because she suffered from alopecia, which developed after she went through a bad break-up. She had whipped the wig off, and continued being intimate with him. She looked weird and he was freaked out, but he could not stop, as they were already in bed together. She was uninhibited in the bedroom and they had a great night together, so he started dating her, not caring that she wore a wig. They went out for three months, during that time certain insecurities began to surface which he found very hard to accept. She grew jealous if he even dared to mention another woman's name. On New Year's Eve they were at her sister's house party, and she got drunk. After midnight he had to take her home. Back at her place, she started accusing him of trying to hit on her sister. He decided enough was enough and started to pack up the few things he had there. She disappeared into another room, and as he was heading out she blocked his exit, brandishing a knife. He hadn't been sure if she meant to use it on herself or on him, but he had wrestled it free from her and promised to stay.

I was shocked to hear that my friend was still with the psycho, but it did make Carmen seem a lot better by comparison, even though she acted weird when we spent our rare periods of time together.

Being away from Clapham, I realize how much I miss the place. Maybe I am becoming a Londoner now, and that fact makes what is coming up all the harder to face.

* * * *

As we lie in bed, I trace my fingers over Jas's left nipple and think about licking it but I really don't want to wake him up. The sleeping beauty is always pushing himself to extremes, so it is good to let him sleep in. My thoughts drift back to the previous night and how we ended up in bed together. We had moved into a quiet corner of the club and Jas was high as usual; he had taken a hit of X and was feeling the effects. He wasn't working that night, and he was not surrounded by hordes of clubbers vying to get a fix. He'd started to hold my hand.

"Ooooh, Nat."

He told me his body had turned electric and every cell was heightened—the slightest touch felt like a thousand caresses. I rubbed his fingers, then the back of his hand, then worked my way up to his forearms. At that point, Jas turned his arms over and I responded by gently rubbing and stroking the sides, which appeared to be even more sensitive. I ran my fingers along his smooth, lightly-tanned skin, feeling the blood pulsing through the veins. Jas's eyes were shut and his head was back, relaxed. I could tell the guy was in another world, in a place of pure ecstasy.

"I love you, Jason," I finally told him, knowing that he did not hear the words, but it was something I had to say. At that moment time stood still for me, suddenly, I was brought back to reality by a tap on my shoulder from a very burly-looking bouncer. He told me I might want to get my friend out of there. I tried to stir Jas from his other world. Jas responded sluggishly, staying in his dream world. I escorted him out of the club closely followed by the bouncer, who made a point of not touching Jas or helping. I gave my destination to a taxi driver; the bouncer, who seemed relieved that we were out of the club, offered to get our coats with the tickets I gave him. As we waited, Jas said, "I love you, Nathan."

* * * *

We are strolling through the market. Tim is taking in the atmosphere; he stops at every stall. I stand next to him, agreeing with whatever he says without really caring or paying any attention. He takes out his wallet, gets some money out, and hands it to the woman in a stall who, gives him a bag. This brings me back to reality. I wonder what crap Tim has purchased that will have to be trashed at some point—judging by the other items on the stall, it will definitely be a trashcan item. However, Tim seems happy with the purchase, and there has not been a lot of happiness in our relationship recently, so I force myself to cheer up. I put my hand on Tim's shoulder and give it a little squeeze, and he turns, looks at me, and smiles. He tells me that he has booked Sunday brunch at a place we used to go to, and that we really like. He is trying really hard, so I play along the best I can. We settle down to brunch over a bottle of wine and discuss our friends—a safe topic. Mentioning my work makes me remember Ged, a major bone of contention.

I just hope that Tim doesn't misread the signs and want to address the giant pink elephant that had entered our lives, revisiting the conversation he had started in Twilight. That night I had dismissed the idea of us getting married, saying I had to discuss it with my parents, but I know it is something that he is going to go on about at some point. As brunch continues, I tell him some gossip I heard about one of the reality contestants from Starz, a show he loves, to placate him. I am mid-story when I cannot speak anymore. I feel physically sick, seeing Ged and some muscle-mary walk in. He spots me, and the two guys come over to our table.

"Ged, this is my boyfriend Tim."

"Bobs, this is a friend who I met last night." Ged winks at us.

"Would you guys like to join us?" Tim asks Ged and his new friend with benefits; the naïve fool probably thinks I could do with hanging out with my friends—which is probably true, but just not with this one guy.

I quickly reply, "They obviously want to sit by themselves, after just meeting,"

But Ged starts to pull up a chair. "We would love to."

* * * *

Carmen is in the kitchen making us both a late breakfast. I go over to kiss her. As I get closer, I see that she has a face on her again so I do not bother. She never smiles anymore, and I know she must be desperately unhappy. I tell her how my parents had said hello and wished she had come too. I had invited her, and when she did not accept I knew she did not care about my family. That had helped me make my decision. She places the food she has prepared down at the place she has set for me, and she sits opposite. Carmen tells me that we need to talk, but I know that already. I care for her as a person but the love has gone. Perhaps we were best suited as a university couple who was never destined to make it beyond that, or maybe she had pushed me away because she could not stand the fact that I was doing really well, or perhaps it was because I had developed feelings for someone else, but it seems like our time has ended.

She says she has something important to tell me. The part of me that cares for her as a person wants to remain friends, so I do what I think is the right thing and stop her mid-sentence. I think it will be easier on her if I do it. "I agree with you. I think we should break up. I still love you and always will, but only as a friend now." I watch the tears run down her face. I know that she will have to go through the pretense that breaking up is more upsetting than it is, to give the failed relationship its adequate sendoff. I go over to her and hug her to offer a last level of comfort, but she pushes me away.

"Get the fuck out!"

I briefly protest, saying we should be civil about it, but I realize that will come later once the shock has passed. I walk back to the door, pick up my unpacked bags, and walk out.

* * * *

The traffic coming back from the airport is terrible, but I do not mind being stuck because I enjoy spending time with Al. Besides, it is partly our fault for getting caught in the Sunday traffic. We should not have stopped off for lunch and a not-so-quick quickie. I am driving Al's car, which she lent to me when she went back to Canada to end it with her sort-of girlfriend. I had offered to pick her up at the airport without her suggesting or expecting it, a gesture that made me realize that I love her. This was so different than when the Bone and I were together, where I had more or less been a glorified chauffeur.

Al finishes telling me about the breakup and how her now-ex girlfriend took it. Even though she did not have the right to be pissed off because she had a husband, she had been. In the time Al and I had spent together, I'd noticed how clingy the ex-girlfriend was by the way she was always calling Al. I hope that it is all over now and there would be no more contact. I tell Al about the kid at the airport, how I'd supported Carmen when she went to get an abortion, and how it had made me feel a longing I did not know I had. I tell her how it seemed so quick— Carmen went into the room and I had waited for her in the reception area. Before I knew it, Carmen was back. It just seemed so wrong. Al tells me maybe after a year of being together we can discuss having a child, which I was not expecting but deep down is exactly what I want to hear.

* * * *

At the club that night my illusion had been quickly dashed, as Jas went on to tell the bouncer who returned his jacket that he loved him too, and said the same to the Middle Eastern taxi driver. The driver had seemed uncomfortable and kept warning me that if Jas threw up, it would be an extra fifty. When we got back to Jas's place, which was close to the club, I helped him into bed and then went to get him some water. When I returned to the bedroom, Jas had stripped to his underwear and said he wanted to be massaged. I sat on the side of the bed and continued to gently stroke him as I had been doing in the club earlier, but this time I included his biceps, chest, and legs. I found myself getting really turned on and decided to leave because I did not want to do anything with someone in that state. As I kissed Jas on the forehead goodbye, Jas had pulled me on top of him. He said he was cold and I could keep him warm. I found myself in my underwear with an erection, holding Jas through the early hours of the morning, while Jas rambled on about his life, friends, the scene, the state of the world, and a miscellany of other incoherent thoughts that entered his head. When he finally passed out, it was about eight in the morning. I might have dozed slightly through some of his random chatter when I was not required to offer an opinion, but I did not sleep much because of how horny I was. Even though I had not taken an illegal substance I felt as high as Jas. As it approached the early evening my erection finally went down. I got out of the bed to use the toilet and to get some food—a bowl of cereal and milk. I went back to the bed instead of just going home and managed to sleep for a few hours.

Now I am laying here thinking with my eyes closed. I hear Jas wake next to me. He whispers something, which I miss because I decide to pretend to be asleep. Jas gently rolls me on my side and hugs me from behind. I can feel he is getting aroused. I turn around to face him and tell him I think I had better go, but before I can say anymore, Jas has locked onto my lips with his own mouth.

* * * *

Tim is standing at the end of the bed. He pulls off the polo shirt he is wearing. I look at his body and realize that he has somehow managed to get more ripped. I find the body in front of me, which I had always adored and actively encouraged, a turnoff, because now I like a lean trim body. Seeing Ged with another guy had really pissed me off. I know I have no right to be annoyed because I'd ended it, but I do not like to think of him with someone else so soon. The brunch had been a very painful experience. I spent most of the time quietly dreaming about Ged, while Tim and the "gymbo" spent lunchtime proving that muscle-bound gay guys really should take a book to the gym.

Tim has stripped down to his boxers and joins me on the bed; he kisses me lightly on the lips and wishes me a good night. I am wearing some pajamas and take them off; I grab Tim's hand and shove it down onto my erect penis. Tim responds instantly, and climbs on top of me. He compliments me, saying he thinks I have lost weight. I feel suffocated with Tim lying on top of me, so I push his head down towards my groin, and Tim starts doing what he does so well. I think about the intimate moments I had shared with Ged, and start to enjoy this experience. After a few minutes I start to climax. After I cum, I open my eyes, and I am disappointed to see Tim.

Something flares up in me, and I punch Tim square in the face. I am not sure why I do it, but it definitely feels good. I look at Tim and see the mixture of red blood from his nose and white semen from his mouth running down his face.

"That's a strawberry shortcake. You have been going on at me for weeks that we should be more kinky."

Tim's eyes are glazed; he does not say anything. He obviously wants more. I push him down face-first on the bed and pull down his underwear. Tim starts speaking, but his words are lost as his face is buried in the pillow. I start to massage his butt cheeks and then shove Gilbert II inside him. I continue doing this until I become hard again and then enter Tim. As I am pounding away, I wrap my hands around his neck and start to squeeze.

* * * *

I knock on the once-familiar door, which now feels like a surreal object, the final boundary keeping me from being able to be. I am not exactly sure what I am going to say because I have acted like a complete twat these past couple of months when I was still with Carmen. Maybe I should just start with "sorry." Waiting for an answer feels an eternity. I know Taylor is in; I texted him earlier asking if I could visit, saying that I wanted to talk. But it is late on a Sunday night, and he might have gone to bed to get ready for work. I start to think I should just leave, when Taylor answers the door, looking a lot shabbier than usual. He is wearing grey track suit bottoms, a white t-shirt, and matching hooded track suit top. He does not have his contact lenses in. Instead, he is wearing his black-framed Tom Ford glasses. It looks like he has not shaved all weekend, and the dark brown stubble on his face has little flecks of light brown interspersed. I like him looking like this, it is more natural. Taylor opens the door wider and lets me in, staring at my large rucksack and the bag with my everyday camera and lenses. As Taylor shuts the door, my heart is beating really fast. I feel a sense of anticipation in my aura as we stand facing each other, having so much to say but not knowing where to start. I decide that maybe it is best to not say anything and just show Taylor how I feel, so before my heart bursts through my sternum, I start to kiss him. Taylor responds.

Finally I feel at peace. We wrap our arms around one another, and I think Taylor's touch is majestic. The kisses are so much more passionate than with a woman. The delicacy when kissing a woman is replaced with a greater intensity, a feeling I want whenever I kiss again. Taylor's hands have already found the skin under my jacket, shirt, and the vest I am wearing. He is gently touching my back. The touch is electric; a pulse seems to resonate from it and spread throughout my body, leaving a warm sensation. If the kissing is this much better, I wonder how great the sex will be. I think I am about to find out.

13

HE ACTS HOMOPHOBIC

The earlier scenes had whizzed past too quickly to be of any interest, but now the outside world is more interesting, and gives me something to look at. The best part of the trip is when more people enter the equation—I hope that there will be someone whose eye I want to catch who will want to catch mine, and the seduction can begin. So far, it had been mainly ugly people or families, so I sit on the subway thinking it was rude that Marco had not bothered to pick me up from the airport. Instead, I had been given clear instructions on how to get to Marco's place because my cousin was too busy working, but it is the principle—family should come before work. I'd preferred visiting with the family when I was younger because Marco had been a more gracious host back then. At least I would have been picked up from the airport.

I start to reminisce about my previous visits to London. They were always fun, as I find English women fall for my charms easily; I had lots of sex on my English vacations. I am worried about my cousin, though; the country seems to have softened him, because he always gets a bit uppity whenever I comment on how all the English women are easy for Italian men, or something similar. I dread to think what will happen if Marco marries an English woman. He is already distancing himself from his roots, and that will mean the end of all the Italian that remains in him.

The tube stops at Hammersmith and another bundle of passengers get on. A woman and two men sit opposite me. I hope the woman is not with the guy next to her, as she is definitely my taste. I will play it cool and watch to see if they are together before I make my move. The man beside her is talking to the man next to him and does not once speak to the woman. I think about asking her some stupid tourist question so she can help me, but get distracted because the two men are being quite touchy. I look closer at the guy furthest away from the woman—he looks like a "fucking omosessuale." Watching them makes me feel sick. I want to say something, to right the injustice I see in front of me. I desperately look around the carriage for someone else who is as disgusted as I am by the two men, particularly the one talking like a woman, but no one else seems bothered. What is wrong with everyone? As I look around panic-stricken, I see the woman glance at me and smile. I calm down a bit and smile back. She looked better when there was a mystery to her, so this puts me off. But as she is offering herself on a plate, I decide to use my tourist line. She looks at me blankly, then the guy furthest away from her answers my question. I just nod. I feel weird, and get off the subway at the next stop, disregarding the instructions Marco had given me.

* * * *

The hot water feels good on my chest, but the massage and soaping of my back is the best part of this shower. I turn around to kiss Taylor. I think we will be happier staying in for the night. I ask, "Are you sure you want me to go to this party with you?"

"Yes, I'm sure, and you know most of them there. Why

are you being so apprehensive, Ricky?" Taylor asks, turning me around so he can wash my front. "We don't have to tell anyone about us yet or tell them that you are gay, if you are worried about it getting back to Carmen."

"That is partly it. Some of them are her friends, and it might be strange if I start hanging out with them," I reply, and start to lather up Taylor's front.

"So what is the other part?" Taylor asks, pausing what he is doing.

"Well, I'm not actually gay."

Taylor looks at me blankly. "How can you say that when you have your hand on my cock?"

"I thought you knew. I have fallen for you as a person, that is true, but it has nothing to do with sexuality."

"Listen to yourself. Don't you think you fell for me because I am a man and because you are attracted to men? What about all the stuff we have been doing these past few weeks?"

"I don't want to sound crude, but I have never taken it up the ass."

"Not being a bottom does not make you straight. What am I? Some kind of experiment?" Taylor starts to raise his voice.

"Calm down. I just left one hissy-fit woman, I don't need another."

Taylor grabs the shower head, quickly rinses himself down, and passes it to me. "I am clean enough already. When you are finished in here, you might want to go to the closet in my bedroom and hide in it for the rest of your life."

* * * *

194

"They are having another holiday, Nat?" Joe asks me. I have taken it upon myself to organize everything for the joint "Joson" (Joe and Jason) housewarming and the just-Joe birthday party, so I know the RSVP positions of all the guests.

"Yeah. Bobs said it was a very last minute thing, as in they woke up and said 'lets have a couple of weeks away' and left. They are due back today and will try to pop by, but he doesn't know when the flight lands."

"So, anyone else not coming that I should know about?"

"I invited Carmen, because I bumped into her getting party supplies and felt sorry for her because she looked like shit. I heard Ricky dumped her—just walked out. So he won't be coming."

"Do you think he's screwing some other girl? You would not like to know how much his sell-out exhibition made him; I bet he is fucking half the Claphamites now. But you are right, we should stick by our dumped sister."

"You know, Marco has one of his terrible cousins over to help his dad travel back to Italy, so he can't stay out late." I look at Joe. I know Marco would have told him personally, but he seems disappointed at hearing the words. "Anyway, I am sure he'll make it up to you. You never know, I mean look at me and Jas."

"Oh, pass me your punch bowl while I throw up in it. I live here too. I haven't been able to miss you and Jas for the past two weeks." He winks at me and goes off to check on the music situation because it is nearly party time.

I feel a little bit guilty about leaving out the fact that I have invited Ben and guest. Joe has not seen her for a while and I know he misses her. I had invited her via text message from Joe's phone, saying he was sorry and really wanted to see her and could she please come. I think it is about time the nonsense ended, and I knew if she hadn't thought Joe wanted her there she wouldn't have bothered.

Just to make sure everyone has fun, I add more alcohol to the punch. What's the worst that could happen?

* * * *

Hearing someone call me gay is just like being in the playground at school, where your immediate response is gut-reflex denial. Plus, I do not like being labeled. I wonder why people have to categorize everything and everyone, and I decide that it is for their own comfort and not out of any humanitarian desire to right the ills of society. After I finish my shower, I go into the bedroom to find that Taylor has nearly finished getting ready. I know that he is not after some record for the quickest dresser— he wants to get away from me.

I cringe at the thought, because I don't want him to leave. "I'm sorry…"

"It's my fault, Ricky. I shouldn't have rushed you. You're young, just finding yourself, and getting used to the idea of who you are now. You don't have to go with me tonight. I'll show my face, pay my respects, and just leave." He gives me a peck on the cheek. "I'll be back soon. Besides, we need some time to make up properly."

He kisses me goodbye, longer this time, and leaves for the party. I put on some casual clothes and boot up my laptop, deciding I will do some work. I have fallen two weeks behind, from having to move all my stuff out of the Phoenix—since when did I start to refer to that place the same way the gay guys do?—and into my temporary home at Taylor's, while I look for somewhere else to live.

There are numerous requests in my inbox for Dick C to do private photography sessions. I ignore them all, and open up the pictures I had taken instead. I take a really good look at all of them, including the naked ones. It had never been a sexual thing with any of them, it was just professional. Once the guys said they were happy with the pictures I'd never looked back, until now—I had forgotten a lot of the faces. Looking back over the pictures objectively, I realize some of the guys are attractive, but I had not been able to admit it then. I think about my fun nights out with the Knights. I always thought it was because Taylor was there, but I liked the places we went to and I thought some of the other guys on the team were cool too. If I am gay, why had I not come out earlier, at university? Was that not the time people came out and experimented?

I open up pictures from my university days and look at my group of friends. One group photograph catches my eye. Suddenly, everything makes sense between two of the guys in the picture. I feel a bit stupid for not realizing earlier that they were a couple behind closed doors, which translated to a close friendship in public. It was a friendship of which I had always been jealous, but it was not the friendship itself, it was because I wanted to be with one of the guys. Then I realize Cambridge University was not the place for me to come out because I was not ready; neither was high school because growing up in the Midlands with my circle of friends, it simply would not have happened.

I think about Carmen and realize I had loved her, but it was a different type of love. She had offered me the security of not having to accept that something I was brought up to believe was wrong. But being gay is not wrong—it is so right. I think about being intimate with Taylor. When I was with Carmen, I could never reach that level of satisfaction and had to finish myself off under the pretense of birth control. But the satisfaction Taylor feels when I am inside him literally grips me so tight I soon cum, hard. Not only the full-on sexual act, but also other acts of affection from a kiss to a cuddle to anything involving nudity feels better with a guy. Suddenly I know I have been in denial my entire life. But that is going to end now. I make my way to the bedroom, strip off, look for some of my best clothes. I do not care about those sort of things but Taylor does, and if I am going to be at the party at his side, I want him to be proud of me. I am proud of myself; finally, I can accept my true nature. Finally, I know there is nothing wrong with being gay.

* * * *

Watching Nat and Jas interact with each other, I see how happy they look. It was a long time coming, but it appears to be worth it for them. Ever since Nat met Jas, all of Nat's friends could tell how he felt about him. It had seemed so obvious, it was hard to understand how Jas never knew. Then, as I got to know Jas, it seemed like he was into Nat too, but he would not make a move. At times I wanted to knock their heads together and say "just fucking get together."

"Hey, Marco."

I turn around and see Taylor. He looks glum.

"Are you still having straight man problems?" I whisper.

"Yes and no. We are now together, but he's not ready to come out yet, which is understandable. He is young and he grew up in the sticks. It's just that I didn't know what to expect; it all took me by surprise."

Shit. He got with his guy; that is two couples now. Should I make it three and go for it with the one I like? But my life is too complicated. Plus, I don't deserve it, but I have been trying to make amends for it all these years and I sort of have. Maybe it is time to finally close that door and move on. I decide that when I get a moment with Joe, I will suggest we go on a date.

I try to reassure Taylor. "Everybody needs to do that in their own time. I always thought the people who rush into it and do it too young or without any support are the ones who become fucked up later in life. Let him take his time; you can support him, and you guys will be fine."

"Thanks. That's what I'm going to do. There is no time like the present. I'm going to call him."

He heads off toward the back garden. At that point, my phone starts ringing. It is Nico, my idiot cousin, who has been AWOL all day.

* * * *

I open the front door to be met by an unusual group whom I assume had just met on my door step: the Terminator and the Stepford wife from across the road (whom we invited out of politeness because Jas had had some run-in with them, but we never really expected them to accept) and Carmen and a female friend.

"Joe, this is my friend Mary. I hope you don't mind me

bringing a plus one."

"No, no. Come in." Rare for me, I take an instant dislike to Mary because she looks evil. She has long, striking facial features, large oval eyes, and not an ounce of fat anywhere on her face including the cheeks and chin. But I do what any good host would do, and start showing these guests around—I have done a lot of cosmetic redecorating since I moved in.

* * * *

"Jas, go get the door."

"Joe is supposed to get it; he wanted to collect all his presents."

"I just saw him take some people upstairs."

I open the door for Ben, Al, and Ricky. I do not bother with the *tour de maison*, even though Joe had told me to show everyone around. I just show the ladies straight into the living room, where everyone has gathered.

Ricky is on his phone. "I'm here. Jas has just let me in. Okay, I'll come meet you in the garden."

* * * *

I make my way to the back garden to see Taylor. Luckily no one else is in the garden with us, so we kiss and make up and must have been pretty lovey-dovey, as I tell Taylor who I am.

* * * *

"Marco, let me introduce you to my girlfriend, Al."

I am happy to see Ben. It has been ages since I last saw her, and I am happy to meet her new girlfriend, as they look good together.

"Ladies, do not think me rude if I suddenly disappear, but I might have to go soon, as my foreign cousin Nico got lost in London chasing after some woman he saw on the tube. I told him to get a taxi to this address, wait outside, call me, and we would go back to my place, but I am not sure where he is. So I might have to leave at any moment."

* * * *

"Kissing an out guy feels so much better," Taylor murmurs in my ear.

"Ha. I'm going inside to get a drink. Are you coming?"

"I'll meet you inside. I just want a moment to myself."

* * * *

"Thanks, Nat."

I have just been talking to Ben and Al, and point them upstairs to chuck their jackets. I have to answer the front door, since more guests ring the bell and the two hosts, boyfriend Jas and birthday boy Joe, are not around.

* * * *

Heading into the living room with a drink feels weird, because I am wondering how Taylor's friends will react to me now I am going out with him. I see the back of Nat's head but don't speak to him as he rushes off to the door.

* * * *

"Ben all your friends are nice, I really like Nat and Marco. When do I get to meet Joe?" Al asks me as we make our way upstairs.

On her way down a long-faced woman slinks pass us. As she walks off in the direction of the garden we check out her arse, peering from the bannister, and both of us say "nah" in unison.

* * * *

Upstairs, I run into Ben and Al. I do not hate seeing

Ben, but I am shocked because Nat never once mentioned she was coming. I had heard, mainly from co-workers gossiping, that Ben has a girlfriend. I want to ask Ben about her and talk to her myself since she is standing in front of me, but I cannot do it. I can't rely on her anymore because she picked the Bone—whom she was meant to hate—over me, when we were meant to be best friends. Plus, seeing Nat and Jas together made me realize even more that I want to be with Marco, and I can't forgive her for betraying my confidence. Why did she have to ruin everything by opening her big mouth? I could have dealt with my feelings as long as Marco never knew, but Marco knowing and ignoring them ripped right through me.

Ben and Al are both smiling at me.

"Joe, this is Alison, Al for short," Ben introduces her.

I shake Al's hand but do not embrace Ben like I usually would have done. How could someone who knows me so well betray me so badly? Ben hands me a gift. It is just bath stuff; the smell makes it obvious what it is, but I love it. We awkwardly stand on the landing in silence; then Al thanks me for inviting them.

"You have Jason to thank. He picked his own guests to invite to the housewarming, and picked Benita. I only invited people I can trust."

"You invited me and apologized for being such a twat."

This shocks me. "That was not me; it must have been the tattooed one, Nat, out of some sense of chivalry. I can NEVER forgive you." Then I have to run off so as not to cry, and I head downstairs.

I am at the bottom of the stairs when I hear Ben tell Al, "Let's go home; these queens can hold a grudge for millennia."

* * * *

My quiet moment in the garden contemplating Ricky is interrupted by the arrival of a woman. She is coming on to me. I am not even flattered. So I head inside. I enter the living room and close the door behind me, not to keep the noise down, but hopefully to hide from the scary woman.

* * * *

Finishing up in the bathroom, I go looking for Mary, who had said she would scout for talent while going for a smoke. As I walk past the front door, someone gently taps on it, so I let them in. I am greeted by a tall, dark, handsome stranger. He tells me how he never likes to miss a party.

"Now I know why my cousin did not invite me—he wanted to keep all the beautiful women to himself," he says as he kisses my hand.

"Pleased to meet you I am Carmen."

Nico, as he introduces himself, follows me through the house to the back garden in my search for Mary.

* * * *

I'm in the kitchen topping up guests' drinks, and it becomes a lot more interesting when I see a stranger with Carmen. The stranger stares intensely at me, which causes me to get a little bit excited. Maybe my birthday will be a lot of fun after all.

* * * *

"We will just say a quick goodbye to Nat, Jas, Marco, and the others and leave," I tell Al as we walk into the living room.

I see Ricky there and feel a pang of guilt. I whisper to

Al who he is. Al looks at him and tells me she would have thought he is gay.

* * * *

"Are you sure you want to do this?" Taylor asks me. Instead of responding in words I go for my tried and tested response of responding physically. I start kissing Taylor in the middle of the room.

* * * *

Taylor and Ricky start making out in the middle of the room. Everyone who knows them stares in disbelief, apart from me, since I suspected Ricky was the subject of Taylor's "straight dilemma." Then the door opens and Carmen, another female, and my cousin Nico walk in. The kissing couple are oblivious to everyone in the room watching them.

All eyes seem to move from the couple to Carmen and her mini entourage. I see my cousin looking on in shock at the two guys kissing. At that point, Joe walks into the room and sees what could only be described as a Mexican stand-off—in one corner are Taylor and Ricky, next to them are Ben and Al, by the DJ turntable are Jas, Nat, and myself, and by the living room door are Carmen, another woman, Nico, and the neighbors. All the other guests seem to have taken a back seat, as they are either unfamiliar with or didn't care about the situation unfolding in front of them.

Taylor and Ricky stop kissing and glance around to get the approval of their friends, but they see Carmen looking like she has been shot. They cannot take their eyes off her to see what other people are expressing. The other woman with Carmen, not able to handle the tension anymore, screams, "You fucking poof, Richard. What the fuck are you doing, you faggot?"

Then Nico speaks up, asking me a series of questions and making derogatory statements in a flurry of Italian: "Marco, che razza di amici hai? Perché sei in giro con queste persone? Batty ragazzi sono disgustoso."

"Not now," I hiss at him, to cut him off.

"Car, I always told you there was something about him I didn't like," the scary woman booms in the silence; someone has stopped the music.

Ricky takes a step forward towards the women. "Carmen?" he says, extending his arms, as he gets closer to her.

"Don't fucking touch her, you queer," Scary says, as she steps between them.

"I don't know what's going on, but I think we should leave," the Terminator tells his wife. "I said from the beginning, they were all wrong 'uns!" The Stepford wife does not make a move to go. Even though she does not know the history, she is enjoying the drama far too much.

Carmen speaks for the first time since entering the room. "You want to know what's going on? My boyfriend of over three and a half years, who has lived with me for the past six months, dumped me a couple of weeks ago without any warning OR reason. Now it looks like he's been fucking THAT," she points at Taylor, "all along!" She clasps her hands to her temples, turns away from the Terminator, and slowly looks around the whole room at everyone's face. "And all these gays have been covering for them."

The Terminator sounds off. "I said they weren't

normal."

"Questo é orribile!"

Ben steps out and comes forward. "Carmen, I didn't know, I just saw them together now."

"You were meant to be my friend, but you were probably wanting to fuck me all the time," Carmen flares up at her.

"We are friends, and I would have told you if I had known," Ben responds.

"Fuck you. You big fat dyke," Scary cuts in. "Why the fuck would she want to be friends with you? Not for fashion tips or make-up advice. She probably felt sorry for you because of how you look."

"She was that stupid tart's fucking friend when she dragged her along to the abortion clinic," Al blurts the words out. All us spectators collectively turn to Carmen, like our eyes are following the ball in a tennis match.

"Yes it's true, I had an abortion to get rid of my gay boyfriend's baby inside of me, after confiding in his gay boyfriend, the good doctor, who told me to do it."

"Malato!!"

"Nico, enough. We are going." I move over to my cousin, so that we can leave.

Maybe because she hates all gay men at that moment in time, maybe because she believes it, or maybe because she is hurting badly, Carmen adds, "Yes, Nico, go before you hear that your cousin probably fucked both of them."

"Gay people are not normal. They should all be shot," Nico says, managing to work out his sentences in English so everyone could understand.

I can't believe my cousin has said that in a room full of

predominantly gay people. "Nico, I'm gay, should I be shot too?"

"We gay people are not different from straight people," Joe cuts in. "All we want is to be loved by our families, have fun with friends, meet someone we can fall in love with, and maybe settle down with a special someone. The only difference is that person happens to be someone of the same sex, but why is that wrong? It is who we are. It's not unnatural; to us, it is normal. We should not be persecuted, we should be accepted by society. It's not like we go out murdering people or committing crimes simply because we are gay. So what is the problem with it? Nothing!"

He is interrupted by Nat and Jas applauding him. Some other people in the room cheer for him too.

Joe looks at Scary. "You have no right to speak to one of my friends in my house like that, so apologize. And she's not fat, she's big-boned." He winks at Ben as he says it. "Carmen, I cannot begin to imagine what you have been through and how you are feeling. But I don't think anyone here knew about this, and I don't think it is about being gay, it is about the breakdown of a relationship after your ex moved on. You should probably speak to Ricky privately."

"Carmen, you were pregnant?" Ricky asks her. He looks wild-eyed and crazy; his body language is definitely saying he is not happy with this news. "Why didn't you tell me? I would have supported you."

She looks at him and starts to cry. At that point, Scary escorts her out of the house without letting Ricky speak to her. Things settle down, the music starts up, and a party atmosphere slowly returns.

* * * *

Ricky has moved into the back garden to hide from everyone else. I join him to comfort him, but receive the cold shoulder. Carmen's abortion story scapegoating me as a doctor involved has achieved its purpose. I know I will have to speak to Ricky once he has had a chance to calm down and will be able to hear me. I open my mouth to say, "I am here…"

"Stay away from me, you poof," Ricky shouts at me, then he punches me. I fall to the floor, nursing my face.

14

HE KNOWS HOW TO PARTY

Looking at Tim as the car speeds through London, I realize I need better light in which to examine him. I take out my phone, hold it to his face and run it down to his neck like a kind of scanner, not liking what I see. There is still some bruising, and under better lights at a house party the eagle-eyed gays will see it too. If it were a club, I might get away with it because the bruises Tim has from two weeks ago are barely visible, and the fresh ones on his body from the trip cannot be seen unless he takes his top off, but Tim knows not to do that.

"There is a change of plan. We will go to Nightingale Hall instead of that address in Vauxhall," I tell the taxi driver before turning back to Tim. "It would be better to go home first to freshen up and then catch up with our friends at whatever club they go to later." He looks disappointed, so I add, "you are looking tired and I thought you would want to get ready properly." I know the vain side of my "giancé" and he will now want to go home first. That is another issue—I have to ensure that Tim does not blab to everyone.

After I got carried away and took my Ged frustrations out on Tim, I'd decided we should go away to give him time to recover mentally and physically, to give the evidence time to disappear, and to stop him blurting out to someone what had happened. Plus, I needed to give myself a chance to get away from the temptation of Ged. On the trip, Tim was quiet for the first few days and was being really difficult. I had to put in a lot of effort to get him to respond to me in any way. One night over dinner, when we had barely spoken to each other all night, we had almost finished eating, and I ended up proposing. Tim accepted straightaway. Some switch in his brain turned off, or on, and I was forgiven. He was back to normal. That night, to celebrate our engagement, while we were making love for the first time since the incident Tim told me I could hit him during sex if I got off on it, but not on the face. So Tim received a few new bruises throughout the week, and I found a way to get over Ged and tolerate Tim. "I know we are both really excited about the engagement," I whisper to him, "but tonight is Joe's night, so if we do go clubbing, we can't tell anyone."

* * * *

Most of the guests have left the party now, and I'm sure it will be remembered for all the wrong reasons. I decide to keep quiet about sharing a spiff with the Terminator in the garden, where I had told him gay people were normal, and that I felt being gay was so normal that I automatically defaulted to thinking everyone else was gay too. After I'd delivered my homonormative theory, the Terminator had tried to kiss me. That I definitely won't be telling my boyfriend Nat, who looks slightly lost as he collects empty bottles.

* * * *

My night with Erica is now at the forefront of my mind. I have not heard from her after our night of fucking. She took a job at a competitor agency soon afterward, and

I had not bothered to contact her. I decide not to tell anyone about it, and hope it does not end up like Ricky and Carmen. I see Jas smiling at me, which confirms that I really don't want to ruin our newly formed relationship.

* * * *

The lovebirds are doing most of the cleaning up, which is nice of them. At least one positive came from the party—I have made up with Ben and met her woman, who seems nice. Right now they are tired and want to go to bed. I understand this to mean "we are a new couple and want to go and have sex with each other." Luckily for me, the bathroom separates my bedroom from Jas's. Nat and Jas had said they would go clubbing with me if I wanted to go, as some of the other guests had gone. I'd said I was all right; I could not take any more excitement for the night. Walking up the stairs, I wonder about Ricky; I am surprised I missed that one because it seems so obvious now.

My thoughts flit to how I had only said a few words to Marco, because he had to run off early to find his cousin who had disappeared—probably to out Marco to the whole of Italy. I am a little bit disappointed that we did not get to spend more time together. Opening my bedroom door, I see the outline of someone sleeping in my bed. Fair enough. Someone got drunk and wants a place to sleep it off. I walk around to the side of the bed to see who it is. When I see the jet-black hair sticking out from under the duvet, I become scared. I pull it back to be greeted by the sleeping Italian. The movement of the covers must have woken him, or he had not been sleeping deeply, because he opens his eyes and looks at me.

"Your little speech downstairs moved me," he says as he pulls me on top of him. He is already fully naked under the covers, and it does not take long for him to get me that way too. I try very feebly to protest, but it is way past midnight, it is my birthday, and I deserve a present. The Italian demands that I fuck him, something that I have never done before because I had always been the lock, not the key, but I do want to try it. I open my top drawer and pull out lube and condoms and start. There is no kissing, sucking, or any general foreplay—we just get down to it.

"Fuck me harder, bella uccellino," the Italian demands as he slides further down the bed to take me deeper inside him. As I get into it, I have to consciously remember not to scream out Marco's name.

* * * *

The night has not exactly gone according to plan. I didn't even get to speak to the birthday boy. I send him a text message: "Happy birthday, let's celebrate properly soon. I can't find my cousin Nico. He's probably found some poor English woman for the night to reassert his masculinity on. M x."

* * * *

It is one day shy of two weeks since the party happened. I want to meet up with Joe and take him out for dinner to tell him how I feel about him. I had decided to do this on the night of the party, but everything kicked off, and now tonight has somehow turned into a group thing with Nat, Jas, Bobs and Tim being invited along too. Maybe there will be a quiet moment when we can speak alone.

Things had not gone as expected. The day after the

party Nico had returned home acting very smug. I assumed that it was because he got laid, and just hoped it was not with Mary. But we talked, and he said he would not tell anyone in the family, or anyone else for that matter, about me. Nico said it was my life and I should do with it as I wanted, and since I was not camp, the word he followed by a limp wrist gesture, it was okay in his book. His reaction had surprised me, but in a good way. He seemed true to his word, because the following day Nico and my dad returned to Italy, and I never got "the call." I considered that Nico might try to blackmail me in the future, but if that time comes, I have resigned myself to just tell everyone, as I had originally intended.

When the entire group are together and seated, I find myself annoyed that Joe is at the other end of the table with Nat and Jas while I am stuck with Bobs and Tim. Once the drinks have been served, Bobs taps his glass with his fork and stands up. Tim stands up next to him and links his arm with his boyfriend's. Bobs announces to everyone that the two of them are now "engayed."

* * * *

Nat and Jas are up toasting the couple. I try not to look glum. I am worried about inevitably having to see Bobs's father again, and the way I am working my way around family members, someone should warn Nat's little brother. I get up and toast the couple. I am really happy for them and I think that Bobs has done the right thing. As we start to embrace, Marco gets close to me, and I feel guilty. I can never tell him that I slept with Nico. For a start, I had promised Nico that I will not, but I also think Marco would not like the news. That night, after we finished,

Nico and I ended up talking.

"When I was younger I used to fuck with other guys. Italian guys like to have sex and girls did not always oblige, so it is fine to make fuck with other men. If both guys are straight, there is nothing omosessuale to it."

"But I am gay, so what does that mean now?"

"Hearing you speak so passionately about being gay, I thought I should try it the other way. I am not a gay because I have never kissed or sucked another man."

"Well, you can't tell any of your family about Marco. He will do it when he is ready. Otherwise I will tell him about tonight."

"I am happy not to say anything, but I have a job for you." Nico pushed my head down to his cock and let me blow him, so he could see if a man did it better than a woman.

In the cold light of a sober day, I am tempted to put the experience down to one of those working ones I would prefer not to remember. But it is difficult to forget the incident, because for the whole time we were together, I pretended it was with Marco. It is my way of saying goodbye to Marco, as I know nothing will ever happen between us. Now I have closure.

* * * *

The engagement celebrations continue the next night. Our group and more friends go to a club. Bobs is buying most of the drinks but promises us that there will be an official engagement party. Jas is working in the club, which is the only problem I have about our relationship. I knew that about him before we got together, and he has told me he has to make money somehow. I have to let it go, so I am channeling all my frustration into setting Joe up. I keep telling Joe that various fit guys are checking him out. They are smiling at him but he refuses to go over and chat with them. I mention that there is a very good-looking dark-haired, tanned guy checking him out. Joe tells me that the guy is looking at me. He is not. I tell Joe to smile at him. He smiles and then turns away, giving the guy his back. I sigh. I do not want to be one of those annoying people who, once in a relationship, has to fix everyone else up, but with Joe I can't help it. I start dancing with Joe, and separate us from the group. Somehow I manage to maneuver Joe nearer to the guy, who meets us half way. As Joe is dancing, he accidentally bumps into the guy a few times—I keep gently pushing Joe into him. Each time, they both look at each other and smile. I find it annoying that Joe keeps talking to me instead of lunging at the hapless foreigner, so I do what any good friend would have done: push Joe hard into the guy, then leave him and return to the group. I sense some hostility from Marco, who probably thinks the pushing thing was too teenager-like. Then I have to stop Marco going over to give Joe his drink and potentially disturbing the pair, who are chatting away. We watch as Joe and his new friend start kissing on the dance floor. I feel elated, grab Tim in a hug, and we jump up and down. Marco is saying something but I can't hear him. Bobs wolf-whistles, but I doubt the couple can hear us.

* * * *

Re-reading my emails, I glance over the confirmation from the budget airline that my flight to and from Ibiza has been booked. I open up the latest installment of the email chain that had started this trip. It was from Joe, sent the Monday after the weekend-long engagement celebrations. Why the fuck do gay men enjoy dragging out celebrations for so long? "Bobim" spent a whole weekend celebrating, and still had their official "do" to go. Now it looks like Joe is hell bent on continuing his birthday celebrations nearly a month after the event. I analyze the email in my mind as I read it. Joe spends the first paragraph thanking Nat for being such a good friend and for helping him meet Jesus. No, this was not a "I had great sex that night and cried out the Lord's name at the height of ecstasy meeting of Jesus." The guy Joe met at the club is Spanish and is actually named Jesus. Joe adds that Jesus is excellent in bed and that they'd spent their entire Sunday there. Jas adds to the email chain that, based on his experience, most Spanish men are well-endowed. *Thanks for lowering the tone, Jason*, I think, *and thanks for providing way too much information, Joseph*. Joe writes that he is the world's best DJ, playing the mega-clubs all summer long in the coolest place ever, and we are all invited to go see him play. So our savior, not satisfied by just pleasuring our friend all weekend long, now wants to save us all by letting us stay at his villa in Ibiza because he has to go there for work. Joe, needing no persuasion, says he plans to go to the opening night and asks everyone to go. "Natson" agrees that they will come. Why do I agree to go? I stop analyzing it because I realize it is childish. I make the rest of my arrangements in silence.

* * * *

Friday night comes, and just under two thousand kilometers away from the sanctuary of Clapham, we find ourselves drinking cocktails on the island of Ibiza. Joe and Jas had flown out the day before and picked out the best restaurants and bars for Marco and me—we have just arrived. A guy approaches our table and asks if we have tickets for one of the clubs tonight. He looks frustrated when Joe says we do. He wants to know which club, then says it is crap, but he can sell us tickets to one of the better ones. Just so we will not be out of pocket, he will buy the tickets we already have. I have to politely tell him we are happy with what we have. When he leaves, we joke with Joe about how he managed to not leap out of his chair and say that his boyfriend got us free tickets, and that it was obviously going to be the best night on the island because Jesus was in charge.

"I have to go meet a business acquaintance now, but I'll see you all in the club." Jas finishes his drink and leaves.

"Wait a minute, don't tell me he came over here to work?" Joe asks.

I feel sheepish. "I don't think it's full-on work, more of a surveying mission. He said the Cow had introduced him to the Vaca and they wanted to talk."

"Who is the Cow? And what's a Vaca? What if he gets caught? What will happen to Jesus?"

"The Cow is what he calls his dealer. A Vaca is the Spanish term for a cow, and Jesus will be thrown out the country if Jas is caught selling drugs because his boyfriend invited the criminal to come to the island," Marco explains.

I laugh. "Joe, he is surprisingly good at his job. It's not what I would have chosen as a career path for him, but it's what he does, and we all know it. If he's caught, I'm sure the lovely DJ Rainbow will not be implicated as a conspirator."

"Ha, you know it's not Rainbow. I know he has nothing to do with the drug selling, but what if the police saw that Jas got into the club from a ticket given out by my boyfriend, DJ…?"

"… big cock!" Marco butts in and laughs. "Josephine, I never knew you were a shallow size-queen."

We order another round of drinks. While we are waiting, Joe asks Marco if he will be on the pull in the club. I stop listening to them and think about what Jas told me about the drug scene in Ibiza and how a good, trustworthy dealer, especially one who speaks English, could do really well—well enough that he would not have to do it for the entire year. He could work one season to set himself up financially, and then get a real job. I am torn; even though I am against Jas's drug dealing, I also want this trip to go well for him.

* * * *

A few hours later, we were in the club; three of us are drunk, while the other is mildly high on some illegal substances. The main DJ for the night is not due for a couple of hours, so the rising star, DJ Jesus, is warming up the early clubbers. The club is not yet filled. It is early in the night, only the beginning of the Ibiza session, so we have more than enough space to move, and are messing around doing stupid dances. The others make me do Essex dancing, Marco has to dance like an Italian trying to seduce a woman with his lothario moves, king of seduction Nat has to work an imaginary pole, Jas takes the piss out of a dance-off, which involves him standing on the spot rotating a full 360 degrees holding his foot at his ass and his hand at his head. He also does some variation of an extreme worm, but he actually makes the moves look good.

After a couple of hours, the music is starting to get more serious—not the better known club tracks, but the emerging tracks for the upcoming summer season. This is dramatically complimented with a laser light show and smoke. When I see the green blanket of light work its way down to us from above, I and the other guys instinctively know what to do. We momentarily stop and thrust both arms straight into the air. Everyone moves their bodies to the rhythm as the wave of light gets closer and the music builds up to a massive, thumping crescendo. The club is starting to fill up more, each clubber feeding off the energy of those around them, but at that moment it feels like we are the only people in the room. Then the magic moment hits. The atmosphere is so charged that each person feels he owns the night. Fingers penetrate the light, causing it to streak open. The music hits the mega-beat and the clubbers really go for it on the dance floor, moving to the rhythm, jumping, hugging, or kissing the people next to them.

Nat and Jas are kissing each other in a long, sweaty manbrace, Marco is catching his breath, and I go to try to catch the DJ's eye to give him a little wave. As I am standing in front of the shrine erected for the DJs, I do not have to try too hard to catch Jesus's eye. The DJ has a bird's eye view of the dance floor and tells security it is okay for me to come up. At first I am astounded that Jesus does not mind being seen with me so publicly after just a week. I think my luck with men is getting better. Recently, I had had a very fit "straight" Italian guy and before that a gorgeous Internet lover, so yes, I can pull good-looking men. I have found the best looking guy here, in my opinion, who is talking to me on a stage for everyone to see. I am no longer hidden away like some dirty secret, which is the way every guy had made me feel in the past. I am shown the decks. Below the decks, I see a little alcove and asks Jesus if that is where his groupies blow him off. He laughs and says other DJs did receive that there, but he is not that big yet. Then I get onto my knees and temporarily hide from the world again, but this time out of choice. I undo Jesus's fly. Jesus bends his knees slightly and comes closer so his bottom half is accessible to me but remains hidden from the crowd. I take Jesus's fully excited member.

"I will be your first."

"You can be my only." Then Jesus starts groaning with pleasure.

* * * *

I am watching Joe, when he disappears under the DJ booth. It is obvious what is happening. I decide we will have to have the talk back in London once the Lord has left Joe. Ultimately, I came out here to make sure my friends are okay and have a good time, but I feel a little bit stupid for following a guy on his "romantic break," expecting something bad to happen so I could pick up the pieces. I tell myself I am in Ibiza, I am horny, I have had a really fun time up to this point, so there is no way I am going to let this little downer ruin my vacation. I decide I might as well make the most of things. The only problem is we are not in a gay club. Of course, this being a mega-club in Ibiza means there are lots of gay men present, but it is not like I could just pick a guy I like and go up to him like I would in any gay place.

I take my top off, not that it makes me stand out because most of the clubbers are topless. It will help if I catch anyone looking. I scan the room for someone I can introduce to Carlo, but the club is getting busier and it is hard to see far. All the guys are either definite nos or are European, which throws off my gaydar. I decide I need a wing woman, someone good-looking, so if we go up to a guy, the guy will give away his sexuality by staring at one or the other of us. Jas and Nat are pretty much occupied, so I go for a walk. After a quick circuit, well, as quickly as you can "wance" (walk-dance) around a crowded club, I go back to a hen party I'd spotted. I single out a fairly attractive member of the group. I give the hen my underwear, which she requests as part of some challenge she has to complete, as I figure I will have them off later anyway. I have my wing woman.

Two hours later, I have just finished 69-ing a Welsh guy on the beach. We are skinny-dipping in the water to clean off, when the guy starts idly talking. I don't listen. I am thinking that I enjoyed the chase more than the end result, which satisfied a need but is ultimately an anticlimax.

* * * *

I realize that both Joe and Marco have disappeared. I want to get to work now that the club is busier, but I do not want to leave Nat by himself. I start to wonder if I should take Nat with me, for I know my boyfriend has a certain charm that people find hard to refuse. With Nat by my side we will be an unstoppable team, but it is a dangerous road, which once driven is hard to exit. I am not sure if I was seriously considering it, but luckily for me, before I have to make a decision, Joe and Jesus join us. I congratulate the DJ on a great set. I had not heard that much of it because I was too obsessed with Nat to actually listen, but what I had heard seems good. I whisper in Nat's ear that I have to go now, and give him a little peck on the cheek.

"Hurry back, Jas, so we can continue this party at the beach…privately," Nat says to me.

I start to walk around the club. It is a new club to me, a different country filled with lots of languages, but it is all so familiar. Instinctively, I know the clubbers who are partying; the signs are all the same. I watch them, and when the time and the client are right, make my move. I do the business in discreet parts of the club—another self-taught technique. The language is not really a problem, as most of the people speak English. Those who do not get by with making a snorting gesture or placing their finger on their tongue. Only the turf is different. Back in Clapham and Vauxhall, I am respected; people know who my Cow is, so they will not touch me. But here, while the Vaca supplied me with the goods and said it will not be a problem for me to sell, it is pretty much dog eat dog.

A guy approaches me and asks to buy some stuff. We go outside to seal the deal, which I welcome because I am really hot inside the club. Besides, it is always safer to do deals outside because once you are out of sight of the bouncer, you do not have to worry about cameras. The guy seems nervous, but pays me up front. As I hand him the tab wrapped in a bit of plastic, something heavy connects with the back of my head.

I am lying face down. I put my hand to the back of my head and it feels wet. Then someone kicks me in the ribs, and another kick on the other side. Stomps rain down all over my body, my head, shoulders, parts of my back, ass, and legs, then more kicks to the ribs. The pain is getting too much, but I am unable to scream out because my face is on the ground. I have already cut my mouth on my teeth. The attackers rummage through my pockets and take all my money, phone, and the few remaining narcotics I have left on me. They start speaking to me.

"Hombre negro..."

"He's English."

"Oi, fucking nigger, stay away from our territory..."

15

HE IS ADVENTUROUS

Mr. Ashton has just finished making a speech when all the guests burst into applause and clink their glasses to us, the happy couple. We raise our own champagne flutes in unison to join in with the people celebrating our love and the new direction in which we plan to take our relationship. I look around "my" apartment into the sea of faces. While the night should have been one of my happiest, the absenteeism gets me down. Due to the relatively short notice for our official engagement party, few of my family including my mother and stepfather had been able to come down for it. I had suggested to Bobs that we postpone the engagement party a couple of weeks to accommodate my family, but then Bobs's parents would have been on a cruise, and as he pointed out, since they had paid for the party they should be present. There was no Skinny or Skinnier. I do not know why they are not present, and I can't check because Bobs told me to leave my phone in the bedroom—it looks rude to be seen calling or texting people in front of all our guests. Then, there are my secret friends, whom I have not been allowed to invite because I have to pretend they do not exist, even though they have gotten me through the hard times. No, this is definitely a party for the Ashtons to show off their money to their friends and extended family, who all seem surprisingly available on such short notice.

I look at all of Bobs's cousins and their partners and wonder how many of them had to do what had been asked of me earlier in the day. In my suit jacket pocket is the document given to me by Mr. Ashton. The thing is light but weighs on me tremendously. Bobs asks if I am all right, and says we have to go do some more photographs. I tell him I am thinking about our missing friends.

"I know, I miss Taylor, Joe, and Jas too. But don't worry about it, once the party is over I have arranged a surprise to make up for their absence."

* * * *

Tonight is the big engagement party. I know I have to be firm and stand my ground, because my friend Bobs has an amazing ability to get his own way. He is staring at me from across the coffee table in disbelief. Even though I am sitting a short distance away and could have reached out and touched him, after I tell him I won't be able to make it to his engagement party the distance between us seems monumental.

"Joe, I refuse to believe that you are actually blowing off my—Tim's and my—party."

"I tried to change my flight so I could make your party but I couldn't," I lie. "I need to get to Ibiza to support my boyfriend. He's playing a longer set that day," I add, hoping the details will distract Bobs from his hurt feelings.

"I will pay for a flight the next day, and speak to Jesus to get you permission to be late." Jesus would have let me do what I wanted to do, but I cannot handle seeing Bobs's father again. My life is going so well at the moment I do not need any reminders of my past, especially seeing the one jerk who has given me my most grotesque memory. I justify that while my ditching the engagement party would temporarily hurt my friend, in the long run it is a selfless act that will save Bobs and his mother from hurt. Even if I could somehow tolerate being in a room with that man, I have no idea how the father would react. He might totally flip out at seeing a former rent boy of his, one who knows his kinky persuasions, one who happens to be best friends with his son. Definitely, the father would not be able to remain cool; he might give the game away, and I do not need the hassle, so I think it best to stay away from the soiree.

In an attempt to pacify Bobs, I invite him and Tim to holiday with us in Ibiza.

"So, you guys seem pretty serious for, what has it been, three weeks?" Bobs asks me.

"Yes, but when you know, you know straight away. He's not like any of the guys I've met before. He's really into me, he's not ashamed of me, and he treats me the way I deserve to be treated. You know, maybe I have found my Tim."

Bobs touches my hand. "If you believe you have found the one who is right for you, then go for it. If you only get to see him on weekends in Ibiza, then go. I understand."

At that, my eyes start to well up with tears, "I didn't want to say this because today is about you and Tim, so don't mention it to anyone else, but I am bursting to tell someone." I don't wait for a response. "I have quit my job, and I have decided to move to Ibiza."

* * * *

It had been over a month since my very public coming-out. I am over it now. After all, I had instigated it, but I had never meant to hurt Carmen. I need to speak to her to apologize and make sure she is okay. I do not want to awkwardly bump into her later tonight at Bobs's and Tim's engagement party, so I decide to try and speak to her now and clear the air. However, she refuses to answer my phone calls and emails, and she is being driven to work in one of her dad's cars, so I cannot intercept her on her way in. When I go to the Phoenix to see her, I am not allowed up. I am stopped at reception and told that Miss Howard has instructed them to call the police if I show up. When I told a naïve concierge that I am going to visit Timothy Douglas, I made it to her front door, but she never answered. The locks had been changed so I could only shout an apology before being escorted out by security.

At the Phoenix, there are a whole lot of caterers going in by the service entrance. They are all uniformed, so I would stick out like a sore thumb. The florist, however, is in normal clothes and seems to be making multiple trips to her van. I start speaking to her about the engagement party, how I am the neighbor, and how I am thinking of doing something special for my girlfriend's birthday. As planned, I help her carry some flowers in while we continue to talk.

I make it up to the floor where I used to live. Now, I just need to get into my old apartment. One of the caterers singles himself out from the group, presumably to smoke, as he smells of cigarettes when I approach him. I give the guy fifty pounds to knock on Carmen's door and ask her if they are making too much noise. He is instructed to get the hell out of here once she opens it. The guy looks suspicious at first, but I explain that it is my ex who is angry with me for cheating (I omit the "with a man" part), and I want to talk to her and make amends. The guy agrees, adding that he will not disappear, however, if the woman does not want to see me. Once Carmen opens the door to the stranger and I appear, she tries to shut the door on both of us, but I put my foot inside and ask her for five minutes. She agrees, wrapping her cardigan around herself and signaling to the guy that she will be okay.

Carmen, like Taylor, has a public face. But she is not on show in the privacy of her own home, and looks rough. The clothes she is wearing are really baggy, maybe to hide the fact that she has put on weight. She catches me staring at her stomach and becomes very defensive.

"What do you want, Richard?"

"To explain and apologize. I want you to understand this was all me and nothing to do with you," I start.

"I actually don't give a fuck. I have already moved on and I want you out of my life."

"Car, you look terrible. Let me help you. We can try to be friends, in time."

"Were you fucking him while you were with me?"

"No, of course not. Nothing happened until we were broken up." I decide not to tell her about the kiss because I do not want to hurt her anymore. "We were so unhappy, I thought you were going to end it with me, and I wouldn't have blamed you. You deserve someone who will make you happy."

"Does he make you happy?"

I hesitate, knowing that she doesn't really want to know the answer to that question. "He told me about the baby and what happened. I wish you had told me. I would have supported you whatever you wanted to do. You didn't have to go through that alone."

She stands up and turns to one side, unwrapping the cardigan to reveal the strained t-shirt she has on underneath which covers an obvious bump.

* * * *

I can really do without my unexpected visitor. Mr. Ashton sits drinking tea. I think about all the times I have been alone with the man, which is never. Before he sat down to have tea, he had checked with the hired staff that everything was going according to plan, and I resent him doing that. After all, this is my home and I am more than capable of managing the staff. Not that I need to; Bobs hired a planner for the evening so I would not have to worry about anything.

"Timothy, if Robert must go through with this nonsense, there have to be some rules."

I do not like the way the stupid wannabe Lord Ashton is looking at me. "I'm not sure I understand." My voice sounds meek.

Mr. Ashton gets up, moves over and sits down next to me. "I know, son. Don't worry." He places his hand on my leg and passes me an envelope. He tells me to read it, sign it, and return it to him tonight. I start to read it. Mr. Ashton gives my leg a little squeeze and gets up to leave.

It is a legal document, which I read several times to understand the gist. Once we are civil partnered, should we ever separate, I could make no legal claim on any of Bobs's money, property, or family wealth. Instead, I would be given twenty thousand pounds cash as a token gift for the affection Bobs had for me. There is also an injunction clause that any private Ashton family or business matters to which I am privy to during the course of our union had to stay just that: private.

* * * *

I look at Nat as he stands at the front door acting like some sort of protector. I want to tell him that he looks like shit, that Jas would never want him to let himself go like this, but think it is better not to upset him further.

"So how is he?"

"He says he is fine, Bobs, and just needs time to rest and recover. But he seems to be in pain all the time. Then there is his mental state: he refuses to talk about that night."

"How are you?" I ask Nat. I can see how being Jas's caretaker has taken its toll. It had only been a short while, but I realize it must have been difficult for him. When Nat does not reply, I prompt him. "Are you sure he wouldn't be better off in a hospital?"

"Of course he would. But he won't go," Nat snaps back. "Sorry. You know, when we found him after he was mugged, he said it looked worse than it was and refused to go to the police or a hospital in Spain. He said he would see a doctor back in England, and since our flight was later that day I agreed. Since he got back here, he has been holed up in our bedroom. I had Taylor look at him, and he said although nothing appeared broken and the concussion period had passed, Jas should go to a hospital and get a thorough work-up. Taylor prescribed him some painkillers if he promised to go to the hospital, but he hasn't gone."

I enter the bedroom. It's murky and dark. I look at the blinds, wanting to go over and open them and the windows too, but I know it is not my place to do so. Jas is lying on the bed. We had visited him once before, when the group had just returned from Ibiza. He was all bandaged up at the time and was totally out of it, but not today. Jas sits up in the bed and turns on his bedside lamp, and I see the extent of his injuries. Jas's torso is still bandaged up, but bruises are peeking out from where the gauze ends. I hope they are just superficial. Most of the swelling on his face has gone down, but it looks like his nose has been broken, and his mouth looks raw from where his teeth had cut through. Looking at this man so visibly hurt makes me think about the times I hit Tim. A cold shiver runs down my spine. I decide not to do it again. I must have been staring for too long or too obviously because Jas interrupts my thoughts.

"You should have seen the other guy." We both laugh, before Jas gets serious.

"You have to take Nat with you, he needs to get out of here. He hasn't left the house since we came back. He called in sick at work and orders whatever we need online or sends Joe out to get it. Please take him to your party tonight. I'll be fine, I'll be better if I know that he is getting better too."

"He won't leave you," I tell Jas. "Not unless you agree to go to a hospital tomorrow and give him peace of mind by getting an all-clear."

Jas nods in agreement. We continue to chat until Nat comes in the room, saying the patient needs his rest. We tell Nat the plan. While Nat is saying goodbye to Jas and hearing his reassurances, I go into Joe's bedroom and sit on the bed. I look around the room and feel a sense of pride for my friend Joe who is going off to follow his heart. I think if only I'd had the balls to do that myself, how different things would have been. But I'd decided to stay with Tim, and will make it work. I am secretly hopeful that tonight's surprise will go some way toward achieving that goal.

* * * *

"She couldn't go through with the abortion. She decided to not discuss it with anyone else except me, but then I dumped her. The next time she met me, I was making out with you, Taylor, so she could hardly mention it then. She blanked me out because she was so hurt, but the time we spent apart made her realize that the baby is the priority. When I apologized, she said she wanted me to have an active role in our baby's life."

Ricky finishes telling me about his visit with Carmen. I sit there patiently listening, not revealing how disturbed I am to hear the update. I had hoped she would be out of our lives for good, but that cockroach has managed to cement her life forever with Ricky's. At first I hope it is lie, but he is holding a copy of the sonogram. I do not understand how she has become so understanding and Mother Theresa-esque. Perhaps she is better at the game of life than I gave her credit for. But I think better than to voice my concerns to Ricky.

"She did say she still felt betrayed and would prefer not to see either of us in a social setting yet," Ricky continues. "So, I agreed that neither you nor I would go to the engagement party to upset her further, especially given her condition."

This really pisses me off. How dare Ricky speak for me

and stop me from going to my friend's party? It is not that I badly want to go, it is the principle of the matter. I want to let this go, because over the past month Ricky has come quite far in terms of accepting his sexuality. So I think it best not to argue and possibly send him backwards on an emotional level, which will give Carmen what she wants. While Ricky is not yet sparkly hot pants out and proud, strolling in a pride march, he has stopped making derogatory references to anything gay. After Ricky hit me I was worried he would go hurtling backwards emotionally, but he'd apologized the next day, saying he did not mean it and was just upset about the baby. He'd joked that we were now even, considering the first time we met. I saw how upset and genuinely sorry he was, so I forgave him for the punch and we moved on. That is, until the bitch's latest stunt.

Ricky tries to sweeten the deal. "If we stay in tonight, you can fuck me, I feel ready to try that." I know he is doing it to keep me on board about missing the party, but I play along. Anal is not everything in a gay relationship and some couples seem happy not to do it, but I like it. In this relationship, I have been the bottom so far but I am desperate to top Ricky. He has allowed me to rim and finger him but never to fuck him; I'd presumed it was another hang-up he had about being gay. But right now I don't care what has caused him to change his mind—I hope this will break the final taboo, and Ricky can finally accept every aspect of his sexuality.

* * * *

The Cow has just left me. After Nat left earlier with Bobs, I had called him over because I needed something from him. Although we are just business acquaintances, he seemed very concerned about my health and well-being. Deep down, I knew it was because with me out of action, the Cow was losing money. That was his real concern. But now our professional relationship has changed. He has been in my house and seen me looking weak and in need of help. This makes me think that once I am back on my feet and make back the money I lost, I will quit this business. But for now, the Cow has come through for me and has quite generously provided me with the thing I had asked for. I normally draw the line at injecting myself when it comes to recreational drug use, but the prescription drugs Taylor had given me were not cutting the mark and the remains of what I had in the house were doing nothing for me—maybe it is my own fault that my tolerance is so high. I decided I needed to go that extra mile, as the pain was too great and I needed it to stop for a while. I also needed the horrific memories of being beaten unconscious to go away. I needed not to feel guilty that I finally got what I deserved for being a scumbag dealer. I needed a hit of heroin. Anyway, if I am going to quit this business and lifestyle, I want to do it knowing I have at least tried everything, so tonight I will mainline.

I get the largest metal spoon we have and tip all the matte-white powder onto it. I add water and lemon juice, so that it mixes and dissolves. I heat it very briefly on the stove, and I smile because both Nat and Joe are always telling me to cook more often. I take a syringe from the pack of ten that the Cow has kindly provided and draw up the contents of the spoon. I sit at the kitchen table, tie a belt around my left bicep, and inject the contents of the syringe into a vein that has become nicely visible. When I have fully depressed the plunger, I withdraw the needle and undo the belt. I feel heat rush from the site of the injection and spread all over my body. I hope the euphoria will take away all my pain and worries, and it does. This is the first time since the attack that I feel no pain. I can relax. I feel a loving chemical safety blanket wrapping around me, making me invincible. The effects become greater, but I find myself unable to breathe. I'm gasping for air.

* * * *

My lover's hands are covering my eyes, guiding me where to walk, I am led to the bedroom. I feel a little bit nervous. Previous surprises have not always been full of happy memories, and my gut feeling is that this one would be the same. Bobs whispers in my ear, asking if I am ready. I nod, hoping that when he removes his hands there will be a puppy on the bed with a bow wrapped around its middle. But I am greeted by a not-so-unfamiliar stranger who is naked in our bed.

"This is Damian, the treat I arranged for us to celebrate properly."

I turn and look at Bobs. "You paid a cocktail waiter to come and join us in bed?" I whisper back.

Bobs looks puzzled. Damian pipes up from the bed, "I am not really a waiter. Bobby paid me to be ready to celebrate with you guys as soon as all your guests left. I have never had a gig at the Phoenix, and I just wanted to see what the place looked like, so I made myself useful. I am really an escort."

"You know how we discussed that when we got

engaged we would not be one of those boring settled-down couples? Well, we have never done this before. It's a way of introducing variety into our love life without cheating, which we might be tempted to do after years of monogamous partnership," Bobs says.

Damian sits up and asks, "Is this happening or not? A threesome in the Phoenix will be awesome, and I promise you guys will get your money's worth."

Bobs responds by grabbing my hand and leading me toward the bed.

* * * *

After a full-body massage and lots of kissing, licking and touching everywhere, I am lying face down with my legs spread wide. Taylor has rimmed me for a while, getting his tongue in really deep, and he is now fingering and lubing me up. Every time he goes a bit deeper with his finger, I feel myself starting to enjoy it more. Taylor is telling me to relax.

* * * *

I am unsure if we should cross this boundary. I recall Bobs mentioning trying this when we were on vacation, but I never thought he was being serious. However, I cannot back out of it because my clothes have already been removed and Damian is sucking my nipples, telling me I have an amazing body.

* * * *

We change positions. I am now lying down on the bed. Ricky is astride me. I thought if he could look into my eyes, he will feel more relaxed. I am rubbing my lubed self against his hole, waiting for Ricky to initiate the next step, while I am gently strumming his hard cock.

* * * *

The three of us are really starting to go for it. I am on my back 69-ing with Tim, while Damian is eating Tim out. When the thrusting permits, he works his tongue on Tim's balls and shaft as it goes inside my mouth. Tim is thoroughly enjoying being sucked off and rimmed simultaneously. I knew Tim will enjoy this gift; this turns me on even more.

* * * *

"Stay still, don't move," I gasp as Taylor's head enters me. Taylor lays perfectly motionless, resisting the urge to move his hips upwards. After getting used to the head, I start to move up and down very delicately. This continues until I push past the initial hurt, hit the pleasure zone, and start to go down a little bit further on Taylor.

* * * *

Finishing a blow job triangle, Damian lays on the bed, telling me I have amazing tits and squeezing my rock-hard pecs. Before he can say anything else, he finds his mouth full with both my cock, I am now sitting on his chest, and Bobs, who is opposite me kissing him.

* * * *

I have now been fully inside of Ricky. He is used to me, and he wants more. I move to the missionary position and grab his legs up by my shoulders, as I continue to fuck him. Ricky is groaning, begging for it harder, as he works himself with his own hand.

* * * *

Tim is now on top of Damian, being fucked by him, while Damian is sucking me off. I am kissing and grabbing Tim, and he is doing the same to me. I move, standing in between Damian's legs, which are hanging off the bed, behind Tim who is in the anal drop position.

* * * *

I can tell we are both close. We move into the spoons position so we can kiss each other deeply. Taylor continues pumping me from behind. His hand is caressing my cock and balls. I feel my body tense, and I cum on his hand. He increases his motion as I tighten around him, and he shoots his own load inside me. After he has finished, he stops moving. We both keep our bottom halves still and continue to passionately kiss each other. Lying there sweaty and satisfied, I want it again once we are both ready.

* * * *

Bobs lubes himself up and is trying to enter me too.

I am full with Damian. "Please no, I can't take any more. "I don't think it will work."

"I can come out and you can finish him off," Damian says and stops humping.

"No, we should at least try. Come on, Tim baby, let's try. You stay inside him, and I'll ever so gently join you," he tells Damian.

Bobs forces himself in too. I cry out in pain, dizzy and swaying but I cannot fall over because Bobs grabs me from behind as he fucks me.

"This is amazing, my hard cock against Damian's. Oh boy, I am going to shoot." He reaches around to finish me off as he cums, but I am soft. I painfully remove myself from the double penetration. I lie that I had cum ages ago.

"I came too, I am going to leave now if you guys are finished with my services," Damian tells us.

I think he is lying, like me; he probably faked it too. He knows I did not enjoy the last part. During the act, he had seemed to be all there in the room with me, and had kept asking if I was okay. When we made eye contact he would have seen the "help me" look in my eyes. Bobs had gone to another place, and he had satisfied only himself, oblivious to my feelings or my pain.

16

HE BREAKS YOUR HEART

The ground feels really cold. I look down at the precision-cut slabs of some rock under my naked feet that I do not recognize. The light from the moon and stars gives the dry parts a blue appearance; the wet parts are a lot darker. It has not been raining, so I wonder where the wetness has come from. As I walk toward the swinging doors, I feel colder. I push the doors open and step inside, where it is freezing. I exhale; my breath is like a mist. I look down at my feet again and see that the black band around my right ankle is covered in a dried red substance, as are both of my feet. I realize the wet substance is not water but blood. I push on further into the sterile environment. I look at an up-front silver table as I walk past. It is highly polished, reflective. I see myself staring back. Not just my feet are exposed—I am completely naked. Even though I am alone, I feel self-conscious. The two souvenirs on my right shoulder from my teenage years are bleeding profusely. I touch them with my left hand, and wipe my hand across my forehead. I have been given a job to do and I am going to complete it. Once I reach the far end of the room, I stretch out my arm and touch the wall to support myself. With my other hand, I tug on the silver handle and pull out the table. It is a gentle tug, but it causes the table to fly out from the hidden depths of the wall. I reach out and pull back the pristine white sheet; lying there is Jas's body with the life sucked out of it, a cold shell of its former owner. I stand there staring at the body. Suddenly, dead Jas opens his eyes and calls out, "Nathan!"

I wake up, being shaken by my bedfellow. He tells me I am having another bad dream. I snuggle up to the warm body in my bed, hoping it will help me sleep, but am poked by the guy's erection. It pisses me off that given everything that has happened, this guy just thinks about sex.

* * * *

The sweat is dripping off her as she runs. She is starting to get weary a bit. This is usually the time I would come in with a motivational speech, or speed up my running on the machine next to her to make her go that extra mile. But today, I just don't have the motivation.

"Are you sure you are okay, Tim? You're very quiet today, You're not being your usual active self."

"Sorry, babes. Don't worry about paying me for today."

"I wasn't asking because I was worried about the money. I was asking out of concern."

"I don't know why you bother, when I didn't even invite you to my engagement party."

"Don't worry about that. I understand. You kept it to family and close friends, not some silly girl who accosted you at the gym asking for personal training sessions." Claire smiles back at me.

"I really wanted to invite you because I think of you as a friend too. But I couldn't, and I feel like shit for not doing so." I try to look apologetic. "You have given me a goal in life, a purpose and direction, for which you will never know how grateful I am."

Claire stops her treadmill. "After that speech, Tim, I will be expecting an invite to your civil partnership. To be honest, I am quite excited. I have never been to one before. But I hope that you are not overdoing it, trying to get even more buff for your wedding. I noticed you were hobbling earlier."

"I am not. Anyway, he wouldn't even notice."

She looks at me and suggests we go to the juice bar. We sit there quietly for a while; she is playing with the straw in some ghastly smoothie I ordered for her. "So, what did you mean when you said he wouldn't notice?"

I look at her, uncertain. I need to get so much off my chest, to talk to someone. Before I can think, I blurt everything out. While I am telling her about Bobs and me, I have a very surreal moment. I leave my body, in a way, and hear myself telling her about the numerous problems we have. I really hear the words; I listen to each one as if a stranger were saying them. When I finish speaking, stop observing and am one with myself again, I feel sick, disgusted by the words I have spoken for the first time. Judging by the look on her face, she feels the same way. She puts down her drink and hugs me because maybe I needed it, or maybe she needed it, or she did not know what to say.

* * * *

It has been a week since I found out about the baby; that day Carmen had told me to come back so we could talk more. I have been really excited all week long, not because I particularly want children at this moment in life or have even ever given it much thought, but it takes a certain pressure off me. After finally admitting to myself that I am gay, part of me realizes the chances of having a biological child are slim. I think about how society demands everyone should procreate, that it is traditional, and those who chose to do otherwise are seen as some sort of deviant. Ultimately, when I eventually tell my parents I am gay, that is the only issue they will have with it—the lack of a grandchild. Now I can tell them I am gay but have fathered a child, so they can live happily in grandparentland. Approaching the Phoenix with a large bouquet of flowers and a cuddly stuffed bear I'd brought for Carmen and the baby, I am thinking how Taylor had not been excited by the news. I wonder if Taylor is jealous that it is not his own biological child, or if he thinks a kid would upset the plans he has for our life together.

I see Maurice as I enter the building. Before he can tell me I am no longer welcome at Nightingale Hall, I announce that Miss Howard has invited me here and any unpleasantness is in the past. Maurice says he has been notified, and was told to escort me up. Maurice opens the door and I walk into my former home. I walk through the hall to the living room and notice that she has started clearing stuff away; the place is looking very sparse. I open the door, walk in, and find almost all the furniture has gone. Mr. Howard is standing by the window looking out onto the common.

"You know, the reason I picked this place for my little girl to live was because of all the faggots. I knew they would look after her, but I never realized my little princess would have stupidly gotten knocked up by one."

"Where is Carmen?" I interrupt him.

"I cannot blame her entirely. I never had you pegged

for one. Right cunning bastard, aren't you?"

"Fuck off," I manage to say. Then I find myself on my knees, the presents drop, and my arm is twisted behind my back by someone who has appeared from nowhere.

"Never speak to Mr. Howard like that!" the enforcer shouts as he bends my arm.

"She's gone, Fairy. Now I have a message for you: do not contact her ever again, do not contact my grandchild ever, do not ever look at a member of my family again. Is that clear?" he booms from across the room. "If I ever see or hear anything from you again, I will get my associate here to break your arm, and there will be no more snappy pictures from you."

On cue, the guy exerts enough pressure to make me scream out in pain. "If you tell anyone about our little meeting, I don't think my associate would be pleased, and by the time he is finished with your face, no woman—or man—will ever want you again."

* * * *

I am hugging Joe in our old office. Knowing he is leaving feels weird.

"Congratulations on the promotion, Ben."

"I only got it because you took yourself out of the running," I tell him. "I'm still shocked that you are going. I'll give you the manager's job and I'll continue as the assistant, if you stay."

"No chance, love. I could never give up my new sex, sun, and sea lifestyle."

"At least you can stop bothering with the fake tan now."

He links his arm with mine, and for old times' sake or

because I have work to do, we walk around the cinema. We walk from the office to the kiosk, checking that the staff there have stocked up everything for the next screenings before the rush begins.

"So I heard your new best friend has skipped town."

"I see the 'gayesdropping' network is as prolific as ever, but I bet I know something you don't."

"When I went to say bye to Bobs and Tim at the crack of dawn this morning, I saw her ordering moving men to haul her stuff out of there. I said 'bye to her. She was innocent in all of this. So, what don't I know?"

"She texted me earlier to say she was sorry for thinking I lied to her, and that she had acted out badly due to her hormones from the baby."

We go into the box office to see what has sold out and whether any seating problems should be expected.

"Really? I just thought she let herself go after she turned the last man to have a go on her gay."

We both burst out laughing.

"Thompson, I am going to miss you. Who else will be as cutting as you and make the mundane so bearable?"

"Whatever, Sanders. You are all loved up in 'dykeheaven,' and you will forget about my existence once you guys buy a cat together."

"Coming from the guy who's moving across many oceans after just two days together," I say, and smile at him, "you will come back and visit Al and me?"

"Of course. And you guys must come to Ibiza."

"I will even do my homework and try to find out where the lesbians go."

"You have a deal."

With that, we go into the smallest screen to make sure the temperature, volume, and quality are okay, and that the crowd is behaving. Then we work our way around the other screens doing the same. He follows me into the projection room. "I know you did not want a party and a fuss after what happened to Jas and all, but I got you a little something." I hand him a gift. He opens it, and when he sees a book on learning to speak Spanish, he hugs me.

* * * *

"Ben, am I making the right decision? I love him, but this is such a big step, I feel nervous."

She is staring at me, a warmth is in her eyes, telling me it will all be okay. "Of course it is the right decision. Why wait around? You don't get opportunities like this ever, so why not go for it when it happens?"

"Thank you."

"Well, you better get going and start your new life."

"I just have one last goodbye to make before going."

"Oi. I thought you saved the best till last."

"I wanted to, as you know you are my bestest friend in the whole world, but this last one has been very hard to face."

* * * *

I am sitting by the hospital bed holding Jas's hand. There has been no change in the week he has been in hospital, and the doctors told me there is unlikely to be any.

"Jason," I whisper to the body on the bed, "It's me, Nat. I have come to say goodbye. When I found you last week I thought you were dead, and a part of me died. Then they brought you here and pumped you full of more drugs, and when you woke up, I felt complete again. But you slipped into this coma and they don't know the reason. They said it might be because your brain was deprived of oxygen for too long or the amount of drugs in your system just shut everything down, but I cannot take it." I start to cry. "Every time I shut my eyes I have nightmares: finding your bloody body in Ibiza, or finding you passed out on the floor, or me having to identify your dead body. I love you, but I am not strong enough to cope with this. I think I love you too much, and it was a love that was never meant to last. No one deserves to be as happy as you made me. Now that you are not in my life, I don't want to go on. I think about cutting myself all the time, but I know you would not want me to do that. The only way I can survive what happened to you is to say goodbye. Please don't hate me. I am doing this because I love you dearly."

After saying goodbye, I kiss Jas on the forehead and walk away from him. I stand at the door for what seems likes hours just watching him, wondering if I am doing the right thing or if I am just being a coward.

"Your friend sounds like a fighter, he could wake up any day," Rod tells me as he drives me away from the hospital. In the aftermath of Jas's overdose, I'd needed someone to be there for me to make sure I would not do something stupid. I had picked Rod because Rod had made it clear how he felt about me; even though I said I was not into sex, he'd persisted.

I do not respond. I think that saying, "a fighter," is a load of crap. How can someone fight when there is no one in there any more? If there is any fighting going on, it is a biological war inside Jas's body with his brain and nervous system trying to achieve normality, but Jas had riddled his body with drugs for so many years, it is a losing battle.

"I have said my goodbye to him and have closed that chapter in my life so that I can move on. Otherwise, I might as well have taken up the bed next to him."

"And you are sure you want me in your life?" Rod asks eagerly.

"Yes. But can you take me as I am and be happy not having a sexual relationship?"

"Of course, I just love being with you, and if that is the condition I can take it. Just lying in bed next to you is enough for me. I love you."

I decide not to reply to those three big words because it would be a lie. Rod is more like a father figure, especially given the age gap between us, and that is what I need the most now. In homage to Jas, I thought it was fair that I never feel happiness again.

* * * *

I am standing at a spot on the common where I hope the majority of the runners go by. I am slightly pissed off that Marco is too busy to fit in a proper goodbye, but then I had said I didn't want a fuss. But surely, everyone who knows me realizes that I want the appropriate amount of fuss given the circumstances. I look up, and see the distinctive shape of the body I had admired for so long in the distance. I wave in an attempt to flag him down, but Marco does not deviate from his trajectory, so I quickly move to where we would bump into each other. As Marco approaches me, I shout out his name. He stops and takes out his headphones but does not come over to embrace me. I presume it is because he is sweaty.

"Hey. I just wanted to see you before I leave to say 'bye."

"So you are still going then?" Marco asks, an accusatory tone in his voice.

I get defensive. "Yes, why wouldn't I?"

"You have only just met the guy, you can't speak Spanish, you don't have a job, you are going to leave all your friends. The list goes on, Joe."

"All my other friends have supported me, even Nat with what he has gone through. I can easily pick up bar work. Everyone out there speaks English. And I love him. Why can't you just be happy for me like everyone else?"

"Everyone else lives in a fairy tale world where dreams come true. I am a realist, so I am telling you, you're making a mistake."

"My mistake was thinking you'd be happy for me, that our friendship meant something to you. I think you're jealous that I have found love while you just sleep from one random guy to the next, lying about who you are so no one can get close to you. You have never been with a person for more than two weeks, so do not judge me."

"Joe, I have to go and finish my run. Good luck with the man in Ibiza."

Then I watch in disbelief as Marco continues running. I watch him disappearing out of my life. I start to walk off in the other direction, wishing that goodbye had gone as easily as all the rest. I figure Marco does not believe in "happy ever after," and I start to feel sorry for him. I have walked about a hundred meters when I feel two sweaty arms grab me from behind and hug me tightly like they will never let me go.

* * * *

I use my left hand to open the front door to Taylor's place because my right arm hurts when I use it. Despite the warning, I fully intend to tell Taylor what has happened. Taylor is sitting on the sofa nursing what looks like a large whiskey. He does not look up when I walk in.

"I could do with one of those," I say. Taylor does not say anything. He just points to a second glass of whiskey already on the table.

"We need to talk, Ricky," he tells me.

"Yeah, I know. You would not believe what happened at Carmen's."

"No, I mean talk about us," Taylor says, still not looking at me. "This has nothing to do with you and Carmen and the baby."

I sit down, pick up my drink and have a sip. Some part of me already knows where this conversation is going, as I had done the same thing myself a couple of months ago. While it had come as a total surprise to Carmen, I had never understood how much of a surprise until now, when I find myself on the receiving end.

"Go on."

"Everything between us is happening too fast. One minute you are straight and we are friends. Then we are kissing. Next thing, you have dumped your pregnant girlfriend and have moved in with me. Now we are in a full-on relationship with talk of co-parenting."

"You don't have to worry about the baby, I am not allowed to see it or have anything to do with it."

For the first time Taylor looks up at me, I look down

into my drink.

"She can't stop you seeing your child, but we can talk about that afterward. I want to talk about us. Can't you see how fast this whole relationship has gone? I was never looking for a relationship."

"But you instigated this whole thing. You kissed me," I plead.

"I really liked you. We had such a great time together and I got a vibe from you, so yes, I kissed you. But don't you see? I never turned you gay—you were always gay. I was simply the catalyst to help you see who you truly are."

"That kiss was the turning point of my life. Until that moment I had not really lived. It was the kiss of my life; it made me see who I want to be. How can you turn your back on everything we have?"

* * * *

I look at Ricky and think about telling him the truth, that I am just a game player, that his thrill and appeal was that he was straight at the time, a man with a girlfriend—that the chase had been a major part of the turn-on for me, and that as long as he tried to come across as a straight man who would not give himself wholly, I was keen. But now that I have got him, the game is over. There is nothing new or exciting to keep me interested; in fact, Ricky has become too coupley too fast. But I decide against the truth for now. "I was in lust with you, and you are a great guy, but I don't want a boyfriend."

"Shall I move out and we just take things slowly? We can go back to being friends, and then date and take things from there."

"I think it is a good idea if you move out. And we can

be friends; that would be nice, as the scene is such a small place. But I don't think we can ever be a couple again. We've been there and done that. It's time to move on."

I finish my drink, get up, and leave the room to let Ricky mull everything over.

* * * *

I look at the food that Tim has served up and am less than impressed. The chips do not look homemade; they resemble something out of a package, as does the sauce that covers the fish. There is no effort made in the presentation; it looks like it had just been plopped on the plate. I catch Tim watching me, as he always does, for the sign of approval that he has done well.

"Is something the matter with your food?" Tim asks me.

"It just looks funny, but I am sure it will taste lovely."

"If it doesn't, there is a number on the package you can call to complain," Tim replies, and casually sips some wine.

I push the plate away from me. "You know we don't eat this sort of food. Why did you not make it yourself? What have you been doing all day?"

"Working."

"Yes, I know it's hard work, keeping this place together and everything, but..."

Tim cuts me off. "No, I mean working as a personal trainer. I have been doing it for a while. I thought you should know, because we are engaged and all."

"See, this is why I told you not to work, because your standards will drop elsewhere."

"You could try cooking, then."

I note the defiance in his voice and realize I have to

reassert my authority. "You have had your experiment with working, but now you can quit. I provide this lovely home for us and I'm too busy to cook for us."

"Not for us. For yourself."

I look at him blankly, not keeping up with where he is going with this.

"This apartment is just yours and will remain that way even IF we get civil partnered, per the instructions from your dad."

"It cost millions. It's hardly fair that you get half when you haven't put in half!"

"That's fine. I don't want it, I am happy to work and be independent. That pissy amount he offered me is less than a year's salary, and I am worth more than that."

"I'll speak to Dad and get that changed. How much do you want, one hundred thousand?"

"That depends—how much did you pay the escort? Because every time we have sex, you treat me like one. That fucking rent boy treated me with more respect than you do. When I said no, he stopped, but you forced me." Tim sounds confident when he speaks, which is quite unusual for him. "You fucking rape and abuse me with your sick perversions, and then you want to know what I am worth."

"Timothy, where is all of this coming from? What's wrong?"

"You are what is fucking wrong. I'm leaving you.

"No, baby, don't say that." I stroke his cheek with one hand and wipe away his tears with the other. "Please, you can't go. We are due to get legally partnered. That is what you want, isn't it?"

"I should have done this years ago. We were fine at university, but when we moved here, you changed. You became obsessive and controlling and took away all my self-worth. I want it back."

* * * *

I stand up to leave. I have already packed my bags and left them downstairs. Initially, I was surprised how little I actually owned in the place. Then I realized I should not be shocked, as it pretty much sums up our relationship. Bobs pleads with me not to go, hugs my legs, and cries into my knees to stop me walking away. He is a heap on the floor.

"Sorry, Bobby, it's over."

Bobs starts pulling at my clothes to stop me leaving. I pick him up with ease. I am so much more physically stronger than him, I am surprised that I had allowed myself to be the victim for so long. As we face each other, Bobs starts kissing me and tries to undress me, so I let him. I love Bobs, but love myself more now. We strip and start to make gentle love to each other. This is the last time we will be together sexually.

* * * *

I remembered the first time I sat on this bench. It was when I first moved to Clapham. Here I am again, this time getting ready to leave the place. I am not sure what has brought me back here, but it seems appropriate because I have nowhere else to go. The Phoenix has a red hue around it as the sun is setting. I am tempted to unpack my camera and take a picture, but I can't be bothered. I look down at my belongings; I have the same bags with which I had when I arrived at Carmen's. Admittedly, they are filled with nicer things because I had made decent money here. The more I think about it, the more I do not regret coming here, or my choices. I have been able to find myself and establish myself professionally. I just wish it did not hurt so much.

"Hey, soldier boy, you look lost again."

I look up at the man who is talking to me.

"You probably don't remember me. The last time I saw you, you were on this bench and my ex made a few lewd comments. If you need a friend, I can help."

I stare at him. The guy puts up both his hands in the air and says, "Nothing funny. I just remember when I moved here and learned that things don't work out the way we think they should. You look like how I felt back then."

"A friend right now would be good, thanks," I say to the guy. We shake hands and introduce ourselves. I pick up my bags. "Where are we going?"

"We can go to my place. I don't live far."

The guy points to where he lives—to the most sought after piece of real estate in SW4 for gay guys—the Phoenix.

EPILOGUE

Bobs sat on Clapham Common near the tennis courts. While he waited, he glanced up at the sun. He was not staring directly at it, but was looking close enough to make his eyes water. He was not bothered about anyone seeing his eyes, which were bloodshot and red from all the crying he had been doing, but he still hid them behind sunglasses. He wondered about the heat from the sun, and what the fire in that star felt like knowing it could devastate everything it touched. Such an immense power appealed to him. He often thought about fire and how people seem to fear it because they were scared about being burned. Really, it was an ally, bringing warmth and comfort, providing a light in dark times, and generating the energy needed for survival.

On one of the courts, he watched a couple he recognized from the scene but to whom he had never spoken. Briefly he watched them trying to play, and thought they were not very good. Suddenly he visualized them being alight, not rolling around on the ground type of alight but embracing and being one with the fire. In his head, the two men on fire were glorious; their delicate skin had been replaced by the illustrious moving surface with brilliant shades of red, orange, and yellow dancing over them. They were the embodiment of power, and no one would be able to hurt them.

Marco tapped him on the shoulder, bringing him out of his fantasy. Bobs stood up and embraced him. They both held on for a little longer than was necessary, but they both needed the hug more than they realized.

"How are you?" they asked simultaneously.

Marco waited for Bobs to answer first. "I'm shocked that it's over. I cannot believe he dumped me and took off."

"Tell me about it," Marco said gloomily.

"Your situation is different. If you had told Joe how you felt about him, he would have stayed for you. You cannot be so egotistical to not see that. He loved you."

"He loves that DJ."

"He fell for Jesus after he got nowhere with you."

Marco got defensive. "He never tried to get anywhere with me!"

"Because he thought you were out of his league; you never let him in."

"I wanted to, but it's just too complicated."

"That's why I wanted to meet up. I think we need to talk about what happened."

"I don't, we promised never to talk about it again." Marco started to feel panicked. He did not like where this was going, so he tried to change the topic. "What are you going to do about Tim? Are you going to try to get him back?"

"I can't. I was such a twat to him, I don't blame him for leaving. Honestly, I am surprised he didn't do it sooner."

"How did the rest of the Ashtons take the news that the wedding was off?" Marco asked, trying to keep the topic of conversation on safer ground.

"My parents seemed really upset. I'd expected it from

my mother, but I never thought that my father would take it as badly as he did. Maybe he was even more upset at having to tell the family that his gay son could not even hold on to a low-bred gay boy."

"It must be really hard for you," Marco told him. "This is not a time when you are thinking straight. Please don't do anything stupid. Maybe you should go on a vacation."

"Actually, I'm going to visit Joe next week." Bobs searched Marco's face for the look of disappointment, but as usual, he was blank, as he had been ever since that day.

"Should we be encouraging him to stay out there by making little visits?" Marco asked bitterly.

"My dear friend, he has been over there for over a month now. He is happy, he has a job, and has made new friends. I don't think he's coming back."

"I am happy for him. What? Don't look at me like that. Honestly, I am."

"You know you deserve happiness too, as do I. But neither of us have allowed ourselves to feel happy since that time."

Marco took out his phone, played around with it, and then took out the battery. He asked Bobs to borrow his phone. Bobs handed it over, thinking that Marco wanted to swap batteries.

"You are sure you want to go there?" Marco asked him, pleading with his eyes for Bobs to come to his senses and not speak of it.

"I think we need to. It is not just about me, but both of us."

"Me, I am perfectly fine," Marco said, pointing his finger at himself.

"Really? You've never had a relationship. You go around serial fucking guy after guy. You lie about your name, your job, and where you live to everyone you meet. Your family doesn't know who you are. You don't let anyone in. And you pushed away the one guy you seemed to really care about. All you had to do was tell him you wanted him to stay, but you just gave him a little hug and sent him on his way. You might as well have introduced him to Jesus, bought him the ticket, and flown him out there yourself."

"I've heard enough of this analysis. Have you ever thought that I live my life the way I do because I am actually happy doing this? It's the way I want to be and it has nothing to do with repressed feelings. What about you, then? You settled down with one guy and played happy families but it blew up in your face. So how can what happened back then have fucked you up when you did the total opposite of me?"

"I wanted to be at peace with myself and I tried to be happy. But I knew I didn't deserve it, so I ruined it. I was angry all the time. I didn't know it, and I couldn't see what I was doing, so I pushed him away. I cheated on him, I lied to him, I manipulated and controlled him, I bullied him, and I physically and mentally abused him. You can't tell me I am not fucked up." Bobs started to cry, uncontrollably.

The gay guys playing tennis stopped and looked over at them.

"He'll be fine, his dog died," Marco snapped at them, waving them off.

"Oh how tragic. I remember how upset I was when

Lady died," he heard one of them say to the other.

Bobs had his arms folded over his knees. He brought them up to his chest and buried his head while he continued to sob. Marco rubbed his back and whispered to him that he was upsetting the queens by bringing up bad memories about their dog dying. This made Bobs smile, and he started to regain some composure.

"Remember what I was like back in school before IT happened? I would never have treated anyone like the way I treated Tim, the man I loved."

"I know. But we have to find a way to forget it and move on. Maybe we should just fuck again," Marco joked.

"In your dreams. Actually, I am happy to leave that as a great memory—one of my few untainted great memories," Bobs replied.

"Sometimes in my dreams, I see it." Marco told him, his tone barely audible.

Bobs nodded. "I dream about it every time I shut my eyes."

"You have to let it go; otherwise, it will consume you." Like the power of fire which consumes everything, Bobs thought to himself.

"We killed three people."

"One of them deserved to die; don't tell me you give a crap about that one," Marco hissed.

All the memories came flooding back to him of the day he and Marco had burned down the building known as Nightingale Hall, the building that rose back from the fiery hell to which they had sent it. Under the weight of his guilt and his grief, Bobs began rocking back and forth, crying hysterically and inconsolably.

THIS STORY TAKES A DARK TURN
AND CONTINUES IN…

The
Degenerate Opportunity

He sees the world as dystopian...
he will change it.

Mark Lakeram

The Degenerate Opportunity

MARK LAKERAM

PROLOGUE

Slowly he began to regain consciousness. All he could see through partially opened eyes was a halo of light. As some of his other senses started to come back to him, he wanted to touch his hurting skull. He tried to move his arms to his throbbing head but he could not, and then the memory of being restrained came back to him. Panic gripped his tormented body, causing all the newly delicate parts to hurt more. He would have started to struggle against his fetters, but his head felt woozy and he lost consciousness again.

A few hours passed before he managed to wake; this time he took things slower and gently lifted up his head to survey his body. He looked up at his arms—each one was stretched out and tied to a bedpost. Then he glanced down the bed at his naked self, briefly stopping at his stomach where the hair was matted and stuck to his skin. Continuing downwards, he saw his legs were spread and also fastened, forcing his body into an X-shape on the bed-prison.

After his visual inspection, he allowed himself to take in all the physical hurt he was feeling. There was the dull ache in his head, his shoulders were sore mainly from the position he was being held in. He arched his body upwards to lift his ass out of the patch of spit, blood and shit that had leaked from him, but this caused him pain.

He started to feel really sorry for himself again, just as he had done since his dream date had turned into his worst nightmare. He was so young and yet he was worried about dying, but more importantly, what would his family say when the details of his death emerged? He had never contemplated his own mortality before this day started. His mind shifted to the events that had brought him here.

* * * *

Being too scared to approach anyone in the real world, he had continued his secret life where he felt safest— chatting to gay men online. At first he was chatting, always in a private dialogue box, to various men; some guys demanded to see pictures before they would even contemplate maintaining the discourse. Others wanted to talk dirty and share sex stories, which he did not feel comfortable with, as he had none at that stage. Then along came Martin Fealy, who he felt a rapport with. Martin was in his mid-twenties, which he found to be exciting because he did not want to be with a schoolboy like himself. Martin was respectful of his age and experience and never pestered him for anything untoward.

They had started talking online frequently. Finally he, Robert "Bobs" Ashton, felt relaxed with Martin. He shared his face picture and full profile with him, but continued to lie about his name. Martin said he could only show Bobs his face in person because of the nature of the work he did, but Bobs's sexual attraction to Martin was provoked by the other pictures he received. Finally, Bobs had found someone he trusted to come out to. So he did.

Telling Martin gave him the confidence to eventually open up face to face with a person, and at the end of that summer he came out to his best friend, Marco. Now he had an actual friend to be his confidant, one who he could go out to bars and clubs with and one who told him not to trust people online—especially someone who would not show his face. Bobs gave up on his online life.

* * * *

There was a noise from the other room, which brought Bobs's mind back to his current predicament. He was not sure what the sound had been, but it could only mean his assailant had returned. This told him he could either do nothing—and be abused and tortured more—or he could try and get away. He decided to stop feeling sorry for himself and to push past the physical pain.

Bobs yanked his right arm hard, as far as the restraint would let him, but as he pulled his limb the knot seemed to get tighter. Maybe it was one of those special knots— one that the more you struggled against, the more it tightened. He switched to his weaker left arm, arched his body upwards and pulled even more against his right one so that he could move his left hand towards the bedpost. It seemed to work…his right hand became numb as the entanglement at the wrist had become very tight now, but his left hand could freely touch the bedpost and attempt to undo the binding. He was fumbling because he was not left-handed and did not have the dexterity in that hand, but mainly because he was scared. After what seemed like a lifetime, he managed to free his hand. He flexed and scrunched his fingers to get more feeling back to them. Freeing his right arm was easier because having one limb liberated had settled him, and since the cross was broken he had more maneuverability.

He sat upright, causing significant pain in his head, but he knew he had to keep on going. He was about to try and untie his legs when he heard the guy directly outside, saw the handle to the bedroom door start to move.

Bobs froze. A sitting duck, still tethered to the bed by his legs. Surely his attempt at escape would earn him a severe punishment.

The door handle stopped moving.

Bobs strained to hear…thought he heard the guy moving off. He did not waste any time. Forgetting everything else, he desperately set to work freeing both legs. Once he had undone the straps, he swiveled his legs together and slid off the side of the bed. This new movement caused him to realize just how sore he was from being held in that awkward position. He looked around the room, picked up a dumbbell bar, and moved over to the door.

He wondered if, when the door opened, he would have what it took to hit another person. All he wanted to do was go home, but he had to remove the obstacle in his path. As he waited for the guy to return his thoughts again drifted back to the events that had led him here.

* * * *

After a night out with Marco, who had copped off with a fit guy and he had not, he went home alone. He was horny as hell, and as he had moved from his bedroom door he stripped off his clothes and got into bed, grabbing his laptop to find some porn to wank to. But just a straightforward wank would not cut it. Or maybe he had something to prove to his friend who could easily pull in the real world? Marco had warned him off, but once online Bobs went back into his old chat rooms. Even though it was late at night, the rooms were busy. Perhaps others were just getting in from an unsuccessful night out, or they had never been out at all and had spent the entire night in front of the screen, or any significant others were asleep, leaving them able to play.

Bobs had scanned through the rooms looking for someone to talk to, when a private message to him came up: *"Hello stranger".* It was Martin, his trusted confidante, the first person he'd ever come out to.

He felt that he had been unfair towards Martin in the way he had stopped going online, never actually saying goodbye or explaining to him that he would not be chatting anymore. His actions had been driven by how he thought others perceived him, and how they were judging him. But he had fancied Martin from what he said, his personality and what he had seen physically of him. So Bobs decided to go for what he wanted to do from the moment they'd first started chatting.

"The folks took away my computer when they found out about me, but it's all sorted now. So did you miss me?" Bobs typed and then stared in the private message box for a reply— Hotstud25, Martin's username, was *"typing".* He waited for the message but Martin obviously deleted it, as nothing came through and the box went back to its default, the process repeating itself. Bobs thought he had missed his chance, when the answer came in, *"Yes".* It was just one word but it was all he needed.

Bobs did not want to waste more time. He quickly typed what he had wanted to type from the beginning of their online relationship. *"I missed you too, do you want to meet up?"*

"Awesome, but look I don't want to get you into more trouble. Don't want any trouble and your parents angrily banging down my

door."

"Don't worry they won't, I haven't told them or anyone about you like we originally agreed."

"Cool. So when were you thinking?"

"Tonight. I could really do with some cheering up."

"Seriously I want to meet you but think we should take things slowly, you're special. Let's get back to chatting and meet when you're ready."

"I'm ready now, soooo horny."

"You are making me horny too with all this talk but lets just chat, we will meet soon I promise. So tell me about what you been up to since you've been AWOL?"

So Bobs had filled Martin in on his night and everything he had been doing since they last spoke, including how he came out to a friend and they had slept together to try it out, but were just going to remain friends. The chat ended with the two having cybersex and giving Bobs the much-needed relief he craved.

This routine continued for a few weeks, progressing to phone sex where Martin would always be the caller, withholding his number. These sessions kept Bobs sated, and he stopped desiring schoolmates as the new year kicked into full swing with A-level module exams. He had started to consider Martin as his boyfriend because he was very caring, not putting pressure on him to meet up, rather wanting him to concentrate on doing well in his exams. Once these were over, Bobs would finally get to meet him. On the day of his final exam, there was just one thing he had left to do and that was to tell Marco, not because he felt he owed it to his friend after he was so negative about his faceless Internet lover before, but because he needed him to provide cover as he planned to spend the night out.

Bobs did not want to be judged again, so when he told Marco he said they had swapped a lot of pictures and talked regularly on the phone—the last fact being sort of true. "As it's the last exam and a Friday, my folks expect me to go out, so I told them I'm spending the night at your place."

"You can spend it at mine—he might just want sex and kick you out," Marco had said, sounding a lot harsher than he intended. "We could actually just both go out and find real people."

"Martin *is* real. And he doesn't just want sex, there are feelings there."

"Okay, I'm just trying to look out for you. So text me after you meet up so I know he's not a psycho. Then later, like the Saturday morning, so I know that everything's good. And if you need to, you can come and crash at my place anytime."

Bobs decided to let the "looking out for" him comment pass, feeling that actually, the opposite was true. Marco was wrapped up in the various guys he'd been seeing. "I promise I'll text you to let you know his picture does him justice, and the next morning I'll fill you in on all the gory details."

"I can come and meet him with you and then disappear when you give me the thumbs up."

"I'm meeting him at his place." Bobs instantly regretted telling Marco this, as he saw his friend's pupils dilate in disbelief.

"Look, he wanted to make me dinner after all the revising I've been doing. He lives in Nightingale Hall—

that really nice building by the common. It'll be fine."

* * * *

Standing naked by the door, Bobs knew it was not fine, and wondered why he hadn't listened to his friend or why his own judgment was so crap that he had trusted this good-looking guy, only to be rewarded with the worst twenty-four hours of his life. The anger in him rose.

Then suddenly the door opened.

Bobs saw his attacker before Martin saw him. Martin walked into the room, naturally looking towards the bed and not behind the door. With all his remaining strength, Bobs swung the weapon at Martin. The bar connected with the back of the guy's head with a heavy crunch, and he dropped to the floor almost instantly. Bobs looked at the body on the floor and hit it again flush across the back; he would have continued to hit him, but he just wanted to get the fuck out of there. He flung the bar down and ran out into the living room, made his way to the front door and started fumbling with the numerous locks on it. Opening the door, he stumbled out into the corridor.

He felt someone grab his shoulders and call his name.

"Bobby…Bobs! What have you been doing?"

A familiar voice roused him out of the shock he felt after his desperate escape. "Marco? Jeez, what are you doing here?"

"I came to find you after you didn't text or answer your phone," Marco responded as he supported his naked friend, who was leaning on him. "Your mum called my house asking what time you'd be back."

With no sort of explanation forthcoming, Marco led Bobs back into the apartment he'd seen him come out of.

"No! Not here!" Bobs said and pulled away from his friend. As he did so Marco noticed his friend was hurt.

"What the fuck has happened to you? Who did this to you?" Marco asked, pointing at the obvious bruises on his wrists.

"It was Martin." Saying the name hurt, not because of what had been done to him, but because of what he had just done to Martin.

"I'm calling the police." Marco took out his phone.

"No!" Bobs shut the door. "Look…you can't. I…think…I think I…killed him..." Bobs tried to justify his words, explaining what had happened to him. As he was talking, they moved back into the living room, where Bobs saw his clothes neatly folded by a roaring fire.

Bobs started to dress as he told his story, saying they'd had sex on the sofa, which was good. Then when they progressed into the bedroom things had started to get kinky, and he had allowed himself to be tied-up. Then events progressed to rough and he wanted it to stop, only then he could not do anything about it. He thought he was drugged maybe, and rough soon became torture, and Martin genuinely seemed to be getting off on subjecting him to various forms of abuse.

Between half-sobs, Bobs told how he'd managed to free himself, club Martin with a heavy object, and hit him again when he was down. "And then I ran out, and that's when you found me."

Marco let him finish telling his side of the story, and felt disgusted for his friend. "But that's more reason why we have to go to the police—he sounds like a right sicko."

"Sounded like, I hit him hard and he went down…I

don't think he's getting up. What are we going to tell the police? I killed my gay Internet friend in a lover's tiff? Can you imagine me telling my father that? You didn't tell anyone I was here?"

"No, I didn't tell anyone. After you didn't turn up back at my place and didn't respond to my phone calls, I came over here. I saw the apartment number for 'Fealy' on the mail boxes downstairs and made my way up, and I was going to knock when you burst out the door."

"So no one saw you?"

"No. But I don't think we can do what you're thinking."

Bobs looked at his friend and then looked at the fire in the fireplace, realized why his clothes had neatly been folded next to it. He picked up a poker and started prodding the fire. "Look, I think he was going to burn all my clothes and do who knows what to me."

Marco joined him by the fireplace. An industrial looking glass jar sat next to where the clothes were. Marco opened it, and the liquid in it was clear but the smell was strong and strangely familiar.

Bobs pleaded with him again. "Let's just go, and we won't tell anyone what happened here..."

His plea was interrupted by a sound from the bedroom.

They both looked in that direction. The door started to open. To keep the evil at bay, both Bobs and Marco instinctively threw what they had in their hands towards the opening door—the poker and the glass jar—and ran out of the apartment.

Neither of them looked back. They just ran, down the stairs—taking a couple at a time—and then out of the building. They ran all the way back to Marco's home. Once safely inside Bobs was able to catch his breath. "Shit! He wasn't dead. Christ, I didn't kill him. Thank fuck!"

"I know…look, call home and tell them you're going to stay here another night. Then go have a bath and tidy yourself up. Then we can work out what to do next, in case he comes after you."

* * * *

Bobs was starting to relax a little bit in the hot, soothing water. Martin did not know his name or address, so there was no way he could come after him, and even if he did, he could just go to the police without having to admit he was gay and what he was doing in a man's apartment.

Marco started banging on the door, shouting. "Bobs! You have to come with me! Now!"

Bobs got out of the bath, panicked at the thought they had been hunted down. He yanked open the door, searching Marco's face for some kind of clue as to what had happened.

"We have to go back to Nightingale Hall. The whole building is on fire! It's all over the news."

Even though he was still wet, Bobs put on his clothes and dashed out behind Marco. Arriving near Martin's building, he detected the smell of burning in the air. They approached the building from the common, and got the first look of the flames licking and destroying what remained of the French Renaissance building. Against the black night the scene ahead was incredible, with the fiery colors enhanced.

Marco spoke in a hushed tone. "I think that liquid I

threw was some sort of alcohol or acid, or something that I've smelt before in chemistry class. That, added to the red hot poker..."

Marco did not need to finish his sentence. "We started this," Bobs confirmed as he continued to watch the destruction ahead.

They moved closer to the barrier that had been set up, to try and see if anyone had been hurt or if the cause of the fire had been established. As the building burned, the devastation was seared onto both their minds permanently. They listened as a reporter next to them spoke on his phone relaying the information to someone else: "Find out everything you can about Martin Fealy, F-E-A-L-Y. The fire killed him. My fireman source said the fire started in his apartment and there were accelerants used. Yes, definitely sinister. Wait, I'll call you back. I think they're bringing out more bodies."

Marco stared ahead, wondering how he could live with himself in the future. Then and there, he made the decision that somehow he had to atone for his part in the fire. Further, he'd have to learn what are the signs and clues to recognize a person who was so deceptive and evil.

ABOUT THE AUTHOR

Mark Lakeram was born and bred in London and considers this intoxicating city his home. That is why his first two novels are set in the city. He wants to write books that breaks the norm. The Scene, fills a void as it is not a run of the mill teenager coming out story or gay erotica that seems to dominate gay literature but is a story for everyone. While The Degenerate Opportunity, explores the darker elements of humanity – taking readers to a dark place.

Learn more at www.marklakeram.com

27530586R00158

Printed in Great Britain
by Amazon